The Majestic Leo Marble

The Majestic Leo Marble

by R. J. Lee

MADVILLE
P U B L I S H I N G

Lake Dallas, Texas

FIRST EDITION

This is a work of fiction, and is not intended to resemble
anyone living or dead.

Requests for permission to reprint or reuse material
from this work should be sent to:

Permissions
Madville Publishing
PO Box 358
Lake Dallas, TX 75065

Cover Design: Jacqueline Davis with
painting by Robert Kuehnle

ISBN: 978-1-956440-93-5 paperback,
978-1-956440-94-2 ebook

Library of Congress Control Number: 2024931136

In loving memory of my brother,
Byrnes Kuehnle

THE OVERTURE

THE OVERTURE

Chapter 1

On the evening of April 11, 1946, the fetus who was destined to be an only child and who would be christened Leo Lawrence Marble quickened in an unusual way. His mother Louisa, she of the towhead blonde hair, full lips, and pale blue eyes, was halfway through the fifth month of his development, and she was sitting in one of the cheap seats in the Majestic Theatre in New York City watching a performance of Rogers and Hammerstein's *Carousel* in its original run.

As a result, the first voice Leo heard through the thin wall of the womb was not his mother's but that of John Raitt as carnival barker Billy Bigelow, singing. The deep, rich tenor notes made him take notice inside the warm, primordial, life-giving sea enveloping his very being. It came to him in a way he could not possibly understand when the voice started singing about gender assignment in life, whether Bigelow would become the father of a boy or a girl and how to handle either event.

The voice seemed more passionate at first about being the father of a boy, at the prospect of teaching him how to dive and swim in the bracing waters off the Maine coast, of just having fun with him as fathers and sons were known to do; but as the seven-minute song progressed, there emerged an equal enthusiasm for fathering a pretty little girl with pink ribbons in her hair—a tintype of her mother; of taking care of her and putting food on the table and watching out for her when her "little boy" suitors eventually showed up with their emotions on their sleeves.

And it was then that Leo's fledgling thoughts turned inward for a second in time that seemed an eternity.

"What am I going to be? A boy or a girl? Is it better to be one or the other? Can I be both at the same time?"

The answer did not come to him, of course, and then the quickening morphed into something else—something quiet and rhythmic and certain, the essence of a heartbeat. Suddenly, there was no further awareness of what was happening on the stage in the Majestic Theatre. There was just that stretch of time during which Leo was allowed a glimpse of what was to come in ways he could never imagine once he became part of the world in which his mother and father lived.

Three-and-a-half more months of quiet, incremental growth passed without awareness of anything more than being warm and cozy. Leo could not hear Louisa Marble's constant complaints about all the on-sale, canned veggies she had to eat in their efficiency kitchen because she and her husband were on a budget.

"I'm gonna give birth to a bowl of peas and carrots," she observed at one point with a wry expression on her face.

"But it'll be our very own bowl," her husband answered in kind.

Joseph Marble, whose rugged features were slightly marred by pockmarks leftover from teenage bouts with severe acne, was writing WWII fighter pilot and detective stories of the pulp fiction variety in his office in downtown Manhattan at Specialty House. Among his novellas were *Red Hot Ice* and *Sultra, the Sumatran Spy*. Of course, his family and friends back home in Beau Pre, Mississippi, thought he had snared such a glamorous job to get published and even be an editor at the New York level after surviving WWII as a decorated pilot. But the position didn't pay as well as people imagined. Living in New York City was very expensive compared to a lazy riverport in Mississippi. His salary didn't go very far after paying the rent on a two-room flat in Greenwich Village that featured a polka-dot toilet seat for their studied amusement. In fact, Joseph had managed to get a free ticket for his wife to *Carousel* from a fellow writer at the office, which was the only way she could possibly have afforded to go. Still, it was all undeniably their big adventure on the heels of their marriage in Beau Pre and honeymoon in the French Quarter in 1945, and the endless supply of peas and carrots were an exasperating part of it.

Leo was finally born with his blazing red hair and pink skin. Down the road, freckles would crop up on his arms, legs, and face. His mother thought that he looked just like a little Buddha when she bathed him in the sink all the time. Meanwhile, Joseph Marble had moved from Manhattan back to Beau Pre, "read for the law," and become a partner in the firm of Carter and Marble to support his family, since his pulp fiction never quite fit the bill. He had given it his best effort but had fallen short.

Leo got through nursery school and kindergarten quickly enough, and even started taking piano lessons in the first grade from his Granny Marble at her music school, the only game in town. Following the untimely death of her husband Sykes due to cancer, Julia Trigg Marble, a short stocky woman with a mound of gray hair piled atop her head, had opened it successfully using her double major in music and math she had received from Randolph-Macon around the turn of the century. Leo took to his rote adventures in sharps and flats, even as he endured being teased on the seesaw at recess for being a "redheaded, freckle-faced woodpecker." His mother told him not to pay any attention to classmates who ridiculed him, that they were just jealous. That it was okay to be different. He remembered those words, and they gave him a certain strength.

Then, at the age of six, it appeared. His parents bought him comic books to read all the time—*Walt Disney Comics & Stories*, *Donald Duck* and *Little Lulu*, mostly. They all had one thing in common: on the back covers were ads for Charles Atlas, the bodybuilder. They were supposed to be slightly comical with a bully kicking sand in the face of a scrawny guy in front of his girlfriend. The solution was to grow the sort of muscles that Charles Atlas had and show that bully "what for." At least, that was the intention.

But that message was totally lost on Leo. Instead, all he saw at his tender age, was a handsome, muscular man who mesmerized him. Though he was far removed from puberty, Leo was constantly aroused by those pictures. He began to fantasize at first. He didn't care about sand being kicked or anything else that was going on at the beach. It would be many years later that he would even know the term pecs or biceps. He did not need to know the names. He only wanted to feel them, squeeze them, and then have Charles Atlas take him in his arms and hold him close. There would be skin contact and warmth and closeness, and who knew what else? He did not think of Charles Atlas as a father. He was nothing like Joseph Marble. No, this bodybuilder was more like an equal of sorts. Not in stature, but in emotional feeling. Yes, Leo had actual feelings for this man.

Soon, the fantasies weren't enough. Leo explored in all his innocence and found a part of him that did "double duty." He knew quite well how to get up at night and pee. But neither of his parents had said anything at all to him about what else *it* was good for. That, he found out for himself—a definite stiffening. At night, when he was securely in bed. In the darkness. He was there. Charles Atlas was there with him. No one else existed. Leo started doing "double duty." Over and over. He would get into a rhythm. Finally, every nerve ending in his body seemed to vibrate, and he would lie there breathless and exhausted. Only occasionally did the thought ever occur to him that he might be doing this because he was "different" and "redheaded and freckle-faced." Could that possibly be it?

Mostly, though, he never knew what to make of it all. What did it mean? Should he bring it up to his parents? Something told him not to. It became his closely guarded secret, even if he did not understand it. But it felt too good to stop.

Once, when Granny Marble had come over to babysit for the

evening while his parents went out to a party, he had succumbed to his urges and sprawled out on the bed naked while fantasizing about his muscular idol. She had wandered in to check on him and, to his surprise, had only said, "Well, if you're more comfortable that way..."

At first, he was afraid she might report his activity to his parents, but apparently she chose not to because neither of them said anything to him about it. For that, he was eternally grateful to her.

During Leo's elementary and middle-school years, he became quite proficient both at playing the piano under the metronome of Granny Marble's guidance— making friends with music notes; and playing with himself under his own guidance, in his own rhythm, entertaining images of someone who was so near and yet so distant. He would be happy with the status quo for several years to come, even though he understood nothing about it except that it existed.

Chapter 2

One winter well after Leo and the piano had become "best friends," he came down with a lingering case of the flu, one that kept him home from school, which he hardly ever missed. His uncle, Dr. Brady Marble with his thick glasses and reassuring smile, was vigilant with his house calls and assured his sister-in-law Louisa that he had "seen much worse around town" that winter and that Leo would recover sooner rather than later, despite appearances to the contrary. Still, it wasn't fun for Leo running a fever, having a cough and the sniffles and being confined to bed.

Just at the point he didn't think he could stand being sick and cooped up another day, his mother came into his room one afternoon with his lunch tray. It was his favorite—a toasted cheese sandwich cut diagonally and a big bowl of tomato soup with an island of nearly melted butter floating in the middle. She propped up his pillows and balanced the tray perfectly on his lap, handing over the spoon.

"I have a wonderful surprise for you," she told him. "Start eating your lunch, and I'll go get it."

Leo blew on his first spoonful and swallowed dutifully. Tomato soup was something that reassured him even when he was well.

His mother entered the room with something that looked like a thin, oddly shaped book with a colorful picture on the cover. But it wasn't a book.

"This is the cast album of the movie of *Carousel* that just came out," she began. "I went down to Miz Lilly's Records and bought it for you." There was a brief pause. "And for me, too."

It was then that she told him that she had seen a performance of the original Broadway production in New York ten years earlier while she was pregnant with him and had fallen in love with the story and the songs. She carefully explained the plot that took place one summer on the coast of Maine with Billy Bigelow the carnival barker falling in love with and marrying Julie Jordan, the sweet, trusting mill girl; and the troubles that followed them up until the very end of their marriage which ended with his tragic death during an attempted robbery.

"I thought listening to the songs might get your mind off being sick and help you get well. As a matter of fact, the first time I ever felt you kick was right in the middle of Billy Bigelow singing about becoming a father. A mother never forgets the first time she feels her baby move like that."

Then she opened the album and put the vinyl 45 on the little record player that she and Joseph had given their son for Christmas the year before.

Leo continued to slurp his soup and munch on his cheese sandwich while the music played. He listened mesmerized as his mother provided an ongoing narration.

"The entire first act is called the *Carousel Waltz*. No one speaks. It's all mimed."

"What's that mean?"

"It's when people move their lips and gesture, but they don't speak or sing."

"Then how do you understand it?"

"The music and the action tell the story. Billy bumps into Julie in the crowd and then gives her a free ticket to ride on his carousel. It's his way of telling her that he likes her. Billy is used to getting his way in life."

Leo loved the sound of the music. It did have a "merry-go-round feel" to it. He imagined the scene his mother was describing by focusing on the album cover picture of Gordon McRae as

Billy Bigelow and Shirley Jones as Julie Jordan. Their names were on the cover in big, block lettering, and he was leaning against her, looking into her eyes as she sat astride one of his colorful carousel horses.

As the album continued throughout his lunch, Leo was drawn ever more deeply into the score. One memorable tune after another delighted him: "If I Loved You," "June Is Bustin' Out All Over," "What's The Use of Wond'rin?" and most of all, the tour-de-force of "Soliloquy" throughout which Billy Bigelow pondered his impending fatherhood. As his mother had predicted, it drew him out of his illness, and he was soon back in school with his classmates. For months after that, in fact, he played the album on his little turntable, practically obsessed with it.

For Christmas the year Leo turned twelve, his parents bought him a hardcover collection containing the entire repertoire of songs from all the Rodgers and Hammerstein musicals—the majority of which were from *Oklahoma!, Carousel, South Pacific* and *The King and I*. His mother had written at the top of the title page: "Buddha plays Broadway." The nickname Buddha, trotted out occasionally, was a leftover from the days when Louisa had bathed her little boy with all his baby fat in the sink. Leo energetically tackled every one of the songs until he could nearly play them by memory. It turned out to be the best gift since his parents had bought the upright for his lessons.

Chapter 3

It was hotter than usual the summer Leo turned thirteen. He announced to his mother that he was going to try out for the Junior Little Theatre's production of *Harriet's Heartthrob*, which surprised her somewhat. His previous experience onstage, so to speak, had been as Rudolph, the Red Nosed Reindeer, in a forgettable, first-grade Christmas production that only a mother could love with enthusiastic but forced applause.

"Well, good luck, sweetie," she told him, remembering the past but not about to bring it up.

When Leo got to the auditions a few days later, he discovered that he was the youngest kid there. All the others were either sixteen or seventeen, which made them seem like adults to him. After all, they were in *high school*. Among the two that stood out the most to him were Melanie Brooks and Dean Forsythe, who were going for the lead roles of Harriet Williams and her boyfriend Billy Carson in this production about teenage summer antics. Leo realized at once that they were going to get the parts, while the only role that he might pin down by default was that of Harriet's Uncle Mike, who had little more than a walk-on appearance. Although he was far too young and immature, Leo did get the part because no one else wanted it or even tried out for it, and he was overjoyed at the opportunity.

"I only have twelve lines, and I'm only in one scene near the end," he told his mother that afternoon. "But you watch, I'm gonna be very good."

Louisa gave him a big hug. "I'm sure you will be. We'll be there cheering you on."

There were only three weeks of rehearsals during July for the brief August run. The Little Theatre building was not air-conditioned, so the considerable time spent there was uncomfortable for most everyone. But Leo didn't mind so much because their bungalow on Orleans Street didn't have air conditioning, either, and he was used to sleeping with a rotary fan blowing across his face at predictable intervals. Fitful sleep, it was at times, but he had grown used to it.

The first inkling of something akin to Charles Atlas and his comic book ads came from watching Dean Forsythe practicing his lines with Melanie Brooks. She was a tall, athletic brunette with an astounding amount of confidence in her looks and presence; he was even taller—the sort of blond with fierce dark eyebrows that somehow seemed to go together. More than that, Dean had a way of winking and flashing his dazzling smile at Melanie during rehearsal that was disarming, and every time he lifted his left eyebrow at her, Leo felt something in the pit of his stomach.

As rehearsals continued, it finally dawned on Leo that he wasn't jealous of Dean, he was jealous of Melanie. She was getting Dean's attention, and Leo wanted to be in her shoes. Then, something began to hurt inside. Really hurt. It didn't feel like an upset stomach or anything close to that. This was something different that seemed to spread throughout his body, leaving him limp with a strange kind of exhaustion. It got to the point that he finally decided to tell his mother about it because he just couldn't keep it to himself any longer, and he thought maybe she would have some insight for him. Wasn't that what mothers and fathers were for?

"I think I'm in love with somebody in the play," he said, the tears flowing while he was lying on his back in his bed one afternoon after coming home from rehearsal.

She stood over him and nodded her head as if she understood.

"Is it Melanie Brooks? She's a very pretty girl. First crushes happen to everyone, you know. I remember mine to this day. His name was Barry Morrison, and I thought he invented sliced bread."

Leo hesitated to say the words but somehow managed. "No... it's not her. It's... Dean Forsythe. They're both seniors, and they don't even know who I am, but, no, it's him, not her."

Louisa appeared to maintain her calm. "I'm sure it's just hero worship, that's all. Boys look up to older boys all the time. It's probably a big brother, little brother type of thing."

"No," Leo said. "It's not like that at all. I know how I feel, and I'm in love with him, and it's not normal."

For that, his mother had no immediate answer and that bothered Leo very much.

"Just concentrate on the play," she said, finally. "I'm sure those feelings will pass. You just memorize your lines, and don't worry about the rest. It'll all work out—you'll see."

The evening the play was over, the entire cast was invited to Dean Forsythe's home for a "let off steam," swimming pool party. It became just that, as everyone dove or cannonballed into the cold water in their swimming suits, and all that pent-up energy rose, thick as fog into the night air, from the surface of the water. Leo pretended to be happy, but he was anything but. The sight of Dean's lean body, exposed to him for the first time, was too much to bear. Although no Charles Atlas, Dean was definitely in shape, so close and yet so unattainable once again.

The most painful sequence occurred when Leo caught sight of Dean putting his arm around Melanie poolside and leaning in to kiss her on the lips. Leo thought he would faint, but he didn't. How he wanted to be on the receiving end of that kiss!

A day or two later, Leo found himself listening to his parents through the louver door at the end of the hallway that led to his bedroom. He hadn't intended to eavesdrop, but just as he was about to turn the knob and enter the family room on the other side, he clearly heard his mother's words:

"He can't be our son and not be interested in girls," she was saying to his father, her tone full of distress. "He can't really have a crush on that Dean Forsythe."

"Let's don't worry about it too much," Joseph said. "It's probably just a phase he's going through. Leo can be very dramatic at times, as you know."

But for Leo, those feelings did not pass, even after the play had long ended. One thing he had gathered by overhearing his parents' conversation behind the door, however, was that he must not disappoint them. They expected him to be attracted to girls, so he would pretend that he was and start dating them. That was the "normal" thing you were supposed to do, and he wanted to be as normal as a "redheaded, freckle-faced woodpecker" could be. Even though a few years back, his mother had told him it was okay to be different. Her words in the family room clearly indicated that she did not think it was okay to be different in this instance.

The next year, his freshman year in high school, Leo began to compile a list and formulate a strategy. He gathered all the info he needed by listening carefully to the other boys in P.E. class as they were all changing or showering and talking about girls the way boys do.

Which ones "put out." Which ones they lusted after. Which ones *wouldn't* cooperate. Why, they didn't even allow a fellow to get to first base, whatever that was! That last category contained the ones that Leo would ask out eventually. He knew they wouldn't put pressure on him if he had to date them, which is what his parents wanted him to do.

Which is what he had to do to prevent them from discovering that he had already developed a crush on one of his freshman classmates. Dean Forsythe may have graduated and fallen into the "out of sight, out of mind" category, but he had been replaced by a new object of his affection, and just as with Dean, Leo had no control over it. His feelings erupted without warning or choice for Coy Warren, now on the football team, with his trademark crewcut, pigeon-toed gait, deep dimples when he smiled—a healthy specimen several inches taller and a lot thicker through the middle than he was. The two of them had been in Cub Scouts together a few years back when they were approximately the same size and doing things like collecting stamps and butterflies for badges, but Leo hadn't had such feelings for Coy then. But now that he had shot up and become a muscular football hero, it was a different proposition altogether. Coy was very different from Dean in nearly every way possible, but that didn't seem to matter. The same kind of feelings had developed without Leo half trying. It wasn't so much a physical attraction as it was an emotional one. Nonetheless, the reality was that there was no conceivable way that he could ask Coy out on a date or for a sleepover without likely getting a bloody nose or maybe his front teeth knocked out. The very concept of dating another boy seemed to belong in another universe.

For the record, Leo tried his best to wait until most of the other boys had showered after P.E. to avoid mutual nakedness or having his gaze stray here and there and possibly reveal something he desperately wanted to keep secret. That, and to avoid listening to the occasional "queer joke" that one of them might crack at any time in the locker room. It seemed to come with the territory, and it was difficult to ignore such unintentional slights; but Leo had become an expert at biting his tongue. He had no margin for error since he had also overheard two of the boys in P.E. on the other side of his locker talking about him after a baseball game.

"Did you see Marble in the outfield?" one of them was saying. "He throws like a girl. Betcha he doesn't even like pussy."

To relieve the burgeoning stress of it all, finally, Leo put his camouflage plan into action, going to his mother with it one evening after she had just finished setting the dinner table.

"Mama, when can I start going out?" He paused briefly and then said the magic words. "Am I too young to ask a girl for a date?"

He could see the delight spreading across his mother's face, could hear the excitement in her voice. "Oh, do you have someone in mind? Come on, let's go sit on the sofa in the family room and talk about this."

Once they were settled, he mentioned a name from his list. "I think I would like to ask Rebecca Bentley out, especially."

Louisa couldn't help but reach over and give him a hug, then drew back with an approving grin. "She's such a nice girl from such a nice family. This is wonderful news."

Nice.

That was the key. But not in the way he knew his mother meant. The gist was that Rebecca was the kind of nice which would involve her not expecting anything of him, other than going to the movies or the drive-in for root beers and potato chips. No kisses, no making out, none of that other stuff the boys in P.E. bragged and snickered about all the time, although he sometimes wondered if they were telling the truth about the things they said they had done. No, Rebecca checked all the right boxes and added an extra one as well: she wore expensive-looking clothes that showed off her wasp-like waist to maximum effect.

"When you get your driver's license next summer, I think," Louisa told her son. He had never heard or seen her so lighthearted. "Your father and I will let you go on a movie date then. I think that's the best way to start. You want to take your time and not rush."

Those were just the words Leo wanted to hear from her. Plus, he was greatly relieved that he had another whole year before he had to start camouflage dating. He could take all that time to plan dates and what he would do on them. Go to the movies, as his mother had suggested, or to the Magnolia Drive-In and order root beers and barbecue pork sandwiches while they sat in the front seat and chatted. He could pick out a subject to discuss and stay on it throughout the date—another movie he had just seen; how excited he was to see the upcoming movie version of *To Kill*

A Mockingbird by Harper Lee, after reading the novel; anything that would keep things on a platonic level and such things as kissing and hugging and all the rest of it he didn't want to know about at bay. The thought of having to kiss any girl on the lips made him wince, while the thought of being able to kiss Coy Warren aroused him in no uncertain terms.

He must never let anyone know about that last part. Not if he wanted to play the game of "being normal."

Leo sailed through driver's ed class the summer he turned fifteen—even the part about learning on standard transmission and letting out the clutch—and coveted the freedom he instantly acquired by being allowed to drive the family car—a two-toned, blue-and-white Ford Fairlane with the futuristic fins. His parents had even given him a model of it as a Christmas present one year. Although the car itself was aging, it was aging well, and his father didn't seem to want to let go of it. Or was there something else involved? Once again, overhearing a conversation behind the louver door between his parents—this time about finances—seemed to have some bearing upon why the Fairlane hadn't been traded in by now.

That aside, the joy of having a driver's license was balanced by actually having to ask Rebecca Bentley out on a date to begin his camouflage. Not that she wasn't pleasant to be around. She was in several of his classes at school, got very good grades and he even enjoyed sharing jokes with her. A blonde with a smattering of freckles, although not nearly as many as he had, she was short of stature, and the rest that the boys in P.E. were always raving about, Leo didn't even notice. To him, she was just a friend in a dress.

Their first date during which he took her to the Beau Pre Cinema went off without a hitch. Leo waited for her to emerge from her bedroom after talking to her father in the Bentley living room about how school was going and the weather and things that didn't matter at all. Once they got to the movie theater, he bought them both a Dr. Pepper at the concession stand, they shared a box of popcorn, and then they settled in to watch *To Kill A Mockingbird*. On the way back to Rebecca's house after it was over, they discussed what they liked about it.

"I thought that little girl that played Scout was so adorable," Rebecca said. "She was just as I imagined her when I read the book. A little bit of a tomboy, but still cute as a button."

Leo nodded quickly. "Yes. She did a great job. I totally believed she was the character in the book."

"And that Gregory Peck is such a dreamboat, don't you think?" she continued.

Thinking on his feet, Leo was careful not to agree with her and let anything leak. Instead, he said, "He's a very good actor. I totally believed he was Atticus, too. I think he has the sort of face that belongs on Mount Rushmore with those Presidents."

At the door five minutes or so later, Leo smiled at Rebecca and said goodnight, making no attempt to kiss her in any form or fashion—not even a peck on the cheek. So, this dating business wasn't going to be so bad after all, and his parents would be none the wiser. He would appear to be a part of their "normal" world.

By the time Leo turned sixteen, he had become a pro at taking Rebecca out to the movies or the drive-in; and as he had envisioned, she never put any pressure on him to go beyond doing things like that. Meanwhile, he continued to have strong feelings from afar for Coy, whose prowess as a running back exploded further his junior year on the football field. There were rumors of him being scouted by LSU, Ole Miss, and other schools for a scholarship. It was a thrill for Leo to imagine the two of them doing simple things like walking hand-in-hand down the school hallways, as boys and girls were allowed to do without anyone questioning the practice. Yet, Leo had a firm grip on reality. He knew that the world didn't work that way, and he sensed there was nothing he could do to change it for the foreseeable future.

Once he had obtained his driver's license, a certain task had also befallen Leo. His father chain-smoked Picayune cigarettes, a habit he had acquired during his stint as a fighter pilot during the War. Mostly at night at odd hours, Leo was asked now and then to take the Fairlane to Jeb Tanksley's Market before it closed to pick up a couple of packs after Joseph ran out while working on legal briefs in his little home study next to the garage. Jeb had hired the firm of Carter and Marble as his lawyers, and thus there was an understanding that Leo could make these nicotine runs anytime they were needed; and the female cashier, a stout woman named Russy, would look the other way where Leo's age was concerned, although sometimes she would joke with him a bit.

"Don't you smoke all those before you get home," she was not above saying now and then, wagging a finger.

He was in fact on one of these so-called errands when he turned on the radio to hear Steve Lawrence singing his chart-topping version of "Go Away Little Girl." Out of nowhere, Leo started accompanying him, and suddenly, there it was—a rich, tenor voice that blended perfectly with the one coming out of the radio. It was like they were a duo. Suddenly, Leo could sing and sing well, although he had never even really tried before, not even during his many sessions at the piano with his sheet music. Nor in church with hymns, nor at summer camp five years earlier during the evening vespers when "Kumbaya, My Lord" was trotted out and boys would put their arms around each other's shoulders—something Leo responded to enthusiastically but did not bother to examine further. It was just an adrenaline experience, and he was content to leave it at that. Group rounds of "Happy Birthday" and Christmas carols were the extent of his singing efforts through the years. Furthermore, neither his father nor mother could carry a tune, so it was a complete mystery to him—and eventually to the both of them—where this talent of his came from. Genes—and when they finally appeared to do their work, whether good or bad—were unpredictable things.

Nonetheless, Leo knew exactly what to do after discovering that he had this particular gift. The next day he called up Granny Marble excitedly and asked if he could take vocal lessons from Mrs. Teeny Mosby—the diminutive woman at the music school with an operatic voice and a towering beehive hairdo to make herself look taller. Of course, he was immediately given the green light by his grandmother, and in no time, he was learning how to open his throat and breathe properly from his diaphragm. His natural talent was being fine-tuned, as Mrs. Mosby was a very good and patient teacher.

One month later, as if some arcane but serendipitous schedule had been put in place, Mr. Lake Campbell of the English and Drama Departments and sponsor of the Chess Club at Beau Pre High School—he of the long, skinny legs and red hair without the freckles—announced over the P.A. system that he would be bringing Broadway to the student body. New York royalties would be paid to have *Oklahoma!* staged seven consecutive times—six times in the evenings and once as a Saturday matinee—and auditions would begin within a week. Leo could already play the entire score of *Oklahoma!* but suddenly, he could also sing it—both the male and female numbers. He decided to try out for the part of the cowboy Will Parker, the sub-lead, and worked up a rousing rendition of "Everything's Up To Date in Kansas City" for the onstage auditions. He thought he was quite good, if he did say so himself.

"You have a very impressive voice," Mr. Campbell told him after he had finished his song to brisk applause from the three-member selection committee sitting out in the audience.

Leo mistook the compliment as evidence that he would be portraying Will Parker, but instead the part went to a senior, Justin Raymond, who had been in the school chorus since his freshman year. Though disappointed, Leo was consoled by the fact that the committee had chosen him to be a member of the *Oklahoma!* boy's chorus—which meant he would be eligible for a line or two here and there, certain choreography and backing up the leads in the group numbers such as "The Farmer and the Cowman" and the eponymously-titled finale.

"There's always your senior year," his mother told him after he'd revealed the results of the auditions. "Consider this good experience for a bigger part—or maybe even the lead when that comes around. Who knows what could happen now that you can sing?"

As it turned out, Rebecca Bentley also tried out for the musical and became a part of the girl's chorus; and Leo was pleased that the two of them were paired as a couple in the group numbers. They were required to smile at each other a lot while they sang, and it lent further credence to the impression he was trying to create that they were an "item"—thus keeping him on the straight and narrow, so to speak, in school gossiping circles. As much as they could, things seemed to be falling into place for Leo.

For good measure, he decided to join the Chess Club, if for no other reason than to make sure Mr. Campbell didn't lose sight of him for future productions. It also gave him the sense that he had at least some semblance of control in his life.

THE FIRST ACT

Chapter 4

The news came over the P.A. system one morning in mid-October during Leo's senior year, stunning him and making him feel like his thoughts were in his mother's kitchen blender.

"This year's musical will be *Carousel*," Mr. Campbell began announcing. "Interested students are invited to try out Friday, the 21st between 4 and 8 in the auditorium. Mimeographed tryout sheets may be picked up at the front desk in the library anytime over the next two weeks, and copies of the play itself may also be checked out there as well. Because there are a limited number of copies available, students may only check them out for one day. We hope for a great turnout and that *Carousel* will be as successful this year as *Oklahoma!* was last year."

Leo could hardly wait to get home that afternoon and tell his mother that he was going to try out for the role of Billy Bigelow. Nothing less would do.

"Ever since you bought the cast album for me, I've wanted to sing those songs on stage," he continued. "I can't believe I'm gonna get the chance now, can you?"

Louisa trotted out a smile for him and said, "It's wonderful." Then she thought for a moment. "Do you know who else will be trying out?"

"No, but it doesn't matter. I just know I'll get the part."

"Your father and I'll be pulling for you, of course," she said. Her tone sounded cautious.

"You'll see. I'll get it," he said, with a finality that could not be denied.

In the days before the auditions, Leo practiced the assigned tryout song, "You'll Never Walk Alone," over and over, both by himself and with Mrs. Mosby at the music school. That part was easy enough, but he decided there was more to consider. He was nothing like Billy Bigelow in that he didn't understand the entire proposition of pursuing girls earnestly and always getting his way in the matter. That was for athletes like Coy. True, his vocal talents would be on display for all of Beau Pre, and that was what he wanted most—to showcase the voice that had appeared out of nowhere to his delight.

As for the acting part, there was a built-in default that no one else knew about. Again, he was hardly the swaggering, macho, sometimes wife-abuser that Billy Bigelow was. But he had a lot of submerged anger because of the fact that he couldn't be who he was in the real world. To get along, he had chosen therefore to play a game, and there was a part of him that was distressed about having to resort to that. He knew he could bring that sort of resentment to the part, which he felt sure would come across as "being macho" to the audience. He even practiced a "handsome scowl" in the mirror. He felt it would pass muster and would be interpreted in the right way. At any rate, it was the best he could offer under the circumstances.

When the time came, the actual audition went well. He was surprised at his lack of nerves. His voice had never sounded better, he hit the high notes without straining, and he thought his dialogue contained the proper amount of swagger in the brief scene that had been chosen. There was only one other boy, Duane Clement, trying out for the lead, and his singing voice was not nearly as good as his was. Duane, however, was known as quite the ladies' man, so Leo wondered if the committee might lean his way because of that.

Before classes began the following Monday, Mr. Campbell announced the entire cast of *Carousel* over the P.A. system, thankfully ending a stressful weekend for Leo. The nerves that hadn't appeared during the actual auditions showed up on a delayed basis, which annoyed him to no end. He knew he cared way too much about winning, but he couldn't help it. When he finally heard his name called, he remained surprisingly restrained as classmates around him offered their congratulations. Interestingly enough, neither Duane nor Rebecca nor Coy were in first period with him, and he did find himself thinking of all three in entirely different ways when the victory was won.

Rehearsals began in November for the early February run, and word soon began to spread in a way that Leo had not considered. Although none of the rehearsals were open to the student body, the girls in the chorus turned into unpaid publicists about Leo's singing and acting. Not to mention that some of them kept coming up to him and asking if it would be okay if they ran their fingers through his bright auburn hair. He didn't get their fascination with it, but he let them do it anyway. On some level, he realized he still thought of himself as that "redheaded, freckle-faced woodpecker" that his classmate had mocked on the seesaw at recess way back in elementary school.

Nonetheless, there was an explosion of flirting to deal with all the time. Leo had also decided that somewhere along the line, he might want to pursue writing stories the way his father had done professionally, since he did get great grades in English on his essays on Wordsworth and his book reports on such literary masterpieces as *Catcher In The Rye* and *The Return Of The Native*. So he took typing his senior year—one of three boys who seemed decidedly out of place among all the girls. He quickly found himself playing the game again when one of the boys named Willie with a bad case of acne whispered in his ear that the reason he was taking the class was just to ogle Miss Paula Graves, the shapely young teacher with long legs who wore tight skirts and who was fresh out of college.

"Wudd'nchoo like to nail her?" Willie tacked on at the end. "Hot little piece. She's got a pair a' legs to wrap around ya."

Without hesitation, Leo said nothing but nodded, even though he did not like the way that made him feel immediately afterward. Like someone straining to understand a foreign language. Like he had done something wrong.

As it also happened, one of the girls in the class was Coy Warren's little sister, Cammie, just a grade below them both.

"This is for you," she told him with a shy grin, handing over a bag lunch she had prepared just before the class began its first timed writing one morning. "It's just a tuna sandwich and some potato chips just in case you get hungry before lunchtime."

Leo wondered if his eyes were widening as much as his brain was straining to remain calm and focused. "Thanks very much," he told her, taking the bag and quickly taking a peek. "You didn't have to do that."

"I wanted to. You're working hard in the play, I hear. You have to keep up your energy."

The irony was not lost on Leo. Cammie was a smaller, female version of her brother in that she was fit and had an ingratiating smile that attracted people to her. But she wasn't Coy. She wasn't a boy. And she certainly didn't know his secret. For her considerable trouble, all Cammie would get, however, was the initial "thank you," even though Leo knew she was obviously wrangling for a date. What she couldn't have understood was that it would have been soul-crushing for him to appear at her house to take her out, possibly even catching a glimpse of her brother there in the process, who would then occupy his every thought every second of his date with Cammie. Leo simply did not want to put himself through that, and Cammie was left guessing as to why her thoughtfulness was not returned in kind.

The flirting started to take other forms as the weeks passed. There were phone calls from girls at random hours at home, some boldly identifying themselves and asking for dates outright, while others did a lot of sighing and giggling anonymously. At one point, he complained to his mother about it.

"Be polite about it, but hang up and tell them you're not interested," she told him. "After all, you have Rebecca to think of."

The most ingenious attempt at getting his attention, though no more effective than any of the others, took place when there was a knock at the front door one Saturday afternoon after he had just come home from rehearsal; and Leo opened it, as his mother was busy in the kitchen and asked him to get it. There in front of him stood two of his female classmates he recognized from their pictures in the yearbooks but otherwise did not know well: Sharon Bitterman and Leslie Waylon. He supposed other boys thought of them as "nice-looking," but their pleasant, expectant faces hardly registered with him.

"We were driving by," Sharon explained, averting her eyes, "and my car got a flat tire in front of your driveway. Can you believe it? What bad luck! Could you come change it for us?"

Leo somehow remained calm, intuitively realizing what they were up to. He was not about to tell them that he did not know how to change a tire. In the eighth grade, he had been forced to take shop—as all boys were required to do—dealing with terrifying jigsaws that could take fingers off and hot, smelly soldering irons that created blobs that looked like liquid mercury. The whole semester had made him nervous and uncomfortable. Meanwhile, all the girls were required to take home ec, and he didn't see why he couldn't take that instead. He wanted to cook like his mother did, but he had said nothing and resigned himself to going along with it all.

"I'll take a look at it," Leo said to them, bravely gathering himself and somehow projecting an air of confidence.

When they got to the foot of the driveway a few minutes later, the car was positioned perfectly in front of it with the right rear tire practically melting into the asphalt. Such a placement, Leo reasoned, could not have taken place by accident. This had taken some clever and precise planning. But he had been put on the spot, no matter what. Thankfully, his improvisational skills came through for him.

"That tire's unsalvageable," he told them, squatting down to examine it closely. He could clearly see the horizontal slit on the right side. "You're gonna have to buy a new one, so let me go and call a tow truck for you, and they'll take you to Beau Pre Tires. Give me your parents' number, Sharon, and I'll call them and tell them to meet you there."

"Well, if you think that's best," Sharon said, the disappointment clearly registering in her voice.

The extra attention Leo was getting also caused a strain in his relationship with Rebecca. They continued to go out on their platonic dates, but she did not hesitate to tell him about all the gossip going on in the little girl's room at school about him. It galled her to hear her classmates making all sorts of lustful comments about him as they primped in front of the mirror. One even asked her the inevitable question.

"Is he a good kisser?" Tammy Powers, a girl who slathered herself with makeup, wanted to know, as she was spraying her teased hair for good measure. "If you ever get tired of him, I'll take him."

"He's not available," she said in a monotone, glaring at Tammy intensely. "He's mine."

That incident, among others, led to a showdown of sorts between Leo and Rebecca. They were on one of their drive-in dates during which he was telling her all about how the rehearsals were going, since she had not made the cut for the chorus this time and wanted to be kept up to speed.

"Why don't you ever do more than just give me a peck on the cheek?" she asked him finally, after a sip of root beer through her straw. "It took you a while even to do that, you know."

He looked straight ahead, thinking quickly while concentrating on a bug that had recently become a smear on the windshield. What he came up with was, "We're good friends, of course."

"That's not what I asked you. Of course we're friends. You're avoiding the question. Is there something wrong with me?"

"So, you want me to kiss you on the lips?"

"That would be nice, yes."

So without further ado, he kissed her gently on the lips and drew back. It actually wasn't that bad. Her lips were soft and tasted of lipstick, and no one's tongue was involved, which would definitely have been off-putting for him. "Was that okay?"

"Yes." Her smile seemed genuine enough. She took another sip of her root beer and continued. "I really wasn't going to bring this up ever, but it's been bothering me. Cammie Warren said something to me the other day in the little girl's room in between classes."

Leo felt his entire body stiffening as a sense of dread crept in. "Oh?"

"Yes. Seems she brought you a bag lunch in typing class recently and didn't mind confessing to me that she hoped you would ask her out. But you didn't. Now don't get me wrong. I'm glad you didn't because of us, but she says you didn't."

"Right. I didn't. I wasn't interested."

Rebecca exhaled loudly. "You understand that I just think she's jealous, that's all. I think both she and her brother are conceited, especially that Coy."

Leo knew he couldn't delve into the truth regarding the matter, so he played along. "I'm sure you're right. She has to know we've been going out for a while. That was pretty brazen of her."

"But… but she said something horrible to me that I just can't get out of my mind."

Leo felt his stomach muscles tightening. "Yes?"

"I don't even know if I should tell you what she said."

"You've gotten this far. Go ahead, then."

Rebecca took a deep breath that seemed to suck up all the air in the car and continued. "Well, she said that she had told her brother, Coy, what she had done for you and that you hadn't responded except to say thank you, so he said to her that…"

Even as she paused, Leo somehow knew what she was going to say next, and every nerve in his body seemed to wake up and tingle. What he greatly feared had come upon him. Did his secret boy crush somehow see through him from afar? How was that even remotely possible? Maybe the way he threw a baseball in P.E. had gotten more play around school than he realized.

"... Warren said that... maybe you were a... homo. I hated even hearing that word. I suppose it's better than queer, but not by much."

An image flashed into Leo's head of being behind the steering wheel of the Fairlane as it sat stalled on railroad tracks somewhere with a train barreling down fast about to extinguish his very existence. He suddenly found himself speaking words way too emphatically at a decibel level that surprised him. It was almost as if someone else, a stranger, was speaking for him.

"I can assure you, I am not a homo. When I fall in love, it will not be with a man. I will take my time until I find the right person, but I think it's very hateful of Coy Warren to say something like that about me. He doesn't know a thing about me."

"I... I didn't mean to upset you. I debated whether to bring it up at all."

Strangely, the exchange altered everything for Leo. In the beginning, he thought there was no saving grace or silver lining in what Rebecca had revealed. Suddenly, he knew that Coy viewed him with suspicion, which meant that his cover might not be working the way he thought it was. Even more confounding was the fact that Coy was correct in his speculation, however randomly it had been reached; and that led Leo to the realization that there was a part of him—the part that wanted to play the game—that was ashamed of his attraction to Coy on some level. That attraction wasn't going to disappear anytime soon, but something new did emerge—a nearly palpable anger toward Coy.

During the run of the play, Leo brought that anger to the surface from the moment Billy Bigelow's first spoken lines to the mill girls, Julie Jordan and Carrie Pipperidge, reached the ears of the audience. That macho quality he needed to project to be effective in the part—initially a resentment of being in the closet but now amplified immeasurably by Coy's accurate speculation—was never in question. He appeared to become the abusive heterosexual that he was not but that all the girls were swooning over. Was that the way the world worked?

The *Beau Pre Press* reviewer hailed him as "in command of the play from start to finish, an excellent actor with an impressive voice, one that had obviously benefited from instruction at the Marble School of Music." Of course, such praise pleased Granny Marble no end, and she took the entire family out to dinner at the Overlook Inn high above the Mississippi River when *Carousel* had been put to bed.

"You really did the family up proud," she declared, just before everyone clinked rims around the table in Leo's honor.

"Let's don't forget that Miz Mosby deserves a little credit, you know," Leo added after the toast.

"I actually did call her up and invited her to join us," Granny Marble continued. "But she had other plans, otherwise she'd be right here with us. I certainly did the right thing when I hired her. She's more than just that hairdo. I have an eye for these things, you know."

The aftermath of playing Billy Bigelow continued to plague Leo, however. The calls did not stop, although there were no more flat tires in the driveway. There were even "love letters" of sorts that showed up at his father's post office box, no matter how often he was seen around town with Rebecca in tow, continuing his camouflage. It got so annoying that Leo could halfway picture himself going to the principal's office and asking to use the school P.A. system so that he could announce to the entire student body: "I am *not* Billy Bigelow. That was not me up on that stage. Furthermore, to all you girls out there—I really am a homo and not interested in any of you. But thank you all for your interest. Meanwhile, stop with the bag lunches and the flat tires."

Of course, that was never going to happen. All he could do about the situation was to ride it out, keep seeing Rebecca and hoping that this *Carousel* infatuation with him would start to fade.

Perhaps the strangest incident of all regarding his reign as the school's heartthrob happened with Coy Warren himself the week after it was all over. One afternoon as Leo was changing his books in between classes at his locker, Coy came up behind him wearing his star athlete letter jacket, jolting him somewhat.

"I saw you in that play," he said. There was a hint of contempt in his tone. "But that outfit you had on made it look like you had muscles. I'm gonna find out right now."

Turning to face Coy quickly, the only thing Leo could think of to say was, "What?"

He did know what Coy was referring to, however. Billy Bigelow's costume consisted of a tight-fitting, long-sleeved, gold turtleneck with a red-and-green plaid vest worn over it. The combination was extremely colorful, almost peacock-like, as would have been the choice of a carnival barker on the coast of Maine in the late 19th century. It also appeared to make his character's arms look beefier than they were.

"Let me feel your bicep," Coy continued, his tone now slightly threatening. "I wanna see if you really have muscles."

Still taken aback, Leo made a bicep with his right arm, and Coy briefly squeezed it, then released it as if he had been handling a piece of overripe fruit. "Just as I thought," he said. "You don't really have muscles." Coy quickly offered his own bicep. "Feel it. That's what a real muscle feels like, Mr. Billy Bigelow, in case you didn't know."

Leo dutifully did as he was told. "Yes, your muscle is much bigger than mine. I don't think there's anyone who would doubt that. You have to have those kinds of muscles to play football as well as you do."

Apparently satisfied, Coy then smirked and walked away in silence with a swagger. But the anger that rose up after finding out that Coy had suggested to his own sister that Leo might be a homo evaporated right then and there. Leo wanted to laugh out loud at first but instead was content with a startling and somewhat ironic revelation.

Beau Pre High School's football hero was jealous of him.

Most likely because he had always had his choice of girls to date and surely still did. But now some of those same girls were making a fuss over someone else without real muscles who wasn't even an athlete. Word got around fast about all matters related to "who was going with who" and that sort of thing. Leo delved into it further: someone who threw a baseball "like a girl," yet who had played the womanizer of all time onstage. Someone whom Coy had suggested might be a homo, who actually was one and had a mad crush on the school's football hero throughout all of it. Finally, Leo couldn't hold in the complexity of it all any longer, closed his locker and walked away chuckling to himself with a swagger of his own. There were unseen benefits to being a school heartthrob after all.

That night in bed, however, some sort of mental shift occurred. It all boiled down to the way Coy had forced him to form a bicep and then made fun of it.

Billy Bigelow would have done something like that, came into his head and set up camp. He could not let go of the notion. Oddly, he found himself wishing something bad would happen to Coy Warren because of his subtle form of bullying. He did not like the way that made him feel.

One month after *Carousel's* run, things did indeed begin to return more to the "normal" Leo so devoutly coveted and plotted meticulously to maintain. But as he reviewed the entire experience when things settled down, he eventually focused on something he had largely dismissed as insignificant, when in fact it was rather remarkable. And like his vocal prowess, he had no idea where it had come from.

Mr. Campbell, who was the director of the play, summoned him to his office one day before first period and after rehearsals had just started and said, "Leo, I'm having trouble making heads or tails of the first act, even though everything is laid out in the libretto."

"You mean the *Carousel Waltz?* The whole mimed thing?"

"Yes. The blocking seems to be eluding me for some reason, and I'd like for you to take over the direction of it, please. I know it's a lot to ask, but there it is."

Leo didn't hesitate, didn't question his director's dictates, and the words came out of his mouth reflexively. "Sure. I know just what to do with it."

And he did know. He coordinated the dark blue lighting with the opening bars of music, knew when the curtains should first start opening slowly, revealing the opening scene in silhouette, followed by the gradual opening of the see-through scrim and then the moment when the entire scene at the carnival would come to life with a bang in full color, so to speak. It all fell into place and worked beautifully, as if a Broadway director had put a hand in the process long-distance.

"I knew you could do it," Mr. Campbell told him after the first run-through, patting him on the back. "I was baffled."

"How did you know I could do it?" came the reply.

"I just knew somehow."

Leo considered long and hard, looking back on it all. From the vantage point of hindsight, how had he known what to do, and how had Mr. Campbell known he could do it? It fell into the category of things appearing when they were supposed to, like Leo's strong vocal talents after years of nothing to indicate he even had them. As for the staging of the *Carousel Waltz*, the newspaper reviewer had even made mention of the imaginative lighting schemes at the beginning of the play. Leo concluded that he had tapped into something he was destined to experience with *Carousel*, and it registered as a mixed bag of lessons he was supposed to learn.

Chapter 5

Leo was standing up rigidly in the balcony of the First United Methodist Church of Beau Pre with Rebecca by his side. They were both staring down at the coffin being conveyed slowly by six pallbearers through the crowded church to the hearse awaiting outside. To call the procession going on below surreal would have been a woeful understatement. After Leo had picked Rebecca up to attend the services in the Fairlane, which his father had given him outright by then, they were mostly silent on the way there. Neither of them had tears in their eyes, but that hardly meant they weren't filled with unresolved emotions. Certainly for Leo, it had been that way since his mother had gotten that unexpected phone call the day before Thanksgiving and told him what had happened.

Home from college as a freshman at Sewanee, Leo was basking in the reunion with his parents and was looking forward to seeing Granny Marble as well the next day at the dining table. He was sitting on the family room sofa when the call came, and his mother took it in the nearby kitchen with the canary yellow phone hanging on the wall. Leo heard his mother gasping at first, then came the words, "I can't believe it. I can't think of anything worse that could have happened."

Leo sat up straight and frowned as the call continued.

"Do they know yet when the services will be?" he heard his mother saying.

There was a prolonged period of silence as she listened further. Leo knew that someone had died unexpectedly, and his thoughts

35

went immediately to Granny Marble, who was in her late seventies but rarely came down with so much as a head cold. The worst that had happened to her in recent memory was the time she had pricked her finger on one of her flowering cactus plants, and the wound had gotten infected. The fleeting thought that "no one lives forever" seemed of little consolation to him at the moment. And he had been so looking forward to telling her all about his decision to major in music theory at Sewanee, as she had done at Randolph-Macon around the turn of the century.

It seemed like an eternity before his mother finally hung up the phone, although Leo wasted no time going into the kitchen to confront what he knew would be bad news.

"It's Granny Marble, isn't it?" he managed, making hesitant eye contact.

His mother shook her head, and Leo felt an immediate sense of relief. But that soon disappeared when the two of them went over and sat on the sofa and she said as evenly as possible, "Coy Warren was killed in a car wreck driving home today for Thanksgiving from LSU. Apparently, it happened just outside St. Francisville. He was trying to pass one of those big trucks on a curve, and there was another truck that he didn't see coming the other way. That was Rebecca's mother, Geneva, and she said that Coy was apparently killed instantly."

Leo was instantly lost trying to process the news. He had not completely buried the thought he'd had back in high school that something bad should happen to Coy Warren for his bullying swagger. In some twisted way, had he gotten his wish? Leo didn't come to for a long while, retiring to his room and lying on his bed staring at the ceiling. The one-time object of his affection was no longer in this world as he knew it. Furthermore, Coy's future had been so full of promise when he had accepted a scholarship to play football at LSU. Tiger supporters said he was going to be the next Billy Cannon and also win the Heisman Trophy.

What to do now with his shock? And even with the hint of guilt?

During Coy's services, the minister had trotted out that old standby that "God works in mysterious ways." Leo remembered a quote from Coy in the newspaper a while back thanking God for helping him win the Mississippi State Championship in Jackson. God, it seemed, was always getting credit for the good things that happened in life; but this minister was suggesting that perhaps God had had a hand in this terrible car wreck and that we as mere mortals had to accept it.

Leo had instantly recoiled at that notion. What if it had all boiled down to Coy's poor judgment? The guy was always full of himself. What if he had stayed in his lane conservatively, no matter what? Would he still be alive? Or did that simply not come into play? Coy had played football with reckless abandon, juking and jerking and taking chances he should never have taken; but mostly being rewarded with success when he lit up the scoreboard with six points.

Not this time. Surely, Leo's dark wish about something bad happening had had nothing to do with it. He came to no definite conclusion about it all and instead concentrated on all the flowers decorating Coy's coffin. They, too, gave him no answers. They were just pretty to look at and did nothing to mitigate all the emotions he was feeling from grief to guilt.

Somewhat wrung out by the sights and sounds of sturdy grown men in their best suits and women of all ages in varying shades of gray and black crying unabashedly in unison below, Leo and Rebecca chose not to accompany the procession to the grave-side ritual at the Beau Pre Cemetery overlooking the Mississippi River and headed home, again in silence. Finally, Rebecca spoke up, sounding thoroughly intimidated.

"Where do you honestly think Coy is right now?"

Leo didn't have to think twice about his response because he had examined that very question from every possible angle over the past couple of days. "I don't know, and I don't think I'm meant to know. At least, not right now."

"But what about what we're taught in church? Don't you believe any of that?"

"Does it satisfy you? Does it make sense of things? I mean, I was okay with being an acolyte in the Episcopal Church, but I'm not sure I really learned anything. In the end, I was just helping out by serving wafers and wine. I didn't think of it as any more spiritual than being a lunch lady in the school cafeteria. That might sound flippant, but I'm telling you the truth."

Rebecca did not answer for a while. When she did, she still sounded anything but confident. "What else is there to believe in? Are we supposed to wander around without any guidance?"

"To be honest with you," Leo said, "I haven't figured anything out yet about my life. Things seem to happen to me, they seem to pop up out of nowhere, and I have to deal with them the best way I can. I'd like to think there was something behind it all, but I just don't know at this point. I'm open to all kinds of possibilities and interpretations, I'll at least say that for myself."

They had finally arrived at Rebecca's driveway, but she turned to him and asked him to shut off the engine for a moment and not to walk her to the door right away.

"Maybe this isn't the best time to bring it up, but I have something very important to tell you," she began. "I haven't mentioned it in the letters I've written to you because, well, I wasn't exactly sure how it would turn out. But now, it's become a thing, so I need to tell you."

Turning her way briefly, Leo said, "What's become a thing?"

She looked down into her lap at her black dress, neatly resting her hands. "I didn't worry about you finding someone else since you were at Sewanee, which is all-male. But Millsaps is co-ed, and the bottom line is I've gotten interested in another boy. His name is Eddie Young, and I really like him a lot. We first met in French class and have started doing things together. I know this may sound silly to you, but he has this way of curling up his lip just the way Elvis does, and it sorta gets to me. I don't think he's actually doing an interpretation. It just seems to happen naturally with him."

Leo actually felt a great sense of relief and exhaled. "I'm happy for you. Really, I am."

She matched his up-tempo mood. "Good to hear. I was worried you might get upset."

"No, I'm not upset at all."

"What I'm gonna tell you is in strictest confidence, and you might not understand this," she continued. "But I was tired of being a "good girl," if you get my drift."

Leo was not about to let her know that he understood completely, that he had counted on her being a "good girl" the past few years, that he had not wanted her to ask for more than the polite kisses he had given her when she asked. That he had never even bought a condom at the drug store or in a men's room somewhere because he was still a virgin and therefore didn't even know how to use them. His father had never even had "that kind" of conversation with him, almost as if he had known it would not be necessary. Tactfully, he did not ask her to elaborate at her end, as he definitely did not intend to do at his. Above all, there was still the matter of protective coloration.

Instead, he tried to sound as philosophical as possible. "After all, we've gone off to different schools, and it was inevitable that we would meet other people. I'm glad you've found someone you're happy with, and I hope it continues to work out for you."

"Thanks for understanding. I'll keep you posted."

Leo walked her to the front door, gave her a hug and said goodbye. On the way back to the Fairlane, he had the overwhelming sense that the chapter of his life featuring Rebecca on its pages was possibly coming to an end.

In the spring of the following year, Leo received a lengthy, rambling letter from Rebecca that made him feel guilty about his camouflage relationship and the toll it might have taken on her. One particular paragraph hit him over the head like a great boulder as he sat on the edge of his dorm room bed wading through it all in between classes:

*... and when I told my parents, they thought the best thing
to do was for me to drop out of Millsaps, which I will do next
week. Once I get home, we'll all decide whether I should keep
it or not. I'm three months in, and I don't show yet. Eddie
denies that it's his, but he's the only guy I've ever been with so
of course it has to be. I mean, who does he think he's fooling?
I felt like I should tell you because I didn't want you to hear it
through the grapevine back in Beau Pre and wonder if it was
true. I hope you understand and don't think anything less of
me because of what's happened...*

That last sentence packed a wallop, and he found himself
gripping the bedspread to steady himself. Think anything less of
her? Far from it. Instead, it made him feel less of himself. Had
keeping her at arm's length driven her into the arms of the first,
Elvis-lip-curling, slick operator that came along? Had he somehow made her feel undesirable and therefore anxious to finally
prove herself as a woman because he had...

He resisted forming the question in his head as long as he
could, but it finally broke through; and he said it out loud for the
first time, though it had never been very far beneath the surface.

"Should I have used her that way?"

The more he thought about it, the worse it made him look
and feel. He had only considered what his platonic relationship
with Rebecca had meant to him, had done for him. It had all
been to maintain a lie. Yet, the alternative seemed entirely unten-
able, too. To tell the world he liked members of his own sex, to
tell his parents, to tell Granny Marble, to tell anyone he knew
might mean the complete destruction of the comfort zone which
he had carved out for himself and inside of which he lived. If
it could be called living. It was more like having a great weight
pressing down upon him—head, shoulders and all. It was like
being underwater and glancing up at the sunlight and oxygen
that existed above, where everybody else could breathe freely and

splash around in the water joyously without thinking about it. Meanwhile, it was a constant struggle for him to keep from sinking to the bottom.

It made him feel like so much sediment. Everything had been problematic for him for a very long time. And now, everything was problematic for Rebecca. At the end of her letter, she had asked Leo to keep everything confidential. For now. Decisions had to be made, and she honestly didn't know how things would turn out. She did confess to him that she couldn't imagine becoming a mother at the age of eighteen going on nineteen.

"I don't really know anything about anything. I'm not qualified to give birth and be a mother. I still feel like a little girl," were the exact sentences she had penned, followed by, *"I really don't think I should have this baby, and nobody can convince me otherwise. I hear people in church talking about ending a pregnancy as a huge sin, but I know they're not going through what I'm going through."*

Leo put himself in her place. He could not possibly envision himself as a father to a child. He hadn't even begun to figure out his own life and what steps to take to make it work better than it had been. How would having a son or daughter to take care of at his age make things better? He knew deep down that it couldn't possibly and that it would be an unholy mess.

But then, he wasn't the one carrying a child. Rebecca was, and her letter had intimated that there was nothing planned about it. So, she was dropping out and coming home to make perhaps the most important decision of her life with her parents by her side; and he would not be a part of the equation.

That was when Leo made a life-changing decision of his own. He targeted the summer between his freshman and sophomore years in college as the proper time to tackle the great weight on his shoulders.

Chapter 6

Shortly before the Fourth of July the summer between Leo's freshman and sophomore years in college, Joseph Marble sat down with his wife and son on the long family room sofa after her delicious dinner of shrimp gumbo and jalapeño cornbread; and then he announced solemnly that the firm of Carter and Marble would no longer be practicing law. Blaine Carter had been diagnosed with terminal prostate cancer and had less than three months to live.

"I'll be on my own soon," he told them. "It may make a difference in how we live down the road."

"Why?" Louisa said, after expressing her condolences about his long-time partner. "Won't you still have the same clients?"

"Some of them have already peeled off and gone over to Bailey, Perkins and Van Camp because they always dealt with Blaine, not me. As you know, he'd bring them into the firm, I'd do the legal work behind the scenes, and he'd handle all the court appearances. I've been pretty much the unseen partner. Blaine's always been the schmoozer and then the slickster during the actual trials. Me, almost never, unless Blaine was sick. I never talked to you all that much about that aspect of our practice because I didn't see any need to. Everything was working fine for us the way it was. We were a big hit, and we weren't about to change the formula."

"Yes, I know. But I must go over and see Leslie Anne soon. She must be totally devastated," Louisa added, referring to her counterpart on the Carter team with whom she was congenial but not particularly close. They did not see eye-to-eye on a number of subjects important to Beau Pre Society, most of which were not of a life-and-death nature, however.

"I'm sure she'll appreciate the handholding. She's got a rough stretch ahead of her. The doctors say Blaine may not even have those three months. He could go fast."

"At the risk of sounding callous about it, can't Blaine ask the clients to stick with you?" Louisa continued.

Joseph's voice dropped to almost a whisper. "He's tried, but he's gotten very sick, very fast, as I said, and Bailey, Perkins and Van Camp have swooped in mercilessly as the big rivals they've always been. It's not illegal to do what they've done, but I think it's damned unethical of them."

Louisa sounded a bit frightened now. "What did you mean by that remark about how we live? We're not gonna have to sell the house and move, or anything like that, are we?"

"No, nothing that drastic, but we'll just have to massage our budget until I can bring in some new clients," he explained further. "No vacation this year, of course. No impulse purchases, that sort of thing."

Louisa's tone had a tinge of resignation. "Clipping coupons and redeeming books of Green Stamps, you mean."

"I think that'll help, yes, although I don't want to frighten you. We just need to be as frugal as we can."

Leo took the news hard but said nothing to either of his parents about his own concerns. His plan had been to sit down with them and reveal that their worries about him in his very early teens regarding his interest in girls were justified; that he had been back then and still was crushing on boys. It was not a "phase." That Coy Warren and Dean Forsythe, the latter whom they already knew about, had been the only objects of his affection since puberty. Perhaps this would be a bad time to let all of that out of the bag with everything so delicately balanced in the days to come.

Back in his room, he plopped onto his bed and considered the plight of his father's partner. He hadn't had that much contact with him, but there had been that cocktail party a few years back among many that his parents had thrown, and Blaine and Leslie Ann Carter had been invited, of course.

Again through the louver door, a habit he could not seem to break, Leo had overheard Blaine holding forth among the guests in the spacious family room with its vaulted ceiling in the midst of telling an awful joke.

"Did you hear the one about the guy...he was walking down Bourbon Street with his fly wide open?" Blaine was saying, his speech a bit slurred. "He was... getting ready to troll for queers."

The punch line met with a sprinkling of laughter among those who had probably had more than one drink by then. It had caused Leo to wince, and then he wondered if his own father and mother were among those who were finding it amusing. He fervently hoped they were not. In fact, he decided that there was no way they could have—that is, if he wanted to be able to sleep at night.

From that point forward, Leo viewed Blaine Carter as the type of person who was part of his problem, but he also concluded that he could say nothing about it to his parents. The short, ruddy-faced man was fond of liquor and cheesy jokes, bought his clothes a size too small thinking that that would hide the fact he was overweight by a good thirty pounds or so; when in fact, it only made his buttons look like they were about to fly off his suit vests at any moment, becoming lethal weapons. Now, after hearing this tragic news about him, there was a part of Leo that wasn't sympathetic at all, although he found himself stopping short of dredging up that old adage that the man had "reaped what he had sown." He really didn't want to believe the universe worked that way. That it was designed to punish or even reward. He saw things as more subtle than that. To him, fire and brimstone was completely wrong-headed, and he firmly rejected the idea he had briefly entertained about Coy Warren that something bad *should* happen to his father's partner.

More importantly, the terminal illness and the dissolution of his father's partnership would send Leo back to the darkness of the closet for a while longer. That, after he had meticulously rehearsed a grand monologue which he thought would cover all the bases for his parents and then some. Well, it would just have to be postponed until the family was not in such a crisis mode. There were coupons to clip, stamps to redeem, budgets to massage and places not to visit with a camera.

For Leo's nineteenth birthday in August, his parents took him out to eat at the Overlook Inn, and it was there that Leo spied Rebecca and her parents getting up from their table way across the room and heading out after the dinner they had obviously just enjoyed. They did not appear to have seen him or his parents; or if they had, they had chosen not to come over for a visit or even acknowledge them with a wave of the hand. He had heard nothing further from Rebecca over the past three months, and he interpreted that as a plea for privacy. She had sworn him to secrecy, but he could still do the math. He had received her "tell-all" letter in early April at Sewanee, and three-and-a-half more months had passed. She would now be close to seven months along and should definitely be showing. But the outfit she was wearing there at the restaurant was decidedly not of the maternity variety. What she had chosen was showing off her tiny waist to excellent effect. She was clearly back to the expensive styles she had always worn.

He decided not to dwell on it mentally, though he did wonder if she intended to resume her college career at Millsaps. Yet he realized that he couldn't contact her about that without the inevitable coming up at some point. Maybe he didn't really want to know. To put himself at ease somewhat, he imagined that the Bentleys had seen him and his parents come into the dining room but had chosen not to approach them to avoid any awkwardness. For his own well-being, he chose not to speculate any further; and, in fact, he never heard from Rebecca again on that or any other matter.

Leo's freshman year at Sewanee had found him trying out for and winning chorus parts in two big musical productions. First semester was Gilbert and Sullivan's *The Mikado,* with its dizzying, rhyme-a-second lyrics; while the next semester featured the more blue collar, straightforward *Guys and Dolls.* During both, his vocal talents had not escaped the attention of the school's Choirmaster, Mr. Harvey Markham, who appealed to him at the beginning of his sophomore year in his office at All Saints Cathedral to "come join God's fold on Sundays," as he put it. He was one of those people who was never without a broad smile on his long, lean face, but there was nothing phony about him, either. Church hymns, he often said to anyone who would listen, were a combination of mathematics and music, both of which were universal languages. They, at least, were not imaginary.

However, Leo told him forthrightly that hymns were not his favorite type of music to sing. "I'm a Broadway show tune kind of guy," he explained further. "I've been playing them at the piano since middle school. You name it, I can play it. I'm especially partial to Rodgers and Hammerstein. Some people swear by Lerner and Loewe and *My Fair Lady,* but I'll always be an R & H man, myself."

"Then you must come over and meet my wife some evening. We'll have you over for dinner. My Margaret was a member of the chorus of the original cast of *Carousel* way back in 1945. She remained throughout the entire run."

Mr. Markham had said the magic words, and Leo felt a huge surge of adrenaline. "I'd love to do that. I played the role of Billy Bigelow in our high school production my senior year. My director even let me choreograph the entire *Carousel Waltz,* and my mother was pregnant with me in New York when she saw a performance of the original run. And here it all is coming up again in my life in a way I would never have expected."

"Margaret could probably answer a hundred questions you might have," Mr. Markham continued. Then that bright smile of his dimmed only slightly and he leaned in. "That's where I met her. I was studying at Juilliard and attended one of her performances. Another cast member introduced us after it was over, and the truth is, I eventually took her away from all those footlights and greasepaint. Of course, she tells me all the time how happy she is being a choirmaster's wife at a liberal arts college like Sewanee instead of still being on the boards. It's quite the change, you must admit."

Leo felt an indefinable kinship with Margaret Markham when he showed up for dinner a week later. He could see why she had been chosen for the *Carousel* chorus nearly twenty years earlier. She had one of those valentine-shaped faces with an easy smile, and her streaked-blonde hair still fell to her shoulders in a most becoming fashion. She was no slouch as a cook, either, offering up a satisfying menu of baked chicken, grilled asparagus, and rice pilaf. Slices of homemade caramel cake with demitasse followed that.

"I don't think I'll ever get the score of *Carousel* out of my system," Leo said, sipping his coffee as the three of them sat around the living room after dinner. "I think it's the best that Rodgers and Hammerstein ever did together. There's such depth in the songs, and the libretto is both brilliant and sad, considering it tackles the big question of what happens after we die. It's the only one of their collaborations that does."

Margaret Markham smiled graciously. "There's that, yes, but I'm sure you have your favorite numbers. Let me guess—"If I Loved You" and "Soliloquy"."

"Half right. The tour-de-force that's "Soliloquy", of course. Seven minutes of singing about becoming a father and what sex the baby will be and all that comes with it. But even though I didn't sing it, I've always been partial to "June Is Bustin' Out All Over". It's so full of joy about the outbreak of summer. Rebirth, I suppose. They say Maine stays pretty cold throughout the spring.

Not that I've lived up there, but so I've been told. Someday, I'd like to experience Maine in June and be that enthusiastic about everything coming to life all over again."

"You're quite the philosopher, young man," Margaret said. Then she put down her cup on the nearby end table and pointed to the grand piano in one corner of the room. "And that was the chorus number that I liked best, too. I just happen to have all the sheet music from *Carousel* in my plantation desk. Would you like for me to dig it out, and maybe the two of us could sing a number or two together? Come on, it'll be fun."

"I'd love to," Leo said.

So, while Harvey Markham looked on approvingly with his customary smile in place, Leo and his wife trotted out "What's The Use of Wond'rin?" for her to sing while he accompanied her effortlessly on the piano. Then, the two reversed roles while he sang "If I Loved You"; and finally, the three of them got together on "June Is Bustin' Out All Over," with Harvey the last to perform on the keys.

After the delightful impromptu singalong had ended, Leo had to fight off the urge to ask the Markhams to adopt him. Instead, he settled for a more mundane question. "What was it like to work with John Raitt?"

Margaret rolled her bright blue eyes and managed a brief wolf whistle. "All of us in the chorus had mad crushes on him, even though we knew he was very married and therefore off-limits. That booming voice of his made us all melt every time, of course, and he was a towering, swaggering specimen to boot. And then, you might not know this, but his understudy was Howard Keel. You talk about a yummy backup."

"I know how crushes work," Leo said. "Believe me." Then he caught himself. "Not that I'm a towering specimen or that I was married, you understand. It was just that most of the girls in our high school went crazy on me. I wasn't ready for it, not by a long shot. The truth is, there was an avalanche of flirtation, and I didn't handle it very well."

The Markhams laughed, and Margaret said, "Everyone should be adored at least once in their lifetime. It's very good for the soul. Harvey and I speak from nearly twenty years of marriage." Then followed the perfunctory "we must do this again sometime" sentiments, and the evening was over at last.

Leo went to sleep that night in the dorm with a single observation stuck in his head: his mother had seen Margaret Markham onstage at the Majestic Theatre nearly two decades ago, and now, here she was in the flesh.

What to make of it, if anything? A brief reminder that he could never be the type of man he had portrayed in *Carousel*? That it was time to search for authenticity?

In the end, Leo decided to take Mr. Markham up on his invitation to join the choir. It was the least he could do for the man for bringing such serendipity into his life. It also occurred to him that in a roundabout way, he was also paying tribute to Granny Marble and her double major in music and math.

Chapter 7

An all-male college like Sewanee relieved the pressure Leo had felt all his life to present that "normal" face to the world. Since there were no coeds, his parents did not expect him to write home about his new girlfriend, or his old girlfriend or anything in-between. For that he was grateful. That said, it also served to present many opportunities from time to time for him to lift the lid on who he really was. For instance, there was that prolonged discussion in Drama Class his junior year on what Robert Anderson's intentions might have been in writing *Tea and Sympathy*. It was familiar territory for Leo because he had actually seen the film ten years earlier at the Beau Pre Cinema with Deborah Kerr and John Kerr playing the leading roles. At that time in the mid-fifties in Beau Pre, the theaters were the first to get air conditioning, and Louisa Marble frequently took herself and Leo to the movies to escape the oppressive heat and humidity. Never mind that some of the films—like *East of Eden* and *Tea and Sympathy*—might not exactly be appropriate for ten-year-olds. In fact, the only thing that stood out for Leo while watching John Kerr portraying Tom Lee was that the character was called a "sissy" for not walking the right way, playing the wrong sport, and apparently not having a girlfriend to write home to his father about.

During the Sewanee discussion, Haywood Laurens, Jr., whom Leo regarded as an obnoxious know-it-all curiously fond of loud bowties, lit the fuse. "It's about the fear of being queer. Really obvious to me. Tom Lee plays tennis instead of being on the football team, and his father worries about him because of that. Tom also likes to hang around with the faculty wives, so clearly he prefers the company of women, but not in the right way."

Leo couldn't help himself. "There's nothing sissy about playing tennis. I think his father was a big, braying jackass who couldn't accept that his son was different."

"Maybe," Haywood said. "But when it comes down to it, don't we all have a fear of being queer?"

Professor Donald Mayhew, a small, balding man who was rather soft-spoken himself, intervened. "That's debatable, Haywood. I don't think we should frame this discussion in those terms. Let's move on. Does anyone else have any insights?"

Leo rose to the occasion. "I think the play is a plea for tolerance for sensitivity in men. There at the end when Tom makes love to his housemother, or his housemother makes love to him if you want to look at it that way, it's quite clear that he likes women in the traditional way and that he had been unjustly persecuted all along for being different. We can't all walk and talk and be the same, after all."

"That's more in line with my thinking," Professor Mayhew added.

"Being different is not the same as being queer," Haywood added. "No two ways about it."

Leo wanted to come back with "Do you speak from experience?" but chose not to say anything further about either Tom Lee's fictional, sexual proclivities or his own, taking note of the intense glare he was getting from Haywood. The thought crossed his mind that maybe Haywood was one of those guys who "doth protest too much" because he, himself, was an expert on the subject of protective coloration. There was always the possibility that the bulk of the discussion was being borne by two closet cases, and the whole thing made Leo feel bad about himself.

Then there was the Saturday evening in the housemother's suite that nearly triggered him into the personal revelation to others that he had been avoiding for so long. As it happened, all the dorms at Sewanee had housemothers in the manner of *Tea and Sympathy*. Each of the retired or widowed women lived in a small suite with a common room where students could come in for cookies, conversation or just to watch a TV program to pass the time. Mrs. Inez Browning, a large woman who seemed to change her hair color every other month and was more than garrulous and good at her job, had been assigned to McCleary Hall with its four-student suites and shared bathroom concept.

On the particular Saturday evening in question, a handful of boys, including Leo, were all watching *The Heiress* with Olivia DeHavilland on Mrs. Browning's modest, black-and-white TV set. Some flighty commentary was being provided now and then by Estes Mulhearn, a short, chubby student whose speech patterns and gestures were decidedly hyperbolic and easy to mock behind his back.

"I think Olivia DeHavilland is the most elegant actress Hollywood has ever produced. And I mean ever," he was saying, waving his hand about like a wand. "Elegant, just elegant. Just look at her, isn't she elegant? I love her dresses and hairdos, too. Don't you?"

Buck Thames, tall and sturdy and one of Sewanee's best athletes who played on both the football and basketball teams, bristled. "Okay, we get it. She's elegant and dresses up all the time. Can you give us a break? We don't need subtitles from your mouth."

Unfortunately, Estes chose to argue. "You don't have to get so snippy about it. I have a right to my opinion, don't I, Miz Browning?"

"Why don't we all just watch the movie in silence?" she said as calmly as possible. "We could discuss it later."

Estes rose from his seat on the sofa in a huff. "I've already seen it, and all I was doing was just praising a Hollywood legend. Plenty of people have their favorite actors and actresses that they admire. And I have better things to do than argue with you, Buck Thames." And with that, he made a dramatic exit, narrowing his eyes and turning back to focus on the entire group one last time. Bette Davis could not have done it better.

"No, Estes, don't leave," Mrs. Browning said.

"Can you believe that guy?" Buck said after Estes was gone. "Is he for real? That wrist of his is enough to make me wanna puke. You'd think he had a one-word vocabulary—elegant. Also, if you ask me, I think he'd had a little too much to drink. I ought to know, sitting there right next to him. His breath smelled like sherry. Gross."

"That's enough of that, Buck," Mrs. Browning said, shaking her henna-rinsed head. "Let's just all finish watching the movie."

Calm settled over the common room again, but Leo was deeply conflicted. Although his personality was nothing like Estes's, he felt a bond with him nonetheless. He wanted to speak up and put Buck Thames in his place but chose not to. Buck was Coy Warren all over again, and Leo thought it best not to dwell on him too much. That brief period of his life had left a very bad taste in his mouth.

Meanwhile, there were several other boys like Estes on campus—*effeminate* would have been the word of choice. And there were rumors swirling around constantly about "affairs" that were taking place in this dorm or that one. The tone of disdain coming out of certain mouths was quite evident, and it had the same chilling effect on Leo that the now-departed Blaine Carter had had telling a "queer joke" at his parents' cocktail party years ago.

None of the gossip around campus stopped Leo from secretly admiring certain boys from afar, however—mostly privileged fraternity types with floppy haircuts and a slightly snobbish aura about them. Especially the boys from Charleston and Savannah and Wilmington and Richmond and other legendary gene pools of the Old South. True, Beau Pre fit that profile in the state of Mississippi, being the oldest city on the river, but those on the Atlantic Coast were even older and more prestigious yet, and Leo found the cachet of their young male residents to be a bit intoxicating.

53

As for Leo's roommates and suitemates in McCleary Hall his first three years, they were all variously boring, uninspiring, and mismatched in any regard whatsoever. He couldn't click with any of them. His freshman year, Rollie Peyton was a Forestry major who was friendly enough but was always talking about his girlfriend back home. Sophomore year was no better; Carl Tomlinson was a biology major who spent most of his time doing lab work and remaining somewhat aloof. Junior year was Ralph Searway, an English major who lamented all the time that he wasn't born in the time of Shakespeare and boasted of being a High Church Anglican. All they basically shared was the small bathroom with two sinks, one shower and one toilet; except for the occasional movie they might see together at Campus Theater. His suitemates were contemptuous, for instance, of the film, *The Group,* when it played there.

"Candice Bergen is super-hot playing that Lakey, no question," Vernon Lowndes, already sporting a beer gut at the tender age of nineteen, declared back in the suite. "Too bad she was a lesbian. What a waste! I mean, no woman can offer what a man does."

Leo had read and enjoyed Mary McCarthy's novel, but decided it wasn't worth the effort to try to explain the character. Plus, no one on campus had made any advances to him at any time under any circumstances, nor had he been really tempted to offer the same to anyone. He concluded that he was worthless in putting out any kind of signal and wondered frankly if anything would ever give him the courage to emerge from the closet before he graduated. Or to his parents. Ever.

Chapter 8

Leo's roommate his senior year was an unexpected freshman surprise. To begin with, he had not received notice from the Dean of
Resident Life all summer that he would even be having someone
in the room with him. Based on his past roommate selection
failures, he had not bothered to contact anyone else on campus
to come and join him at McCleary. He was hoping that he could
have his room all to himself, therefore.

When he walked into his room that first day back and saw
this gangly guy who had made up the bed that had been his for
the past three years, he recoiled visibly. "Who are you?"

Managing a timid smile to accompany the blush that came to
his cheeks, the boy said, "I'm Greg Lightman, your roommate."

Leo made no attempt to disguise his annoyance. "That's my
bed you just made up, you know. And I wasn't informed I even
had a roommate."

Sounding thoroughly apologetic, Greg said, "I wondered
why I hadn't heard from you all summer. They sent me a letter
in June telling me you were a senior. And I thought to myself,
'Good, someone who can show me the ropes.' I really thought
I'd caught a break."

"Well, I didn't get any such letter," Leo told him. "That's
why you didn't hear anything from me. Must've been a glitch
on their part." Leo paused and realized that neither of them
were responsible for what was happening at the moment and
decided to soften his tone.

"Would you do me a favor and take the other bed, please? I'm used to that one you just made up with those linens and plaid bedspread of yours."

"Sure," Greg said, sounding eager to please.

Leo began putting some of his things into drawers and watched his new roommate transferring the linens from bed to bed out of the corner of his eye. Greg was about the same height as he was, only not particularly filled out yet. His hair was a much darker shade of red than his, but there were no freckles on his face. To the casual observer, the two boys might have even come off like brothers, even though Greg had dark brown eyes, and Leo had inherited his mother's blue eyes.

After the roommates had settled in completely an hour or so later, mostly in silence, they sat on the edge of their beds and eyed each other somewhat awkwardly.

"I didn't mean to sound so abrupt with you a while back," Leo said. "It's just that you really were a surprise to me standing there like it had always been your room. I've made a lot of memories here these past three years, and I guess I came off as a bit territorial. Seniors can get like that, I guess."

Greg managed a smile. "I understand. I guess I shouldn't have been the first to arrive and make decisions about the sleeping arrangements. Maybe I should have waited for you to show up."

That seemed to finally break the ice, and Leo said, "Listen, I'm really not a bad guy to live with. I write a column in the *Sewanee Purple* in which I try very hard to find humor in college life if I possibly can and refrain from making too many comments about how bad the food is in the cafeteria. Believe me, it's the same old thing every day of the week. We've even had food fights to protest, turning over tables, making bunkers out of them and throwing some unbelievably hard biscuits at each other. Also, I've changed my major from Music to English and back to Music, and I don't snore. At least, not that I know of. I've had a roommate or two that did, though. I don't think they were ever aware that I would reach over and hit them in the face a couple of times with my pillow to make them wake up with a snort and stop. You don't make all kinds of noises, do you?"

Greg nodded and kept smiling. "Don't think so. I guess you'll tell me if I do, though. As for declaring a major, I don't have any idea yet. I wonder how many freshmen actually do. I talked a little bit to the two guys in the other half of the suite, and they said they're gonna take it all one step at a time. Looks like you've got three freshmen on your hands."

Leo winced slightly and said, "That's why I think Sewanee's liberal arts approach is the way to go, unless you're determined to become a doctor or a lawyer. Then, the path is pretty clear."

What was not clear to Leo was how much effort to put into his friendship with Greg. There was the obvious difference in age, no opportunity to take the same classes, and only a couple of hours at night after dinner in the cafeteria to catch up on anything that might be going on in their lives. True, the Vietnam War came up now and then, especially their opposition to it. Watching the latest reports on the evening news with Walter Cronkite on Mrs. Browning's set kept them well-informed on the latest, and they realized that at least their politics were the same.

Despite all that, however, a bond began to form slowly between the two through pop music. At bedtime, Leo would tune his radio to WLS in Chicago, and they would listen to the Top 40 hits of 1967-1968 together, discovering that they liked the same tunes. Two in particular seemed to have been produced just for them. The first was "I'd Like To Get To Know You" by Spanky and Our Gang. The beguiling lyrics and melody invited anyone listening to get closer to someone else they knew; and Leo was sorely tempted to ask Greg if the song made sense to him that way and if they should do anything about it. Yet, he did not follow through. And then there was epic "McArthur Park" by Richard Harris, the unlikeliest of recording artists. The high notes he tried for amused both of them to no end, as did the psychedelic lyrics promoting leaving cakes out in the rain and other cryptic, hippie-flavored images.

"I can't believe that's a song," Greg said with a snicker the first time it came on the radio. "Do you think he was on LSD when he recorded it? I wonder if he did it on a dare."

"Richard Harris is a classic actor, not a singer," Leo said. "Apparently, no one's told him any different."

Funniest of all for Leo was the sound of Greg singing "McArthur Park" in the shower before their day began. When Greg switched from his regular voice to falsetto there at the end, it never failed to bring an affectionate smile to Leo's face.

Affection.

Leo felt it building as the semester progressed but did not know what to do with it. It was there in the very center of his being just begging for more attention. There were times when he wanted nothing more than to throw back his covers, move purposefully to Greg's bed to lean down and kiss him gently on the lips. Finally, between Thanksgiving and Christmas holidays, he made up his mind that he was going to level with Greg about his feelings for men in general and even go so far as to ask if they might explore any feelings the two of them might have for each other. Greg never talked about a girl back home or anything like that, nor, of course, did he. He was going to use "I'd Like To Get To Know You" as his jumping off point and go from there.

When he got to his room following his afternoon Art Class that particular day, Greg was not in the bedroom or the small study room, though he usually was at that hour. That left only the bathroom as a possibility, so Leo knocked on the door.

"Hey, Greg, you in there? If you are, I'd like to talk to you about something when you get through," he said.

"I'm in here, but I'm looking at myself in the mirror and crying," Greg told him. "I'm not sure I'll ever be through."

The door opened slowly, and Greg stood there facing him, his eyes bloodshot, his cheeks pink and wet with tears.

Leo reached out reflexively and took his hand. "What the hell's happened to you?"

"I... I just got a long-distance call from my brother in

Lexington. Preston said my mother died this morning of a heart attack. My mother's gone, Leo, she's gone."

Instinctively, Leo led him into the bedroom where they sat next to each other on Greg's bed. "I'm so sorry, Greg. I can't imagine how you must feel right now. If there's anything I can do..."

"I don't know what I'm gonna do," Greg continued, not bothering to hold back sobs between sentences. "My father died ten years ago, so now I'm by myself. I don't even know where I'll live or who gets the house, even though Preston said I would be welcome to come live with him and Sherrie. That's his wife."

Leo thought for a moment and said, "Do you know yet when the services will be?"

Greg looked down at the bedspread and shook his head, his eyes half-lidded. "Preston said in a couple of days. I'll be going home to Lexington, of course, but...but I wonder if I'll be coming back. What would be the point? What's the point of anything anymore?"

Finally, Leo knew the moment that had eluded him for so long had arrived, but he was conscious of wording things carefully considering Greg's precarious emotional state. He definitely would have to discard the little revelatory speech he had prepared based on the Spanky and Our Gang lyrics. "You have my friendship, Greg," he said instead. "This won't change that."

Greg caught his gaze, and Leo knew a definite connection of a different caliber had been made. "Thanks, Leo. That's very sweet of you to say."

"I mean it."

"Yes, I know you do." Greg exhaled but kept the intense eye contact.

"In just a few months we've come a long way since that first mix-up about the beds. I still regret the way I acted," Leo added.

Greg managed a hint of a smile, and his body posture straightened a bit. "Thank goodness for WLS late at night, right?"

Leo nodded quickly.

Then he braced himself, leaned in and gave Greg a gentle

kiss on the cheek. He could taste the salt of his roommate's tears when he drew back slightly, and Greg's eyes, which had been half-lidded up until that moment, widened significantly. "I like you as more than a roommate, Greg. I want you to know that, whatever else happens from here on out. No matter what you decide to do after your mother's funeral. But for what it's worth, and if you can manage it, I hope you'll come back to Sewanee so we can at least finish out the year together."

Then the two boys hugged and remained physically connected that way for nearly a minute. It did not feel awkward for Leo, and he sensed that Greg was having the same reaction. What pleased Leo the most was that he hadn't actually had to use the word *homosexual* in his revelation to Greg. That seemed a clinical and distasteful approach dumped upon him by others, whereas what he had actually said expressed heartfelt emotions that came from deep within. He didn't see how that could be wrong, especially since his roommate was in perhaps the biggest crisis of his young life. Far from something to be ashamed of, Leo felt that what he had expressed was akin to a much-needed lifeline.

"I can't go to Lexington with you, though," Leo said, after they finally broke apart. "I've got exams this week."

"I understand. I'm supposed to take them, too. Just don't worry about it."

"But I'll worry about *you*."

"I'll call you after I've talked things over with Preston, and they read my mother's will."

Suddenly, Leo felt that his life was on hold as much as Greg's was.

Two days later, after what felt more like two weeks, the call came through on the second-floor phone out in the hallway, and Leo leaned against the white wall with all the numbers, names and brief messages scribbled on it, hanging on Greg's every word.

"Preston and I will sell the house together, and I'll move in with him temporarily," he was saying after briefly describing the services in strained fashion. "He says I can do some odd jobs for him at his insurance company until I can find something better. But we'll split the money from the sale of the house, so I'll be okay financially. Maybe I'll come back next fall, but I just don't have the will for school right now. I wish I did, but I just don't."

Leo felt an old, unwelcome feeling in the pit of his stomach. He had hurt just that way when he had experienced his first mad crush on Dean Forsythe in the Junior Little Theatre play at the age of thirteen. Now, he was twenty-one and just as heartsick. He had to make a plea.

"But, Greg, what about our friendship? Won't that make any difference to you?"

There was a long silence. Then, "We'll always be friends. What you've told me will always mean a lot to me. But you have to understand that something happened to me when my mother died."

"But if you wait until next fall, I'll be gone. After I graduate, my draft deferment will end, and who knows where I'll be? And what about your draft deferment? Have you thought about that and possibly ending up in Vietnam? We've talked about how much we both hate the war many times."

"I'm already 1-Y," Greg continued. "I have this hearing loss in my right ear. They'd only call me up for a desk job if they needed me."

Leo took the phone from his ear for a second and frowned at it as if it had done something wrong. "What hearing loss? You never even told me anything about that."

"Why should I? I certainly didn't see this coming."

Accepting his point reluctantly, Leo couldn't believe this was happening to him. Just when he'd stepped out on a limb, it was about to break and send him hurtling helplessly to the ground. Or back to the closet?

"For what it's worth, Greg, I think I may be falling in love with you," Leo said, not as a ploy but as a true expression of where he really was.

"If I told you that I'm at a point where I just can't handle that at my end right now," Greg said, "would you believe me? Don't get me wrong, I'd like to reciprocate, but... Leo, I'm a mess. I told Preston I'd like to start seeing someone again. I mean, my psychiatrist. I needed help back when my father died."

"I guess you didn't mention that, either."

"There's a lot you don't know about me. I'm not just someone you listened to Top 40 hits with before we went to bed. I come with a history of big problems."

"Same here," Leo added, but it didn't make the trend of the conversation any easier to take. Then an idea flashed into his head. "Will you at least promise me this? Will you come back down to Sewanee for my graduation in June? Do you think you could manage that?"

Greg didn't hesitate and said he would, which made Leo feel a bit better about things. But there was an overwhelming sense of loss on his part when the conversation ended, and Leo walked slowly back to his room. How ironic was it that he hadn't wanted a roommate his senior year to start with, and now he would have the room all to himself.

Chapter 9

Three weeks before his graduation, Leo received a newsy letter from his mother in which she told him that Granny Marble was coming along for the ceremony, too. Just as she had witnessed her own son Joseph receiving his diploma wearing his elegant black gown in 1940 in the manner of Oxford University across the pond, she would now be back in 1968 to applaud her only grandson experiencing that same grand tradition. The continuity made Leo very happy. What made him frown was the paragraph during which his mother wondered out loud if he intended to invite a girl from Beau Pre up for graduation. Even though she knew quite well he hadn't seen anyone since he and Rebecca had "broken up," so to speak. But she chose to mention her anyway:

> *"Rebecca has a job here working at one of the antique shops on Franklin Street. She sold me a beautiful sideboard last year, in fact, and as far as I know, she's not seeing anyone. I know you're not either, being at Sewanee and all, so I'm sure she would love to come up to join you for the festivities. Think it over, why don't you?"*

At that point, Leo put the letter down and set his jaw firmly. The moment had finally arrived. Greg was still coming down to be with him for the ceremony at All Saints, and it was time to level with his parents once and for all. Then he had a second thought:

just his parents, though. He would leave it up to them whether or not to tell Granny Marble. Maybe that was a generational bridge too far to handle.

His parents arrived the day before the actual ceremony, booking two rooms next to each other at the old-line Sewanee Inn: one for themselves and one for Granny Marble. As for Leo, he had been staying at Middleton Hall where students who wished to remain on campus for the five days between the end of the semester and graduation day were living. Only a handful of boys fell into that category, so the dorm was nearly empty and roaming the hallways had a spooky quality to it.

However, Greg's arrival to stay with him overnight made up for the loneliness instantly, and the two quickly settled into Leo's makeshift room. Underweight to begin with, Greg looked even leaner than when he had pulled out of school before the Christmas holidays last year. His cheeks looked particularly gaunt.

"It's great to see you, but you need to be eating more," Leo said, pulling back after the two sat on his bed and kissed each other gently on the lips while hugging tightly. "Greg, you've got to take better care of yourself."

"Yes, I know. Preston and Sherrie keep telling me the same thing at the dinner table. My appetite's just not there. I go to my sessions every week, but Dr. Lindstrom says it may take at least a year or more for me to get some sense of normalcy back."

Normalcy.

It was a concept that Leo had been struggling with, attempting to achieve it nearly all his life since being called a "redheaded, freckle-faced woodpecker" on the seesaw at recess so long ago. Yet, he had never come close to it, as emotional hurdle after hurdle had presented itself.

"I'm treating you to dinner tonight in the village," Leo continued. "It's just a hamburger joint that some of us would go to when the cafeteria food would get totally out of hand, but by all that's holy, you're gonna eat a good meal in front of me if I have to spoon-feed you."

Greg smiled as the two of them held hands. "You're gonna spoon-feed me a hamburger? Now that I wanna see."

Then Leo methodically outlined his plan. "I told my parents I'd meet them at the Sewanee Inn tonight after having dinner with a friend, but I didn't tell them it was you. They didn't see why we couldn't all have dinner together, but what I'm going to tell them later this evening seemed to me like the perfect formula for indigestion. I have no idea how they'll really take what I have to say, but I've decided to err on the side of caution where you're concerned before I do tell them. All they know is that you left school because of your mother's death, and I haven't had a roommate since then. Greg, my parents may or may not have guessed who I am on some level and may have been in denial all this time for all I know. At any rate, I want to clear the air finally for the first time in my life. I can't go on living in the closet."

"I understand," Greg said, nodding. "I don't know if my mother knew about me, either. I'm guessing she thought she was better off not knowing, since I never had a social life involving girls. I was too young to be dating when my father died, of course, but my mother did ask me now and then if there was anyone special at school. High school, I mean. I never lied to her, though. I always told her there wasn't."

Leo sounded resigned. "Once you start lying about everything, it's difficult to stop. It's endless. It takes up all your energy. But no matter what happens with my parents later today, I know you'll be there for me at All Saints tomorrow. And we'll have tonight together right here in this room."

"So how did dinner go with your friend?" Louisa was saying, as she and Joseph sat on the big floral couch in their Sewanee Inn suite staring at their son in the expensive leather armchair across the way. "They had perfectly delicious prime rib on the menu here tonight. I still don't see why we all couldn't have had dinner together right here at the Inn. You're being very mysterious about all this, you know."

Uncomfortable with the question, Leo shifted his weight briefly and drew himself up. "That's what I wanted to talk to you about. The friend in question was Greg Lightman, my ex-roommate."

Instantly, Louisa's tone became solicitous. "Really? I still don't understand. We would love to have met him and gotten to know him a little bit. How's he doing, by the way? It must be awful what he's going through."

"He's seeing a psychiatrist, and he's lost some weight. Not that he needed to, you understand. He was a string bean to begin with. He's staying with me tonight over at Middleton Hall."

Joseph frowned and spoke up. "I agree with your mother. Why didn't you just bring him with you?"

That required a deep breath, after which Leo bravely forged ahead. "Because there's something I need to tell you both. Actually, Mama, I tried to tell you years ago that summer I was in the Junior Little Theatre play. Dean Forsythe wasn't just a phase you said I was going through. Or a bad case of hero worship, as you suggested. I really had a mad crush on him that never went away until he was out of sight, out of mind, and he wasn't the only crush like that. As I got a bit older, I felt the same way about Coy Warren that I felt about Dean, only more deeply since we were the same age. My feelings for boys only got more intense. And now…"

The brief pause Leo took to suck in more air gave his mother just enough time to interrupt. "You feel just that way about Greg, is that it?"

Leo nodded, making a mask of his face while his parents exchanged furtive glances. "I've never been interested in girls. Never at any time. Not as anything more than friends. It just wasn't there. I had no choice in the matter. I can't explain it better than that."

Then his father started grabbing at straws. "What about Rebecca back in high school?"

He'd rehearsed that response many times over. "I dated her to try and fit in. I did it to please both of you. My relationship with Rebecca was strictly platonic. The truth is, I would rather have dated Coy Warren. But I knew that was ridiculous and impossible, of course. The point is that this is who I am. It's who I've always been, and things aren't ever gonna change any more than my red hair and freckles are gonna change."

Then his mother started tearing up.

"Please don't cry, Mama. A long time ago you told me that it was okay to be different."

"I… I didn't mean different *that way*," she added, making no attempt to hold back her sobs. "Besides, I've always thought that you would make a wonderful father."

Caught off-guard, Leo said, "What made you think that? When have I ever expressed any interest in the subject? Maybe some people in this world aren't meant to reproduce. Maybe some aren't meant to get married, either. There are a lot of bad marriages out there among your friends, to hear the two of you talk. Not to mention messy divorces and the fallout from that, especially when there are children concerned."

"I'll grant you all that. But I was thinking about how wonderful it would be to have grandchildren to spoil. All parents look forward to that. You're our only child."

Somehow, Leo found the courage to continue. "I'll always be your only child. But realistically, I can't see grandchildren happening, not the way things are set up for me."

Joseph put his arm around his wife to console her and said, "About Greg…are the two of you making some sort of plans together? Is there more we need to know?"

It was a painful question for Leo to answer, but he managed. "No. My draft deferment ends this summer, as you know. I have to face that and the possibility of Vietnam before I can even apply for a job. Greg's under psychiatric care up in Lexington until further notice. Tonight will probably be our last night together."

Louisa gathered herself enough to push the envelope. "Have you two... been... I mean... well, you know what I mean, don't you?"

Even though Leo thought that tonight might be their first—and maybe last—time to become intimate with each other, he decided not to bring up the possibility and to spare his mother's feelings instead. After all, there was no guarantee that he and Greg would make such a decision, given the definite parting that lay ahead of them and the emotional weight of it all. He could even envision the two of them being satisfied with just going to sleep in each other's arms. So, he gave his mother a simple, "No, we haven't. Not the way you mean."

That seemed to placate her, and she stopped sobbing. "I'm at least grateful for that."

"Don't be. You make it sound like there's something wrong with the way we feel about each other. This is gonna be hard for us, Mama. Everything seems to be star-crossed. We never seem to have gotten off the ground." Then an odd-looking grin broke across his face. "I just realized I said star-crossed. Sorry, it's all the Shakespeare courses I've taken up here."

"You've always had a flair for the theatrical, son," Joseph said with a hint of a smile. "You came out of the womb that way, gestures and all. Is Greg coming to the graduation ceremony tomorrow? Will we get to meet him then?"

"Yes, he'll be there. But for Granny Marble's sake, let's don't say anything more than he's my ex-roommate who's come down to see me graduate. There's nothing out of the ordinary about that. Let's please don't make a big deal out of this."

"That's definitely the way to go," Joseph added with some authority. "Your grandmother is very opinionated about a lot of things, as you know. Politics and religion and anything in-between. No reason to disturb her image of you as a Sewanee music major who took after her and can sing and act to boot. She says business at the school picked up even more after that review the paper did of your performance in *Carousel*. She was so proud of you."

Leo felt a certain sense of relief when the tense visit came to a close, and his father said, "And we're proud of you, Leo, too, no matter what." Hugs followed to seal the deal, and the world suddenly seemed less threatening.

Back in his room later, Leo summarized his conversation with his parents, and Greg said, "I like the idea of us going to sleep in each other's arms. It's kinda sweet, and maybe we shouldn't try to go any further than that. At least, I'm leaning that way."

"Your thinking being?"

"That this is going to be hard enough as it is. In a perfect world, we'd find a way to explore this friendship of ours and take it to another level. But instead, we've got problems all over the place, and neither one of us knows what's going to happen next. For instance, are you gonna be a conscientious objector when you get your draft notice, or are you gonna trudge on down there for your physical like a red-blooded American boy?"

The question took Leo completely by surprise. "I hadn't even thought all that much about that yet. Yes, it's crossed my mind, but I've been so focused on us and coming out to my parents."

"Well, it's coming right at you," Greg said. "Your draft notice, I mean. Unless you're planning to run up to Canada and hide, you're gonna have to deal with it. I'm covered with my 1-Y. And even if I weren't, there are my psychiatric issues that would do me in."

Leo shrugged. "I can't think about that right now."

"So it's been a long day for both of us. Me, driving down from Lexington, and you having that showdown with your parents. I'm all for a little kissing and hugging and a lot of rest for your big day tomorrow."

That was what they ended up doing, in fact. Leo could not help but notice the difference between the forced kissing he had done with Rebecca and the arousal he was feeling with Greg. He wanted to have his lips against Greg's and linger there for as long as they both felt the surge of adrenaline it was producing. The last thing Leo remembered before drifting off to sleep was how nice it was to experience even a hint of what loving and being loved by someone who was not his mother, father and grandmother was like.

Chapter 10

As expected, Leo's draft notice arrived in late June and ordered him to report to the MEPS in Jackson just after Labor Day for his physical. It created a serious quandary for him that he didn't know how to resolve no matter how many ways he examined it on his own. But the hugs and reassurances he had received from his parents after coming out to them at Sewanee a few weeks earlier gave him the courage to address the matter sitting across from his father one evening after dinner in his smoke-filled, legal study.

Leo began with the issue of becoming a conscientious objector. "Greg asked me how I felt about it that last night at Sewanee. But the deal is, Daddy, that although I oppose the Vietnam War, I don't want to go that route or run off to Canada and hide. I've done enough running away from things in my life. That's not the solution to anything, at least not for me. I mean, you didn't run away after Pearl Harbor. You went into the Army Air Corps and followed orders."

Joseph put out the last of his cigarette and smiled at his son approvingly. "That I did."

"And you came home safely after winning the Distinguished Flying Cross in the Pacific."

"Right again."

The conversation came to a dead halt with Leo averting his eyes.

"What is it, son?"

Finally, Leo broke his silence. "Maybe it hasn't occurred to you, but it has to me. I don't need to be a conscientious objector to get out of this."

"Do you want to get out of it?"

"Yes and no. I think the war is wrong, and I don't want to be a part of it. LBJ's not trying to win it or shut it down, either one. But there's a whole other issue I need to discuss with you, and I feel that I can now that I've told you and Mama about myself. I could report for the physical and just tell them I'm homosexual. Wouldn't that disqualify me right off the bat?"

Joseph was squinting now. "I hadn't even thought of that."

"Do you see where I'm going with this, Daddy? How would they know I was homosexual? How could I prove it? Be some outlandish parody of a person prancing around? I don't want them to think I'm making it up just to get out of military service. It seems to me that any guy could go into one of these physicals and claim the same thing and be lying outright. I wouldn't want to be a part of something like that, either."

"Very admirable of you, son."

"There's more, though," Leo continued, squirming a bit in his chair. "Does the military even want homosexuals to enlist? How would I be treated if I got in and then they found out? Would I be court-martialed?"

Leo watched his father light another cigarette, take a drag and then lean toward him. "What I'm gonna tell you is to be held in strictest confidence between the two of us. I've never told anyone else about this." He pointed to a black-and-white picture of his fighter squadron bunched together somewhere in the Pacific Theater which he kept on his desk. "Take that photo and look at it closely."

Leo reached over and grabbed it. "What am I looking for?"

"First row, guy on the extreme left. Rather jaunty-looking and very likable. His name was Stanley Wickes, but we all called him Wickey. One night back on the base when both of us had had a few neat shots of good rum and were stumbling around outside under the palm trees for the hell of it just to get some fresh air, he swore me to his secret because he said he liked me, and then he let it all out. 'I got past 'em. I like men… but I kept quiet about it when I enlisted… I… I don't act on it, though, and I hope… you don't think I'm coming onto you by telling you this…'"

With widened eyes, Leo said, "Wow! How in the world did you react to that, Daddy?"

"I put my arm around his shoulder and told him that his secret was safe with me. I think the truth is that there are probably way more homosexuals in the military than people would ever believe. To get in, all you have to do is not mention it and then do your job like everybody else. I'd say it's probably the same for most other jobs. It's just all hidden below the surface. It's a matter of protective coloration."

"Yeah, I know a bit about that." Then, Leo wondered if he dared ask but went ahead anyway. "Daddy… have you ever had… a homosexual experience, or even wanted to?"

"No. At least I didn't consider that one time a homosexual experience for me. I didn't quite finish my story about Wickey. I think the rum we'd both had was doing the talking for both of us when you come down to it. Once I'd put my arm around him and it'd been there for a little while, he looked me straight in the eye and said, 'Could I kiss you on the cheek, Marble?' I said he could, and he did. Then, I even kissed him back—on both cheeks. A second or two later, we kissed each other on the mouth just briefly. It just seemed like the next thing to do, even though I clearly don't remember thinking about it that way. It didn't seem wrong at the time, but I do admit we were drunk. But, let me assure you that I've always been about the women. Your Granny Marble can vouch for that."

Leo felt a strange surge in his loins that didn't seem to make a lot of sense to him and took a deep breath to center himself. "Were his lips soft?"

"Yes."

"So were Rebecca's when I would kiss her. I really didn't like it all that much, though."

Taking another deep drag, Joseph continued. "But that brief little incident with Wickey aside, I do know what it's like to be different." He pointed to the pock marks on his face. "As you know, these came from the world's worst case of acne when I was fifteen. I haven't really gone into it too deep with you before, but nothing the dermatologist did seemed to work, and these scars were the result. The whole thing put a dent in my social life there for a while. I felt like a pariah. I was on the outside looking in, and I knew people were talking about me behind my back. Or at least I thought they were, whether they were or not."

"I know all about that," Leo said, feeling closer to his father than he ever had before.

"It didn't stop your mother from falling in love with me later on, though. Or me from falling in love with her. She didn't see these tiny scars. She just saw me, and for that I will be eternally grateful to her."

Leo took a few moments and then said, "About Mama. From all of her tears, I know she took my little session up at Sewanee harder than you did. Maybe she still does?"

"The one thing you have to remember about your mother is how important family is to her," came the immediate reply. "Growing up in the Protestant Orphanage made her different, too. She was literally dropped on their doorstep, as you know. Unlike you and me, she never knew who her parents were, and so, marrying into my family changed everything for her. She and I have talked about it, and she's told me more than once that she thought everything would be ideal for her once we exchanged our vows. That she could put being an orphan behind her and finally belong to something." He stubbed his cigarette and blew the last of the smoke toward the ceiling. "But life just doesn't work that way. Everyone has their challenges, appearances to the contrary. There really are no silver spoons."

"I guess not."

"So. What have you decided to do about your draft notice? If you want me to represent you legally as a conscientious objector, I will. If you want to tell them that you're homosexual and see what they say, we can go that route. Or if you just want to go through with the physical without bringing that up, we can try that, too. No matter what, I'm driving you to Jackson to report and will be there for you when it's over."

Leo sat back in his chair, and the smile on his face surprised him. "Can I think about it a while longer?"

"Take all the time you need."

Leo understood completely why standing around with a roomful of other naked guys, briefs around their ankles, produced no element of arousal at all. He remembered well how he would try to wait out his other classmates for the communal shower in high school P. E. class to avoid glimpses of their packages and rear ends. And they of his. Not that he hadn't become an expert at maintaining straightforward eye contact in the locker room, no matter what.

But the physical exam these potential recruits were all enduring came off as entirely clinical to him. He felt exposed and vulnerable, wanting to cover himself with his hands, and he couldn't imagine that the rest of them weren't having the same reaction. Plus, the room was freezing cold. The phrase "sides of beef hanging up in a locker" came into his head and stubbornly wouldn't leave. Beef that came in a variety of colors—white, brown, and black. Then he thought about the nightly images from Vietnam on the TV newscasts with Walter Cronkite's commentary and allowed himself to shudder. He was, in fact, a number standing in line for a doctor to draw blood and perform other required rituals such as touching his groin and making him cough to determine fitness, possibly for mortal combat.

At one point, a very skinny white boy with curly blond hair at the head of the line fainted dead away while his blood was being drawn, bringing everything to a halt temporarily. The lad was brought back to life, so to speak, with smelling salts, and it was then that something Leo's uncle, Dr. Brady Marble, had told him during his checkup before he matriculated at Sewanee re-emerged.

"Some people can't watch their blood being drawn or get queasy at the sight of blood in general. They can pass out. The medical term is vasovagal syncope. So I always tell my patients to look away just in case they might have it."

And Leo did just that when his time came a few minutes later, not wishing to tempt the embarrassment of fainting.

Back in his briefs as the ordeal continued, he was outfitted with a pair of earphones in another cold room to take what was described to him as a hearing threshold level test.

"We'll be transmitting a series of tones to you. Press the red button in front of you at your seat whenever you hear one," he was told by a different doctor than the one who had drawn his blood. Then, it began.

A very high tone.

A low tone.

A lower tone.

A higher tone.

A still higher tone.

Something in the middle.

There were gaps between the tones, some longer than others. His index finger was getting a workout.

It went on for several minutes. For some reason, it began to annoy him. He felt like a monkey in a lab experiment.

Fully dressed again after it was finally over and some time had elapsed, Leo heard the verdict from a tall guy with a buzzcut wearing fatigues and sitting behind a table laden with a thick stack of papers. He took a single sheet off the top and scoured it quickly.

"Mr. Marble, we're gonna classify you I-Y. That means we'll call you up only if you're needed for a desk job. But you do not qualify for infantry. You have a hearing loss in your left ear.

You might want to consult a physician. Did you know about it before now?"

Leo blinked and told them that he had no idea, that he thought his hearing was just fine. Greg popped into his head, but he didn't even try to make sense of it at that moment. Oddly, he didn't even feel a sense of relief.

His father took him to a downtown Jackson cafeteria chain for a much-needed lunch, since Leo had been fasting and hadn't eaten breakfast; and then they began discussing the fallout.

"Has anyone in the family even worn a hearing aid?" Leo said, dipping his fork into the beef tips over rice he had chosen as he had moved his tray along the line. A small cup of green beans and a square of pepper cornbread supplemented his main course.

"Not that I know of. But then, we don't know anything about your mother's family's genes. That will always put us at a disadvantage."

Leo put down his fork and briefly pointed to his ear. "I didn't see this coming. I've never had a problem hearing anything."

"That test said otherwise. So I guess you're not destined to be a part of the military."

"I didn't have a real desire to be, of course. Not the way you did."

Joseph nodded as he swallowed a bite of his fried chicken breast. "Just about everybody jumped on the bandwagon after Pearl Harbor back then. There was a stigma attached to not wanting to do your part to defeat the Nazis and the Japs. Women took jobs in factories or joined the WACs. If you did nothing, people thought there was something wrong with you. Today, things aren't so cut and dried. I agree with you that it's a mess over there in Vietnam."

Over his afterthought dessert of blue Jell-O cubes with whipped cream—a cafeteria chain staple—Leo was still thinking about the hearing loss that he and Greg shared. Despite circumstances to the contrary, were they somehow destined to be together? Was there a resolution to whatever it was that had developed between them after all?

As if on some kind of inexplicable cue, a letter from Greg arrived two days later, even before Leo had had a chance to sit down and write one of his own about the draft physical and how the subject of his homosexuality thankfully hadn't even come up. The core of Greg's message was nothing short of stunning:

> *... and I have Dr. Lindstrom's go-ahead. When I told him what I was proposing to do, he said he thought I could handle it. He wouldn't let me go otherwise, so there's that. He thinks a change of venue would be good for me right now after all these months of seeing him. Nearly nine months, in fact. He says that there's no limit on grief or the time it takes to heal but that the best way for me to get out of this long depression I've been in since my mother died is to go out there and do some good things for other people. I know it doesn't pay particularly well, but money's no object now since Preston and I sold the house. Did you ever think your ex-roommate would become a bonafide member of the Peace Corps? Kenya, here I come, after I get all my shots, that is...*

Leo re-read the letter and then bounded into the large backyard that he'd been mowing since junior high. He needed to walk around, think things through and dissipate some nervous energy. Was that the answer? Should he, too, volunteer for the Peace Corps and ask for the same assignment Greg had managed to wangle? Was their future overseas?

Kenya.

As a practical matter where his enthusiasm was concerned, it might as well have been Mars.

It might be the answer for Greg, but was it right for him? Because he'd had to wait on finding a job because of the draft physical, he was still unemployed and living with his parents as he had before his college years. Yes, he had a diploma they had paid for but no clear direction for the years ahead.

That evening, he decided to share Greg's letter with them both, hoping that it might produce some sign he could interpret and follow.

"I'm glad you're not going to have to go to Vietnam, but I certainly never envisioned Kenya as the backup," his mother said as they sat down to her shrimp gumbo at the dinner table. "What if that doesn't work out for either one of you?"

Leo took a swig from his water glass and said, "I haven't said I'll definitely join the Peace Corps. I'm just running this past both of you. Just call it my trial balloon."

"My comment would be that nowhere in that letter you read to us did Greg invite you to join him, if I recall correctly," his father said. "Unless you left something out."

"No, I didn't. And... he didn't... invite me."

"Maybe you're reading more into this friendship with Greg than is really there," his mother added. "You really haven't known each other all that long." The remarks came with something of a forced smile.

"Maybe."

"He's been through a lot," she continued. "As the old saying goes, everyone needs to find themselves. But they're supposed to do that on their own. For that matter, have you given any thought to what kind of job you'd like to apply for? That is, if it's not going to be the Peace Corps?"

Leo actually came up with a plausible answer. "In this past Sunday's Jackson paper, there was an ad for an opening for a writer for the New Orleans *Times-Picayune's Sunday* magazine. I clipped it and saved it. Before I heard from Greg, I thought it might be something I could look into. I took two creative writing courses from Andrew Lytle at Sewanee and wrote a column for the *Purple*. I do know my way around a sentence and understand print as a medium. I can do more than sing."

"That sounds like a great opportunity," his mother said, perhaps a bit too enthusiastically. It was quite evident where she stood on the Peace Corps possibility. "It would be a whole lot easier to visit you or for you to visit us if you were in Louisiana. As you know, your father and I spent our honeymoon in the French Quarter, and it was magical for us. Did we ever tell you that we ran into Joanne Dru and her husband Dick Haymes at Pat O'Brien's that weekend?"

Leo's brow furrowed. "Who and who?"

"A little before your time, I suppose. Dick Haymes was an actor and singer back in the 40s and Joanne Dru was his wife, and she was also an actress. His picture, *State Fair*, had just come out, and they happened to be sitting at the table next to us sipping on Hurricanes. We recognized him and timidly started up a polite conversation, and then they both invited us to join them, which they certainly didn't have to do. We went our separate ways for dinner, but it was fun chatting with Hollywood stars for a while. They went out of their way to be gracious."

Then Leo remembered. "Some of the *State Fair* numbers are in that Rodgers and Hammerstein songbook y'all gave me a while back. 'It Might As Well Be Spring' and 'It's A Grand Night For Singing.' I like them both."

"Then take it as a sign," she said. "Go ahead and apply for that job and if you get it, you can try to rent a courtyard apartment in the Quarter. You'll love the atmosphere. Meanwhile, you and Greg can keep in touch writing letters about your various experiences. If this friendship between the two of you is really meant to happen, it'll survive being apart for a little while. You're young and have your whole life ahead of you."

Leo knew exactly what she was up to but thought she might have a point anyway; and he was doubly glad that he and Greg had decided not to make things more emotionally complicated by taking their relationship any further there at the end when they had had the chance. So, he went ahead and applied for the position the next day, writing back to Greg that the ad had said it would be another month before final interviews took place.

"Maybe it's a long shot, but so was your idea of going into the Peace Corps," was Leo's last sentence before his customary signoff of *"Friends forever, Leo."*

THE SECOND ACT

Chapter 11

Beau Pre and New Orleans did have a lot in common, although they were in two different states. They were both Mississippi River ports about 150 miles apart with similar immigration patterns, historical architecture and laid-back attitudes, and Beau Pre was even two years older than New Orleans was. But it was also twenty-five times smaller. Although pleasantly surprised by toughing it out and eventually getting the job with the *Times-Picayune*, Leo was having a bit of trouble adjusting to the pace of life in the Crescent City, as it was often called because of the dramatic bend in the river where much of it was laid out.

He had been unable to find a place to live in the Quarter that he could afford, so instead he had settled for renting the upstairs of an older camelback in the Uptown Carrollton area. His landlords, Gabe and Susie Landry, were a short, plump retired couple who were very solicitous of him, particularly after they found out he was working for the *Sunday* magazine.

"We read the magazine every week," Susie said. "We love it."

"Who knows?" he had told them after signing the lease with an ingratiating smile. "Maybe I'll be doing a story on y'all one day."

"Us?" Susie said, blushing. "What kind of story would be about us? We're just plain folks."

"A story about landlords all over the city. Might be very interesting."

Susie rubbed her hands together and squealed just like a little girl.

85

The logistics of getting from place to place in New Orleans had to be learned quickly. With all the stoplights and busy, one-way, divided boulevards featuring towering palms in the medians, veteran drivers knew all too well to add an extra twenty or thirty minutes to run any errands or just get to work on time. Leo had managed to get a good trade-in price for the Fairlane that his father had given him and which was on its last leg; and he was now driving around in a used 1967 red Volkswagen Beetle. He missed the extra room inside, of course, but he didn't have to fill up nearly as often. And besides, red continued to be his favorite color for some things.

He liked his workplace environment. Spread out as a series of cubicles on the second floor of a sprawling building just off the interstate, there was an anonymity to it that encouraged efficiency while making time-wasting gossip difficult. That said, there were plenty of opportunities to make friends in the lunchroom which featured a cafeteria specializing in New Orleans favorites like red beans and rice (on Mondays), jambalaya, po-boys, muffaletas and bread pudding. Most of all, Leo and his Royal typewriter took to each other immediately, and he gave himself full credit for his decision to take typing his senior year in high school with all those girls who had fawned over him to no avail.

His editor was Arthur LeBlanc, a middle-aged man with a formidable mustache, gravelly voice and a shock of graying hair. He also smoked a pipe at his desk throughout the workday, causing the pleasant aroma of rum to hang in the air. There were two other *Sunday* staff members: a fast-talking, wise-cracking photographer named Chase Knowles with the energy of a puppy who looked like he might even be in high school but was pushing thirty; and another writer maybe a few years older, quite rangy, and well-dressed with a perfect patrician nose and deep-set, dark eyes, who had shortened his blockbuster name of Hugh Howard Henningham into Three-H.

"He thinks it's cute, but I think it's the worst nickname ever," Chase told Leo over lunch in the cafeteria that first week on the job. "It reminds me of a hemorrhoid cream. Of course, when you really get to know him, you'll get a whole new notion of what boring is. He'll go on and on about his wife and daughter and all their social activities and their Mardi Gras Krewe until you want to excuse yourself to go outside and scream. Just a warning because I can guarantee you he'll put in an appearance. Or two. Or three."

It did not escape Leo that Chase was definitely the kind of guy that talked about people behind their back and that he therefore needed to be careful what he said around him. But despite Chase's warning, Leo soon found himself trapped in the lunchroom a day later when Three-H sidled up to him with his tray and said, "Mind if I sit with you? I'd like to make you feel welcome. It's my specialty."

"Of course, not," Leo said, even though he wanted to be by himself on that particular occasion.

Chase had not exaggerated on the subject of their co-worker, however, as the man launched into what amounted to an unsolicited and convoluted family history—both his and his wife's in between bites of his shrimp po-boy. "Lydia is a Duval, and I am a Henningham," he was saying at one point. "Our parents had always wanted us to get together, you see. So, we ended up pleasing them and saying our 'I do's.' It was the social event of the season, if I do say so myself."

Leo retained little of the litany that Three-H trotted out as they ate, making the necessary non-committal grunts and nods to appear engaged. He trusted that once he had been given the full Three-H family treatment, he would be spared in the future, despite what Chase had said. If this was the worst he had to endure on the job, Leo figured he was home-free.

Then came his first assignment. He was paired with Chase to do a story on the Greater New Orleans Tourist and Convention Commission, headquartered in the heart of the Quarter and whose primary mission was to bring conventions to the city throughout the year. He was delighted to discover that Chase's suggestions for shots exuded professionalism, and the questions that he himself had prepared to ask people created some memorable quotes. When all the interviews were done and photographs taken from all angles, Leo realized with a great deal of satisfaction that he could do the job he'd been hired to perform.

When he turned in the copy, Arthur LeBlanc said, "This is good stuff, Leo. I like the way you profiled the head honcho as the go-getter he is. People here think of tourism as out-of-towners drinking, eating, and gawking at strippers in the Quarter, but the real money is in filling up our hotels with conventioneers. After all, Mardi Gras doesn't go on all year."

Nonetheless, it took Leo two weeks to realize that something important was missing in his new life, and it wasn't Greg who continued to exchange newsy letters with him. What had temporarily vanished was his music, his show tunes, his playing and singing at the piano. He missed it terribly. The upright his parents had bought for him was back in Beau Pre in the living room collecting dust. Neither of them had ever learned to play.

But rather than ask them to go to the trouble and expense to ship it to him, he set aside something from his first paycheck, drove to Werlein's on Canal Street and put a down payment on a mahogany spinet that he could call his very own. Soon, he was having his own impromptu recitals, and he even invited the Landrys up once to hear him sing selections from the Nat King Cole songbook he had also treated himself to. They applauded vigorously after he'd rendered "Blue Gardenia," "Teach Me Tonight," and "That Sunday, That Summer" to perfection.

"You ought to be on the TV with the way you sing," Susie Landry told him, giving him a playful wink. "Maybe you oughta go out to Hollywood. They don't have enough redheads out there."

Her comment did resonate with him somewhat. He had, after all, taken music courses galore and had continued to act and sing in plays at Sewanee. But for the time being, he had committed to the written word and his ability to communicate with others;

not to mention that he hadn't even begun to explore all that New Orleans offered.

For instance, his parents had given him a list of their favorite restaurants that they'd raved about all these years that he must try for himself. Two—Galatoire's and Arnaud's—were in the Quarter, while the third, Commander's Palace, was in the Garden District on the other side of downtown. After parking his car in a nearby garage, he was on his way to his first visit to Galatoire's for lunch. He was going to try the Trout Marguery his mother said she always ordered, and then he saw a sign on the door of one of the two-story, brick and lacework buildings that he passed.

NEW ORLEANS GAY RESOURCES COALITION, it read. There was a phone number beneath it.

He made a mental note to enter that door on another visit after memorizing the number. That was the thing he had also noticed lately. The word *homosexual* had apparently fallen out of favor and been replaced by *gay* to describe men and women who were attracted to members of their own sex. Not that he wasn't familiar with the term lesbian or that he had never heard the word gay used before. But more often than not, he had grown up with *queer* and *fag* and mostly *homo*, which Coy Warren had thrown out there to defend his sister's honor. Perhaps things were changing just a bit; but at any rate, he needed to investigate and discover what these 'gay resources' were, and if they might help him in some way.

A few days later after calling to determine the organization's hours and set up an appointment, Leo climbed the steep stairs behind the New Orleans Gay Resources Coalition door and briefly caught his breath on the second-floor landing. There was no sign of a receptionist to greet him, but another door with a transom to his right had a sign in bold block lettering which read KNOCK BEFORE ENTERING. Immediately after he did so, a deep voice from within said "Come in."

89

Leo entered but made no effort to advance at first. There before him, behind a large desk covered with all sorts of paraphernalia in a small, cluttered room with a couple of uncomfortable-looking chairs, sat Henry the Eighth. Or at least Leo's recollection of how that royal historical figure had been depicted for centuries. The man's plump face was framed by ox-blood red scalp and beard hair, and when he stood up, it was very obvious from his girth that he enjoyed eating as much as that notorious ruler had.

"I'm Terrence Dennery. You must be Leo," he said, as the two men shook hands. "You're right on time. Please, have a seat. We're always glad to welcome newcomers to our organization. As you've gathered by the lack of a receptionist, our staff is lean, unlike myself."

Always a fan of self-deprecating humor, Leo cracked a smile and said, "As I said over the phone, I can't wait to hear about all the services you provide and if I can't fit in somewhere."

Terrence immediately pointed to the simple, black, rotary phone on his desk. "That's our main service right there—our gay helpline. If it rings while we're here together chatting, I'll have to excuse myself and take it, although more of our calls tend to happen during the evening hours than at any other time. We man it twenty-four and seven for those who need counseling, to provide someone who will just listen to them, and give recommendations for clinics and health services and information on the dates and times of our bi-weekly social meetings. Some of our members including myself take turns hosting in their homes and apartments because we don't have the space here, as you can see. The meetings give people a chance to get to know each other, discuss issues and compare notes, and even form lasting friendships, although we don't consider ourselves a dating service. We discourage people from trying to use us that way. Eventually, we hope to attract some high-profile speakers and celebrities to address us. I'll end my spiel by saying that as a private organization, we exist on contributions from our members. I inherited some money from my parents, enough to get the Coalition started and keep it running for a while." He paused, giving Leo a hopeful glance. "Contributions are not a requirement to join, of course, and there are no dues. We realize that some who come to us aren't exactly swimming in money."

"I'm doing okay for a first job," Leo said and then described his work at the paper.

Terrence seemed impressed. "Ah, the magazine. I read it all the time, and I think they dig beneath the surface and reveal what New Orleans is really about. All the layers and cliques. Maybe you could suggest an article on this organization to your editor some time."

"I can certainly keep that in mind." Then Leo zeroed in on his goal. "Do you have any shift openings for the helpline? Mine would have to be evenings because of my job hours."

Terrence looked pleased and handed over a small piece of paper he'd placed in his shirt pocket. "I've written down two possibilities for you—one on Wednesday evening and one on Sunday evening. I could use the relief for either one, as I end up taking up the slack when we don't have enough volunteers. I wish it were otherwise, but there's not a line forming out on the sidewalk to join us. There are still too many people living in too many closets, and it might surprise you who some of them are at all levels of society. If it were easy to be gay, an organization like ours wouldn't even be necessary."

Leo didn't even have to think about it. "I know all about the closet. I'll take Wednesday then. I have two days off at the paper, and Wednesday is one of them."

The phone rang, and Terrence said, "Perfect timing. You can listen and watch me in action."

Terrence gathered himself and picked up the receiver on the third ring. "New Orleans Gay Resources Coalition. How can I help you?"

There was a prolonged period of silence during which Terrence listened intently while rolling his eyes.

"Is that it? Are you through?" he finally said to the caller. After a brief pause, he hung up and cocked his head smartly. "You might think I staged that one for your benefit, but the truth is, you'll get your share of crazies calling up. The approved procedure is not to engage them for the most part, as you observed. If it gets too rough, you can either hang up or tell them that the call is being recorded in case they have any intention of calling back. That almost always works."

"What did whoever that was say?"

Terrence filled his ample chest with air and cleared his throat. "It was a man. Most of our prank callers are men. I suspect teenage boys whose voices have just dropped when you come right down to it. So, paraphrasing here from that call, 'Is this Queers, Incorporated? How much will you charge to suck it for me? Not that I'd spend good money on you. Or do you do it for free? I bet you'll do it for free, won't you, you sick bastards?'"

"Wow!"

"Oh, that was relatively mild compared to some," Terrence added. "Expect your share of prank calls with foul language. But don't get distracted by them. For every one of them, there'll be one from someone in need of genuine help. It's those people we're trying to reach. We're a somewhat new group, so we're still trying to get the word out."

"Sign me up," Leo said, feeling not the least bit intimidated by what had just happened.

"Done." Then Terrence leaned forward, reaching into his shirt pocket again and handing over another slip of paper. "Our next social gathering will be at my apartment on Metairie Road a week from now at 8 p.m. Here's the address with some directions and my phone number."

Leo glanced at it and said, "Should I bring anything?"

"Just yourself, unless you're involved with someone. They're welcome, too. Otherwise, I provide the refreshments, and the rest is up to you. It'll be well worth your while."

"This is very exciting. To be able to meet people like myself openly without sneaking around. Straight people take that openness for granted. If they only knew."

Terrence's tone grew more solemn. "A word of caution, though. The Coalition isn't a cure-all for navigating the gay subculture. Mr. Right may not come along. For instance, I still don't have a partner, and I've been trying for years. It's more difficult for guys who are overweight like me. Believe me, I've tried to slim down, but I just can't seem to get over the hump. Plus, I'm over the dreaded thirty. There's a bit of relentless youth worship going on out there that can't be denied." Terrence sighed but managed a smile at the same time. "Heigh, ho. What else is new?"

"You got that right," Leo said, standing up to shake hands. At the door, he turned and added, "By the way, where do you get your hair cut? It looks great, and I've been looking for something more than a traditional barber since I've gone with longer hair."

"Look up Long May She Wave in the Yellow Pages," Terrence said. "Great little unisex salon. The owner is Mara Lehmann, and she does my hair. She's also a member of the Coalition and what they call these days a lipstick lesbian. She never leaves the house without looking like a fashion model. It's just her thing. Tell her I sent you, and she'll take good care of you. You'll never want anyone else to touch a strand after one appointment with her."

The one thing Leo had not shared with Arthur LeBlanc or his other co-workers was information on his private life. During his final job interview, he had not been asked in person if he was married or single, so he saw no reason to delve into it. He considered that checking the single box for tax withholding purposes on his application was sufficient. Despite the fact that he had come out to his parents, he did not yet feel comfortable enough to lead with the information in daily life. He was, in fact, technically still a virgin, his physical needs being taken care of by certain nocturnal episodes common to pubescent boys all the way up to grown men. For the time being, he chose to keep his involvement with the Coalition submerged; at least until he got to know everyone a whole lot better. After all, he did not need or want to know about the private lives of his editor, Chase, or Three-H, even if the latter kept volunteering family tidbits to anyone in the workplace he could corner. It seemed a compulsion with him, and what was worse, he had a tendency to repeat the same things over and over. The man definitely needed new material or at least to tone down the old.

Leo did think it was somewhat curious that Chase never mentioned a girlfriend or a wife, since he was talkative about almost everything else. Not that he was interested in Chase as anything more than a friend and co-hort. But having been in the closet himself for so long growing up, he couldn't help but wonder if that might be going on with Chase. It wasn't exactly radar, or even gaydar as some called it, but Leo sensed something.

Behind the scenes, Leo became used to his Wednesday shifts on the helpline. The profanity didn't phase him, and he would write down PRANK in the log he was required to keep instead of wasting his time with details like—*caller wanted to know if we gave queer lessons and how much they cost;* or *caller wanted to say that we needed to find Jesus unless we wanted to go to Hell and burn there for all eternity.* The so-called theological callers sometimes outnumbered the cussers and jokesters, which was interesting in and of itself. He concluded that they all had too much time on their hands and needed to get lives.

It wasn't much easier, however, for him to connect with the occasional person who obviously had nowhere else to turn and desperately needed a ray of hope. Particularly if that person was hanging by a thread. It was a tough job, and it took him a while to adjust to every aspect of it.

For instance, there was his first legit call from a young man who identified himself as a junior in high school but would not give his name. Of course, Terrence had made it clear that no one was ever required to volunteer a name if they chose not to.

"I'm on the track team, and I have this crush on a teammate," he began. "He doesn't know. Nobody knows. I'm sure I'd be kicked off the team if anyone found out. My parents don't know. They're so proud of me for running track in the first place, especially my dad. I mean, I was too small to play football, but as soon as I got on the track team, his whole attitude toward me changed. So I don't think he'd be so proud of me if he knew I was a homo."

"You don't have to use that word, you know," Leo told him. "It's a term of contempt."

"But that's what they'd call me. I hear the term used all the time at school in the locker room. What I want to do is quit the team so I won't have to be around Will anymore..." Then the boy panicked. "Oh, no, I said his name..."

Hang-up. Dial tone.

There was too much of that, but every once in a while, someone would stay on long enough to get an address or phone number for the help they needed. Leo decided that was enough for him for the time being. He knew very well that things would not change overnight.

Chapter 12

Over the next few years, Leo adjusted to the rhythms and patterns of the Crescent City while honing his craft at the magazine. At the same time, he considered his sessions at the piano with his show tunes to be nothing if not therapeutic; and the Landrys never turned down the recitals he rehearsed for them every now and then. In return, Susie would knock on his door and present him with a covered plate of homemade Napoleons, which he adored.

"You need to put some weight on," she would always say to him. "These'll help."

Venturing out of his apartment when the mood struck him, Leo knew that there were plenty of bars and discos in the Quarter where gay men like himself could go to meet, drink, dance and possibly get involved with each other. The jumping off point for almost all of them was eleven o'clock in the evening or even after midnight. That was a separate world that came to life from then until dawn, full of loud music, layers of smoke and liquor in the veins. Joining the Coalition enabled Leo to familiarize himself with their locations and what kind of clientele they were set up to serve.

Midnight in Motion featured a gigantic, metallic ball that rotated on its high ceiling and threw off bits and pieces of the rainbow as its patrons worked out to Barry White, Diana Ross and Love Unlimited on the darkened dance floor below. It became Leo's favorite place for the occasional night out because it allowed him to work up a sweat without committing himself to anything further. In addition to being a good singer, he was a dancer with many moves that others envied. But they misunderstood if they thought Leo was 'advertising.'

Nevertheless, he still hadn't found anyone who came close to stirring up the feelings he had begun developing for Greg at Sewanee. Perhaps it was the letters he continued to receive from Kenya that kept him from pursuing anyone on this side of the pond. Those letters were full of enthusiasm about simple projects like digging trenches and learning how to give injections to school children and a host of other ordinary things that Americans took for granted:

> *I can't get enough of this, Leo. It's difficult to explain, but the smiles I get are my big payoff. They are so grateful for our help. I truly made the right move in coming here and leaving my heartbreak behind.*

Despite the great distance between them, Leo was happy that his roommate had fallen in love with his job, with Kenya, itself, possibly more than he could with any single person; and there were far fewer mentions of the friendship they had barely begun to explore at Sewanee.

Meanwhile, Leo was finding an equal amount of contentment with his assignments at the magazine and even daring to entertain the possibility of becoming the editor, replacing Arthur LeBlanc somewhere down the line. Of course, Three-H had seniority over him in that regard, and he didn't relish the idea of having to report to him and to endure even more long-winded family updates. More often than not, he tried to stay in the moment and let things unfold.

Then came that extraordinary visit to Midnight in Motion one night. "Love's Theme" was playing over the sound system, and Leo was standing on the fringes watching the dancers while he nursed a club soda with a slice of lime floating in it. A couple of epic, bourbon-spiked, eggnog hangovers at Sewanee had convinced him that alcohol was not his friend. Nor was sleeping in his dorm room with a trash can nearby something he wanted to experience again. He could take it or leave it, so leave it, he did. He was focused on a young woman who was dressed exactly like Alice of Lewis Carroll's literary masterpiece, and she was slow dancing with a man wearing a top hat in the manner of the Mad Hatter. Or maybe it wasn't a man, but another woman dressed like a man. Whatever the case, they made an interesting couple, and one of Alice's most famous comments popped into Leo's head.

Curiouser and curiouser.

He was completely mesmerized by the two of them until someone tapped him on the shoulder from behind. Turning around quickly, he was astonished to discover Three-H standing there with a longneck in his hand.

Over the music and the noise of the throng, Leo said, "What are you doing here?"

"I might ask the same of you, but I already know the answer," came the reply. "I saw you from across the room a few minutes ago, and at first I thought about leaving so you wouldn't even know I was here. But then I thought, 'what the hell! My dream has come true.'"

Straining to hear in his compromised ear, Leo said, "Do you want to move to someplace quieter? The dance floor is tough competition."

So they headed to a large special room off to one side of the bar where people could have conversations without yelling and possibly get to know each other better. There were already two couples there when they entered, both male. One consisting of a white guy and a black guy, was seated on a sofa in a far corner, holding hands and making intense eye contact; the other couple—two very tall white guys wearing boots and leather vests—was standing in an opposite corner and engaged in a liplock.

Leo and Three-H found a spot on another empty sofa, and the conversation picked up where they had left off.

"What did you mean about your dream coming true?" Leo said.

"You mean you honestly didn't know I've had a crush on you all this time?"

Leo drew back, honestly puzzled. "How would I know that? You've never said anything to me, and all I've ever heard from you when you come up to me is raves about your wife and daughter. By the way, are they made up?"

Three-H took a swig of his beer and suppressed a small belch. "No, Lydia and Hannah are real. I'm very much married. But it isn't what it appears to be. I've always liked the boys from the get-go. I just did what my parents expected of me, mostly for social reasons. My parents and hers considered it a match made in heaven, and they'd been oohing and aahing about it since Lydia and I were in high school and started going out. I was just trying to fit in, and Lydia was naive—still is to some extent. She thinks the amount of sex we don't have is normal."

For some reason, Leo decided to pluck his lime slice from his drink and suck on it briefly before returning it to its bubbly little bath. The puckering sensation somehow enabled him to steady himself, and he pressed on. "So you're saying you have a marriage of convenience?"

"To an extent. I do love my wife in my way and my daughter as a father is supposed to. Don't get me wrong."

"You talk about them enough. So, do they know about you?"

"No, and I want to keep it that way."

"Then why did you take a chance and reveal yourself to me? As you said, you could have left without my ever knowing you were here."

Three-H managed a wink, which Leo found disarming. "Like I said, I've been dreaming about how nice it would be if you were my boyfriend... on the side, of course." He finished off his beer and set the bottle down on the floor, but it didn't stay balanced and fell over. He made no attempt to set it upright, however, and watched it roll a short distance before coming to a halt. Only then, did he continue. "What I'm trying to tell you is that I've had my eye on you since you came to work for the paper. In a perfect world, I thought to myself, you would be just like I am, and now, here you are."

"Yes, here I am."

"Do you come here often?"

"Do you?"

Three-H narrowed his eyes. "I don't get the chance that often. Lydia has to be out of town visiting relatives and Hannah has to be at somebody's house for one of those girlfriend sleepovers, you know. Otherwise, I'd have to account for my whereabouts if they were around. I'm extremely good at doing that, I have to say."

Leo took another sip of his club soda and decided to tackle things head-on. "This is beyond ironic. Here I was thinking that Chase might be the one in the closet. He was the one I thought was hiding something."

Three-H nudged him playfully with his elbow. "I know his story. Don't ask me how I found out. It's complicated, but it's the truth. He doesn't know I know that he's been having an affair with a married woman for years; and she's highly placed in social circles just like I am. In other words, she keeps him in a fashion as payment for services rendered. Her husband, it seems, just can't perform for whatever reasons."

Leo decided not to hold anything back. "And is that what you're proposing to do with me?"

"You have to understand that I never thought I'd be having this conversation. It was in the 'too good to be true' category. Maybe I'm still a little giddy that it's actually happened."

"That may be, but you didn't answer the question."

It took Three-H a while to respond. "It would have to be by mutual agreement, of course. These things usually are."

"That would be a no-go. I'm sorry to inform you that what you are proposing would be completely one-sided. As certain shallow people are fond of saying in the gay subculture, 'You're not my type.' Not that I would consider the arrangement even if you were."

"That's pretty brutal," he said, his dark eyes downcast. "I was hoping for a friendly arrangement of some kind. That's the only reason I decided to tap you on the shoulder."

"Sorry, but I see no reason to beat around the bush. I spent too much time in the closet to play games at this point in my life. Let's confine our friendship to work."

The silence that followed was awkward. Some might have even called it painful. Finally, Three-H said, "Will you... keep my secret? I've sorta crawled out on a limb here. It took all my courage to even approach you."

Names and words moved along the front of Leo's brain like a ticker tape: *Lt. Joseph Marble... Wickey... Pacific Theater... dark rum and dark secrets never to be revealed...*

"Don't worry," Leo replied with the suggestion of a grin. "I understand exactly who you are, believe me, and I could have been exactly *where* you are as well if not for getting fed up and taking a stand. Let's just agree that this clandestine meeting of ours never happened. I think that'll be best."

"Sorry that it can't be otherwise."

"I'm not." Then Leo softened his tone a bit. "I guess you wouldn't consider coming to one of our Gay Resources Coalition meetings. I've found it to be a very helpful support group since I joined a few years back. All kinds of people come to sort things out. You'd be surprised."

Three-H made a sweeping gesture. "This is about as brave as I'll get. Although I will admit that I know about your group and I even called up that helpline once a couple of years ago. I described my situation completely... but anonymously. I did find it therapeutic, but as you can clearly see, I haven't done a damned thing about it."

Leo searched his brain quickly. "You probably didn't talk to me. I might have recognized your voice unless you were trying to disguise it. You probably talked to Terrence, our founder, or someone else. But believe me, the married man with the gay lover on the side is far more common than you'd think, especially here in New Orleans. Kinda like the married man with the mistress on the side. Lots of people out there who want to have their cake and eat it, too."

"Like the married woman with the stud on the side like our Chase?" Three-H added with a wink.

Leo's chuckle was pleasant enough. "Looks like the staff of *Sunday* is full of secrets which we all intend to respect."

Three-H thanked him, gave him an awkward hug and then left the room, disappearing into the energetic throng.

Not long after that, Leo received another letter from Greg. Oddly, it didn't surprise him since he had been reading between the lines for a while. To some extent, it was even a relief:

... and what I discovered was that I had been holding back out of loyalty to you. Or really, my memories of all that. Sewanee was all very sweet and innocent. Top 40 hits in the dark in separate beds. But when I met Yaro, I knew there was something real there. I think at first he was as reluctant to get involved with a white man as I was to allow my feelings to develop for a native Kenyan. But his skills as a primary teacher broke down all those reservations we had about each other. When I watched him with the schoolchildren in the classroom, the past suddenly didn't seem so important anymore. The way their faces lit up when he got through to them on something or other. I hope you'll understand that this new development doesn't lessen my affection for you, Leo. We'll always be dear friends. But we live so far apart in different worlds and have for several years. I'm just going to let this happen, even though Yaro and I have to be very careful. Homosexual behavior here is a punishable offense. People have been jailed or even killed. So, what else is new? Yaro could lose his job teaching if he were found out. One or the other of us will rent a cheap hotel room

here in Nairobi, and then the other will sneak in later. We can't afford to be seen together in my Peace Corps digs or his place the way people talk over here. Your letters about New Orleans make America seem like it's light years ahead, but I know that's not universally true…

Greg had enclosed a selection of photos of Yaro: here was one with him standing at the blackboard in his classroom. On the back were the words printed in block letters: MY BEAUTIFUL MAN, YARO PALA. Another showed him leaning on a hoe in the middle of a patch of dirt. YARO IN HIS SHAMBA (VEG. GARDEN) read the inscription on the other side. The Kenyan was tall, muscular, and lean with a wide, confident smile, and Leo could see why Greg had fallen for him. At the same time, it was obvious that Greg was moving on with his life emotionally and was no longer tied to something that had never even gotten off the ground; even though he and Yaro were risking everything by plunging into their love for each other.

Leo wrote back immediately and gave his complete blessing without hesitation, even though Greg hadn't asked for it. It was very liberating, but he felt compelled to add a P.S:

Promise me you and Yaro will continue to be careful.

Chapter 13

Over the next year and a half, Leo began to take a different attitude toward the social gatherings of the Coalition. The residue of his eternal yet also ephemeral relationship with Greg had finally been wiped away; that sense of betrayal that had been looking over his shoulder for so long was gone now. Although there was no one currently in the membership that had seriously interested him, he looked at everyone in a new light. His conversations were longer now, less guarded, more probing. He stopped finding fault with the most insignificant things like a snort after a laugh or the word, "Right?" tacked onto the end of too many sentences. He made a deliberate effort to dig deeper and to stop avoiding what amounted to leftover closeted behavior. He had come to realize that his upbringing still had a very strong hold on him, despite his considerable efforts to neutralize its power. Too many "queer jokes" had taken their toll during formative years. And if no one in the current configuration suited him, perhaps he should keep an open mind about any newcomers that might wander in. Maybe his Yaro would come along. With no strings attached.

And then one evening at Terrence's apartment, before the discussion of the selected topic of Job Security and Coming Out To Your Employer had begun, Leo was nursing his usual club soda and chatting amiably with his flawlessly-groomed stylist and confidante Mara Lehmann, when he received a tap on the shoulder. A sudden rush of transformative memory had him halfway expecting to see Three-H to be standing there when he turned around. Instead, he was surprised by the presence of his former high school teacher, Chess Club sponsor and *Carousel* director, Lake Campbell.

Leo's jaw dropped, and he couldn't speak.

"I'm sure you didn't expect to see me here," Mr. Campbell said, extending his hand.

After Leo had made the perfunctory introductions all around, the polite small talk was over and done with, and Mara had flitted off to someone else, teacher and student found a corner in the cozy living room and began to catch up with one another.

"What happened was simply that I outgrew Beau Pre and moved down here about six months ago," Mr. Campbell began in between sips of his white wine spritzer. "I'm working for the parochial school system—St. Michael's, to be exact. Once I got settled in, I started exploring this fine old city and all it had to offer, and when I found out about the Coalition recently, I called your helpline and got the info for this meeting."

Leo's gasp was nearly inaudible, but it was there nonetheless. "I wonder if I was on the line at the time you called. Was it possibly during the evening one Wednesday?"

"No. Last Saturday morning, I think it was."

"Then it wasn't me." Leo found himself moving into a comfort zone quickly and continued. "I had no idea you were… gay, Mr. Campbell. I mean, we all knew you weren't married back then in high school, but that didn't mean anything to any of us."

"Please, although I'm nearly old enough to be your father, I'd like for you to start calling me Lake now. Time usually puts compatible people on a more equal footing."

Leo was amused and flattered at the same time. Adulthood by any other name was surely upon him now. He also noticed for the first time that he and his former teacher might possibly be mistaken for father and son. They both had red hair, although the older man's was darker with the first touches of gray at the temples, and their faces were more alike now that Leo's mass of freckles had started to fade somewhat into a ruddy complexion.

Leo held out his glass, and the two of them clinked rims, taking celebratory sips. "Okay, then… Lake, it is."

"Of course, I had no way of knowing you were gay, either, Leo. You were a good actor and singer, best in the school as far as I was concerned, but that didn't mean anything, either. Except that I somehow knew you were just right for the role of Billy Bigelow, and I even had you in mind when I chose *Carousel* for our production your senior year."

"Really?"

"Yes. Of course, you had to come through at your audition. But you did, and I also somehow knew you could block and direct the entire first act the way you did. It was just one of those things that happens now and then, and you know not to question them when they come along."

The two had refreshed their drinks and had run through a spate of recent mundane events by the time Leo decided to truly compare notes. "When did you know you were gay… Mr… uh, Lake?"

"Of course, that term wasn't in fashion then," he began with a contemplative smile, "but I was very young. It was definitely before puberty, though. And my first crush hit me like the proverbial ton of bricks. He had no idea, and I had no choice in the matter. It just happened."

Leo thought of Dean Forsythe and managed a thoughtful smile of his own. "Same here."

The newly-christened Lake started shaking his head. "If I could wish one thing and have it granted, it would be that people would understand that we—you and I, that is—didn't wake up one morning and consciously decide that we were going to be attracted to the same sex. Like we just threw a dart and hit that particular bull's-eye on the board on purpose. We just woke up one morning, and there it was."

Growing even more comfortable with their exchange, Leo said, "Did you camouflage date in Beau Pre? I know I did."

There was a burst of laughter. "Absolutely. I asked out two of the single teachers—Pamela Kaiser and Jeanine O'Neal to cover my tracks, even though I wasn't seeing a guy at the time, and I had no interest in those innocent ladies sexually. That went over quite well in the teacher's lounge. The dating part, I mean. Maybe too well. Some of the married lady teachers were always trying to set me up with their nieces or daughters or girl cousins or whatever. They would actually ooh and ahh about these introductions they wanted to make. I was assured that they all came with the requisite great personalities, as the description always seems to be."

"Protective coloration on your part," Leo said with a mirthful expression on his face. "I know all about it."

"Do you remember Mrs. Wayland, the heavy-set, opinionated Bible Club sponsor?"

Leo recalled only too well. " I cringed every time one of her members held us all captive for two minutes every morning over the P.A. system. Sermon after sermon about the salvation we desperately needed and the evils of drinking and all the fire and brimstone your little heart could ever desire. I halfway expected lightning to come out of the speakers. I tried to block all those rants out the best I could, but it was difficult."

"Laveta Wayland was the judgmental terror of the teacher's lounge, butting into everyone's business over coffee and doughnuts," came the reply. "I'm sure she thought she was being maternal and looking after everyone, but that wasn't what she was hired to do. At least I don't think that was in her job description. I can imagine how she would have reacted if she'd known I was gay. I wouldn't have put it past her to have gone to the school board after my job, if not script a two-minute rant about me over the P.A. system, complete with scripture to back her up."

Then Leo highlighted what was going on in Kenya with Greg and Yaro.

"I think you're right to tell them to be cautious. Some African nations criminalize homosexuality. I'm very interested in tonight's discussion topic on coming out to your employer. Or not, as the case may be. I work for the parochial school system here, as I said, so I'm thinking I'm better off keeping my private life to myself."

"Is there anything to tell? Are you seeing someone now?"

There was an enthusiastic nod. "Ignacio lives in Mexico City where I first met him on vacation, and now I devote all my summer vacations to him. We spend a blissful three months together, Christmas holidays and whatever else we can squeeze out. I keep telling myself that one of these days I'll convince him to move to America permanently. Or he'll convince me to become a Mexican citizen. Right now, it's a standoff." He paused to chuckle to himself. "I guess you could call it a Mexican standoff."

"Wow. Lots of foreign intrigue among my friends," Leo added.

"That's because gay people are everywhere. They always have been. Always will be. We aren't something new that just showed up on radar for the first time in human history. Despite what some people would have you believe, our presence does not signal the end of the world or the 'end times.' We've been there from the beginning."

Himself now an experienced journalist, Leo said, "Has anyone ever told you that you're quite the wordsmith? You should bottle that rousing speech and go on tour."

Just then, Terrence interrupted the healthy and well-lubricated interaction around the room to call the evening's discussion to order, and everyone quickly complied, taking seats on folding chairs and the one available sofa. Soon, there was a lively exchange after Terrence set the tone with a prepared speech and then invited the small crowd to contribute their anecdotes.

"I definitely agree that it depends upon the circumstances and the type of job you have," Mara Lehmann was saying. "For instance, at my salon, Long May She Wave, I employ several stylists from different backgrounds, and among them is my great friend, George Kinsey, our transplanted Californian and the only male in the establishment. He keeps me in stitches all the time. Now, I don't want to sound like I'm promoting stereotypes, but I don't think anyone would object to a man being a hairdresser. There are people out there—and I don't want to know them, let me assure you—that think all gay men are hairdressers or drag queens. A lot they know. However, what if you're a gay man and you get a job with a powerful law firm? Or you're a police officer? Or a fireman? Do you have to keep quiet about it? Should you have to keep quiet about it? Does it make a difference in the performance of your job?"

"Thank you for those questions, Mara. They get right to the point of our discussion tonight," Terrence added, standing in the middle of the room as the imposing figure he was. "Things like religious and political beliefs are not supposed to be a part of hiring people. I trust we've gotten past that in our country, but perhaps I'm being naive. But what about people's private lives? Should it matter if someone is married, divorced or single and still looking for Mr. or Miss Right, no matter who they happen to be? Should that be part of the decision-making process? I firmly say, 'No!'"

Lake Campbell's hand shot up. "As an experienced teacher, I have to say without question that there are people out there who would object to my being gay and also being in the classroom, even though that has nothing to do with my ability to teach English or Math or any other discipline. They are acting out of fear and ignorance when they entertain such objections. That said, there are certain things that aren't appropriate to bring up in the classroom anyway. It's always been that way."

"Good point," Terrence added. "I don't recall any of my married teachers in high school or college spending any amount of time talking about their husbands or wives, or even their children. Oh, it might happen here and there, but as an aside, not the focus of the job at hand."

Leo decided to speak up. "Then, are we talking about a problem that doesn't exist? Are we debating a straw dog here?"

"No, I think it's a real part of the world we live in," Terrence said. "But I do think it is incumbent upon us all to be prudent about reality. I've found that I need to get to know someone really well before I delve too deeply into my private life with them. As a rule of thumb, I think that's a good idea for everyone. In general, people don't like too much unsolicited information."

"I agree with that," Mara said. Then she gestured toward Lake Campbell, sitting on the sofa beside Leo. "I just can't imagine someone really going after teachers, though. I had some good ones and some that were not so good. I'm sure we all did. But it never occurred to me to worry about what they did when they went home at night. They were never a part of my homework assignments in that way."

"Ugh...homework. Who invented it?" Leo added, causing an eruption of laughter around the room.

"We can all agree on that apparently," Terrence said when the room went quiet again. "As for our subject at hand, I think it calls for vigilance and courage and not idly standing by when some people out there give in to their darker nature and promote persecution. Let's never forget that we all have a right to exist in the universe without apology."

Then, a wave of impromptu, light applause brought another Coalition discussion to a successful end. Leo, in particular, felt a deep satisfaction that he had been reconnected with a pivotal person in his life.

Chapter 14

As the months went by, the friendship between Leo and his former teacher grew substantially in time spent together and insights shared. It was also platonic, akin more to what a father and son might enjoy. There were dinners in the Quarter and the Garden District from time to time, but the two men were careful to go Dutch so as not to cross a line of obligation. Leo shared parts of Greg's letters, and Lake read snippets of those from his Ignacio, while also sharing pictures of his handsome Latino man. Throughout it all, Leo felt like he was in school all over again, gaining in confidence through someone he would always trust.

One Saturday, after treating themselves to a dinner of turtle soup and crab cakes at Commander's Palace, the two headed to Leo's camelback for an evening of piano playing and a game of chess to top it all off. Leo sang "I Have Dreamed" and "We Kiss In A Shadow" from *The King and I,* both of which spoke to love anticipated and guarded in haunting, R & H fashion.

"If anything, your voice has improved with age," Lake said, after applauding softly. "Have you thought about doing any regional theater down here? I think you've still got it."

Leo rose from his spinet and shrugged. "It's crossed my mind a time or two. I'd have to plan it around my work schedule, though. Anyway, let's play chess."

They adjourned to the dining room table to set up the board with its carved ivory pieces. Leo chose white, while Lake took black.

"My father taught me the game when I was twelve, and it was part of the reason I joined your club," Leo said, as they sat down to make their first traditional moves with their pawns.

"What was the other part?"

"To get your attention for the next musical."

Lake smiled while shaking his head. "You didn't have to do that. You were on my radar from the moment you tried out for *Oklahoma!*"

"I thought of it as my backup plan, my insurance policy," Leo said, bringing out his knight.

As the game progressed, he launched into a chess story about his father and his Uncle Brady. "They were drinking Brandy Alexanders during one of their marathon games, and by the time they got to the checkmate, they'd lost count of how many they'd downed. I forget who actually won, but when it was time for them to get up from the table, they couldn't do it. They couldn't move. All that brandy had frozen them in place. Daddy said they switched to something lighter for their future showdowns."

"I'm not sure chess and hard liquor exactly go together," Lane said, laughing out loud. "You need all the brain power you can muster to get to checkmate."

Leo pointed to his club soda off to one side. "That's why I always stick with this."

Lake had just castled when the phone rang seconds later, and Leo excused himself, moving quickly to the kitchen counter to answer it.

"Leo," his mother said at the other end after his perfunctory hello. "I have some not so good news." Her voice was trembling, her breathing heavy.

"What's wrong, Mama?"

"It's your father." There was another awkward pause. "He's been diagnosed with lung cancer. It's no wonder, since he's been smoking since he was a fighter pilot, as I don't have to tell you. I kept telling him to do something about that cough of his. It's not as bad as it could be, though. They say they caught it in the earlier stages, and it's operable. They're gonna remove it and then do radiation treatments."

Leo had heard all the words, but they didn't seem to be registering with him. He thought he ought to be feeling something, but he wasn't at the moment. His response was on some kind of cruise control. "That's a good thing, then. When is his surgery?"

"This coming Friday at Beau Pre General," she said, sounding as if she were getting a better grip on herself. "They have an excellent oncology staff, and your Uncle Brady will make sure Daddy gets the best care possible with all the friends he has there. I was wondering if your schedule would permit you to come up, and you and I could be his cheering squad. Not to mention that I could use some handholding."

"I won't have any trouble arranging my schedule. Arthur will understand. He's pretty good about these family crises. I'm as good as there."

"Thank you, my little Buddha. I love you," she said.

"I love you, too, Mama. All my love to Daddy. Try not to worry too much. See you soon."

Seated back at the dining room table, Leo repeated the gist of his phone call to Lake as calmly as he could, who then immediately suggested they forget about the game and move to the living room sofa.

"Are you really okay?" Lake began once they'd settled in. "I know the 'C' word freezes people up immediately, but it sounds like a mostly good prognosis."

Leo reached over and took his hand. "It's just beginning to hit me, and I feel guilty."

"Why?"

Leo took a deep breath and described all the cigarette runs he'd made for his father once he'd gotten his driver's license back in high school. More runs than he could possibly count.

"You were just a good son following orders. That was his choice, not yours," Lake pointed out. "It wasn't yours to question.

I'm sure he wouldn't have allowed it. And that was all before we knew what we know now about nicotine."

"Yeah, but don't they call that enabling? Isn't that the hot buzz word these days?"

Lake squeezed Leo's hand hard. "Stop. This isn't worthy of you. The fact is, you can't take people on this way, not even your parents. Their journeys aren't the same as yours. The right thing to do now is to support your father... and your mother by going up to be with her the way you promised her you would."

"I'm afraid it's a fault of mine—feeling guilty about things I have no business feeling that way about. I seem to want to go there all the time. Maybe that's what happens when you spend too much time in the closet."

"You're out now. Remember that."

"You're right, of course." Leo lowered his voice. "I don't suppose... that you could come with me to Beau Pre."

Lake loosened his grip and said, "I can't. I have my classes. If it were on a weekend, I certainly would. Just concentrate on your father getting well and forget about the rest."

"Good advice," Leo added, finally withdrawing his hand. "I need to get my house in order. Seems I've been trying to do that for a long time."

Lake put his arm around Leo's shoulder and said, "I'm no different. And don't let people fool you when they say they've got it all figured out. Most of them are bluffing and pulling a feint. A big, fat feint. Of course, it's my belief that there are signs we can follow if we're paying attention. What I mean is that there are certain constants that crop up in our lives. Certain strains and themes just like in a good symphony."

Leo's smile had a serenity to it. "Like music and singing and connecting with people who have red hair? But there has to be more to it than that."

"Keep an open mind," Lake added. "Change is also inevitable. You never know what's coming down the pike."

*

Leo and his mother were sitting together on a long, Naugahyde sofa in the waiting room of Beau Pre General. Joseph Marble had been in surgery for an hour and a half, and the hospital coffee his wife and son were drinking to try and deal with their anxiety wasn't helping. Probably because it wasn't very good coffee.

"This is nasty," Louisa said at one point, putting her paper cup down on the table in front of her sporting stacks of well-handled, popular magazines curling at the edges. "No amount of sugar and cream can save it. It's just too weak."

"Stop drinking it, then," Leo said. "And take one of your pills."

"I want to be alert. I haven't slept well the past couple of days."

"I haven't, either," Leo admitted.

"Your Uncle Brady keeps saying that the prognosis is good," she continued. "That we have every reason for optimism since it's Stage 1. Well, actually between Stage 1 and Stage 2. Maybe I didn't mention that."

"I'm sure he's telling us the truth."

Louisa looked at her watch, and her mouth hitched to one side. "It just seems like it's taking forever. I just want it to be over with and know that he's come through."

"Uncle Brady said it would be at least a couple of hours. We're not there yet, Mama." Then he remembered something he had been meaning to ask her. "Why isn't Granny Marble here?"

Louisa rolled her eyes but managed a smile. "Oh, that. I talked to her over the phone this morning, and she was in one of her pontificating moods."

"She was pontificating about Daddy's surgery?"

"I can quote her exactly. She said, 'No son of mine is going to die before I do. That's the natural order of things.'"

Leo let that sink in briefly. "I can just hear her now."

"Sometimes I wish I had her confidence about life… and death. I give her credit. She rose like a phoenix after your grandfather died, and here's that dreaded word *cancer* coming into her life again. Like father, like son. I know she prefers to work things out by herself. It's my belief that she's one of those people that likes to shed tears behind the scenes, and then once she's dried her eyes, she comes back with a vengeance."

"The Marble School of Music is proof."

"She also mentioned that your uncle had assured her the operation was a pretty routine one, all things considered, so she had some help with that confidence this time around." Louisa checked her watch yet again and then continued. "Speaking of your uncle, I wish he would come out and give us another update."

"We could talk about something else to pass the time," Leo suggested.

"Why don't we?" she said. "Do you still hear from Greg? Is he still with the Peace Corps?"

Leo nodded and brought her up to date on the friendship with Yaro, including the necessity of the two of them keeping things hidden as a result of Kenya's rigid culture.

"That's not all that much different from here in this country," she added. "I've been reading up on things since that time at Sewanee. I feel it's my duty to keep up. Still, I can't help but worry about you sometimes. I just can't help it. I'm your mother. It's my job."

"I appreciate it, but I can take care of myself, I assure you."

"Are you… seeing anyone?"

"Not the way you mean. But I've written to you about the Coalition and the work we're doing. I think it's my best bet for finding someone who's serious about a relationship. The discos are just for dancing, and I don't much care for the pick-up bars. That's not who I am." Then he told her all about Lake Campbell reentering his life on a platonic, almost fatherly, level.

"Mr. Campbell was… is gay?" she said with astonishment on her face. "I would never have guessed."

"It's not something it's wise to lead with, Mama, the way things are in general. We've discussed the subject of openness at one of our Coalition meetings. I'm just curious, by the way. Have you and Daddy…" The question came to a halt.

"Have we what, Leo?"

"Have you and Daddy told Granny Marble about me yet?"

She smiled and reached over to touch Leo's hand gently. "We still don't think she's ready to deal with it. I mean, here's someone who goes on and on about the natural order of things regarding who should die first. Your Daddy and I still think that decision to come out to her is up to you. Personally, I think not disturbing that world she lives in that's set in stone is the way to go. For some people, not knowing is better."

"I have to admit that it makes sense in a roundabout sort of way."

Then Louisa gave a sudden gasp of remembrance. "Did you see that story on the news last night? There's this Save Our Children campaign that that singer has started up because of some teacher discrimination ordinance that passed down in Miami."

"This is the first I've heard of it. What singer?"

"Oh, you know the one. She was runner-up to Miss America a while back or something close to that. She's had some hits over the radio. 'Paper Roses' was one, I think I recall. I've got her name on the tip of my tongue. She does commercials for orange juice."

"Anita Bryant?"

"That's the one."

Leo frowned while trying to make sense of what his mother had told him. "What does saving children have to do with a discrimination ordinance?"

"I can't remember all the details. You and your Coalition will have to look into it."

"Knowing Terrence, he'll have already jumped on it, and it'll probably be the subject of our next meeting."

Still, Leo thought it was prescient the way he and Lake and the Coalition had been focusing on a controversy that was just waiting to happen. And now, it finally had.

After what seemed more like twenty-four hours, Dr. Brady Campbell finally entered the waiting room in his white coat and a reassuring smile on his neatly trimmed, salt-and-pepper, bearded face. "Everything went well. He's in the recovery room, and then they'll move him back to his bed. Take a deep breath and relax, folks. The hard part is over."

Both Leo and his mother jumped up, and she moved quickly to give her brother-in-law a hug. "Thanks, Brady. So, there were no complications?"

"None whatsoever. They got all of the tumor. It's important to catch these things early before they spread. You were right to stay on him about that cough and get a checkup. You probably saved his life."

Louisa waved him off and flashed a gracious smile. "Think nothing of it. Came with the marriage vows."

Leo stepped up, shook his uncle's hand, and said, "When can we see Daddy?"

"As soon as he gets comfortably settled. Shouldn't be too long, but you'll have to make this first visit a short one so he can get his rest and start healing up."

"Gotcha," Leo said, while his mother nodded enthusiastically.

Ten or fifteen minutes later, the trio was joined by Granny Marble, who walked in looking supremely collected and wearing her favorite, lavender church outfit with the ruffles which always reminded people of an orchid in bloom. She began by greeting and hugging everyone and then said, "I told Brady to phone me as soon as he knew the outcome. I'm happy to visit my son now and every single day until he's out of the hospital to help him recover. I wish things had gone that way for my precious Sykes."

Brady moved to his mother and drew her to his side once again. "We all understand, Moms. You had it pretty rough with Popsy. You were truly blind-sided."

"When I first heard about your brother's diagnosis, I kept telling myself that it wasn't right for me to have to go through this twice in a lifetime. I was so angry, and I figured I was just not fit company for the rest of you." She paused to point out her signature outfit. "But now I'm dressed for the healing I know will take place, and I can't wait to lean down and give my first-born a kiss on the cheek."

"We're all looking forward to that," Louisa added.

It wasn't long before the four of them were taking turns kissing and caressing Joseph's hand as he lay in his telemetry bed.

"Don't bother to tell me I look just fine," Joseph managed in strained tones. "I know I'm groggy as hell... and I barely know where I am... but it sure is great to see all of you here together."

"All you need to know is that you're in good hands," Brady told him, standing to the left side of the bed.

Joseph cracked a smile. 'Yeah, I know. It's all over but the radiation."

From the right side, Granny Marble switched into her most authoritative mode. "You are hereby charged with healing quickly. That is your assignment, and we will all show up to help you with it."

"Yes, ma'am," Joseph said, his grin broadening.

Soon after, an officious young nurse entered the room and cut that first visit short.

As Leo walked out and down the hall, he briefly entertained the notion that he might carve out some time at the music school before he left for New Orleans to discuss with Granny Marble the reality of his private life. But it was just a flash, and he soon thought better of it. There was his grandmother, walking ahead of him with her certainty intact, the rightness of her world restored, her lavender plumage fully on display like that of an exotic bird. He decided that he could not take that away from her. He also remembered what Lake had said about people being on different journeys and that it was mostly folly to try and disrupt them head-on, even with the best of intentions. A person could only take on so much, and people were only capable of so much input at one time.

Maybe there would come a time when Granny Marble might be entrusted with the truth. But this was not it.

Chapter 15

Leo began following the Miami-Dade Ordinance controversy as if it were the very oxygen he breathed. He followed every AP story and evening newscast with a fervor he had rarely experienced. Nothing else mattered deep down in his core where he lived. He talked to Terrence and Lake over the phone daily about the latest developments and never failed to get worked up in the process. By the time the Coalition met to formally discuss the Save Our Children campaign at Terrence's apartment, he had a difficult time keeping his temper.

"How can she be saying these outrageous things and getting away with it? How do you get from an ordinance protecting everyone from discrimination in employment to claiming that gay teachers in classrooms are somehow recruiting their students? How can people be falling for that? That we're vampires who swoop down on our pupils in the darkness of the cloakroom? Nobody recruited me into my attraction to other men. It was just there. I believe it showed up when it was supposed to—at a very early age. Certainly no teacher of mine had anything to do with it." Leo's already ruddy face had turned nearly crimson, and he had made fists of his hands without realizing it.

Lake spoke up while gently patting his arm in an attempt to soothe him. "I hate to tell all of you, but there are some parents at St. Michael's who have expressed their support of her positions to our Headmaster, Father Babineaux. Not a lot, mind you, but enough to get his attention. Some have even asked for a clarification from the church. I think the sad truth is that Anita Bryant has opened up a fearful can of worms here."

"She can't possibly win, though," Leo said, not bothering to lower his decibel level. "She's made this thing up out of whole cloth about teachers, and I just can't see the majority of people thinking it has any merit. What happened to common sense?"

"As a teacher I can tell you that all of us understand quite well that any sort of intimate relationship with any student is grounds for immediate dismissal," Lake pointed out. "There have always been lines that shouldn't be crossed in the classroom and after hours as well. If this were really going on as Anita Bryant claims, there would be widespread firings in school systems already. Yet, there is no evidence of this anywhere. She's manufacturing a hypothetical, and somehow, people are paying attention."

Terrence stepped in. "The bad news is that she's leading in the polls down there. We can't deny that, much as we might dislike it. At the present time, there's not much we can do about it here in New Orleans. We'll just have to wait and see how the election turns out."

Terrence paused to open the small, black appointment calendar he was holding in his hand. "Which brings me to this. The election is one week from now. I realize that we may get some extra calls on the helpline that night because of the results one way or the other. Therefore, I want to make it clear that if you think you're not up to handling things that evening when the results are in, you don't have to feel guilty about excusing yourself. Leo, I see that's your usual shift, but if you want to bow out, I'll take it for you."

"Not necessary at all," Leo said, waving him off. "I'm confident that the voters of Miami-Dade County will come to their senses and keep a perfectly reasonable ordinance on the books. If I get some angry calls about it, so what? I've gotten angry, prank calls before, so I'm an old hand. Count me in, Terrence. I can take it."

"I thought you'd say that, but I wanted to give you the option."

"Thanks, but I'm cool with taking my shift."

After the meeting had adjourned, Terrence asked Leo to linger a few minutes so they could talk, and Lake said as he was heading out, "I'll wait for you outside."

"I know you're confident that the voters of Miami-Dade County couldn't possibly repeal that ordinance," Terrence began. "I applaud your trust in the better nature of human beings."

"That's the way I see it, yes."

"As a result, you expect the helpline calls to be from people who are pissed off and that you think it'll be business as usual for you."

"I've been doing this long enough, so, yes."

"But what if the opposite happens, and somehow the ordinance is repealed? Are you prepared to face a bunch of jerks rubbing it in? That's my real concern. You're so certain that this Save Our Children campaign won't succeed and that people will come to their senses, as you said. But there's a chance they might not."

Leo clearly registered annoyance in his tone of voice. "This is overkill, Terrence. I can handle it. Thanks for your concern, but I can't see that this is worse than anything else I've had to face over the years. I've had a lot of things thrown at me, and I'm still here."

Terrence gave him one of his Henry the Eighth bear hugs and drew back with a smile. "And I'm so glad you are, my friend."

"It's mutual," Leo said and then headed out to join Lake.

Leo brought his portable black-and-white TV with the rabbit ears for his helpline shift so he could catch election return updates on WWL. Lake had made one last pitch to lend moral support by accompanying him to the Coalition office.

"I don't need you to hold my hand," Leo had told him. "But thank you anyway."

The shift began at 5 in the afternoon and would continue

until midnight when Pauly Dixon, a Quarter bartender with a tattoo on his right forearm that read STONEWALL, 1969, took over. As usual, Leo opened the call log and prepared himself mentally for the phone to ring.

The first call came around 5:15, but there was nothing but silence on the other end after Leo said hello several times. Those he always marked as SILENT HANG UP with no other comment. He always wondered whether those were examples of callers working up the gumption to ask for help or to call him out in no uncertain terms. He would likely never know.

Then, at 5:19, the first prank call of the evening: "God will punish you." Then a dial tone. Leo just put down the one word PRANK and rolled his eyes. Business as usual, indeed.

There was an update on WWL as the first returns rolled in, and Leo hung on every word and graphic. The Save Our Children Campaign had an early lead, but there were many more precincts to count, the reporter said. Leo took it in stride, exhaling loudly. Early returns were often deceiving.

The next half hour went as follows:

5:45—PRANK
5:48—PRANK
5:53—PRANK
6:07—PRANK
6:13—PRANK

Never mind that the messages behind those calls—not written down—were petty and predictable:

"How many guys have you sucked off today?"

"There is still time to repent if you accept Jesus. Or else you'll burn in Hell."

"Does your mother know you're a queer?"

"You people disgust me. They oughta round you all up and put you in prison."

"Is this the beyond help line? Because you fags are beyond help."

None of the comments bothered Leo, as he had long ago

become deadened to them. Then, a further update from more Miami-Dade precincts showed the Save Our Children Campaign widening their initial lead. Leo frowned and then rubbed his forehead. Surely this would turn around at some point. Maybe the right precincts just hadn't reported yet. Leads changed hands all the time.

At 6:33, the first call referencing the vote in Florida came through: "Hey, fag, looks like God is winning in Miami this evening. Have you been keeping up with the vote?... What's the matter—cat got your tongue?...Yeah, you should get the message and shut up forever... What? No cute, faggy response?... Yeah, I thought so. See ya. Wouldn't wanna be ya."

Leo's training not to engage served him well for a short while, but the certainty, the optimism he had expressed to both Terrence and Lake was starting to drain away. It began to look like the ordinance was doomed, and the Save Our Children campaign was going to win. More calls came in after every TV update, each more virulent than the last. Leo had never handled this many prank calls in one sitting, and as it became increasingly obvious that the ordinance would be repealed, he began to hurt inside; the same kind of hurt he had felt when he had fallen for Dean Forsythe at the tender age of thirteen and knew how impossible the situation was. And how impossible the situation with Coy Warren was. That neither could possibly end well. Things out of his control began to eat at him as they had back then.

He hurriedly called Lake, and it all came pouring out.

"I feel like I've been rejected," he began. "I never thought I'd take this so personally, but I am. I was so sure the ordinance would survive. I just couldn't believe people would buy into that outrageous campaign. Everything is upside down. I feel sick inside."

"Listen," Lake said, "I'm coming down there. You can't go through this alone. Don't be stubborn about it. I won't take no for an answer."

"You win. I have no intention of arguing. I do need you down here."

Twenty minutes later, Lake walked in, and the first thing the two men did was hug, trying to give one another an infusion of strength.

"They're driving you crazy, aren't they?" Lake said, pulling back while shaking his head.

The phone rang, and Leo pointed to it. "It's been that way all evening. Off the hook. They've come out of the woodwork."

"Let me take this one," Lake said. "You need a break."

Lake picked up the phone and listened patiently, saying nothing. Then he hung up and said, "A rant about the ordinance being rightly repealed and thanks be to Jesus and all the rest of that stuff."

Leo handed over his pen and gestured toward the log. "Just write down the time and put PRANK."

By 10 o'clock, the final verdict was in. The ordinance had been repealed, and the vote wasn't even close. Save Our Children had won 70% to 30%. That qualified as a political landslide in anyone's book.

"Are my instincts that far off-base?" Leo said, after logging in another prank call praising the ordinance defeat around 10:30. "Is that how most people feel about us? Not us as in you and me, but everyone who's like us? I thought maybe things were starting to change after the Stonewall Riots. That was nearly a decade ago."

Lake could only shrug. "There have been some changes, just maybe not as fast as you and I would like. And I definitely didn't expect that big of a margin."

"Wait...are you saying you expected the ordinance to be defeated? I got the impression Terrence felt the same way at our meeting last week. He was so solicitous of me."

"He was only going by the polling."

"Which turned out to be totally accurate," Leo added. "I guess I was in denial."

"You were hoping for the best. There's nothing wrong with that," Lake said. "But let me say here and now that you can't take this personally. That would be entirely the wrong thing to do. This is a point in time that won't be remembered fondly in the future, I suspect. Don't give up, and most importantly, don't give up on yourself."

Somehow, Leo got through the last hour with Lake's help and was never so happy to see Pauly Dixon walk through the door to spell him.

"Horrible news, huh, fellas?" Pauly said, running his hand through his dark, shoulder-length hair and then energetically shaking his head from side-to-side in dog-like fashion, as if that could erase the sadness etched across his normally smiling face.

"The worst," Leo said. "Get ready for one helluva night."

Pauly walked over and glanced at the log. "No legit calls, I see."

"Nope, just abuse."

"I came by to lend some moral support," Lake said. "And if it gets too bad at any point, just shut it down, go home and get some rest. There are limits to what people should put themselves through. We're not here to be punching bags."

Pauly managed to smile. "I'll keep that in mind."

Outside on the sidewalk, Lake turned to Leo and said, "Do you want to spend the night at my place in the guest room? I'll be glad to have you."

Surprised by the invitation, Leo said, "You and Terrence worry about me too much."

"We care about you."

"I know that. All of us at the Coalition care about each other. But I think I need to go home and start working on accepting what happened tonight. Nobody can do that but me."

"I'll let you go home by yourself on one condition," Lake said, putting his arm around his friend's shoulder. "That you call me if you need me."

Leo agreed, and with a final quick hug, the two headed in opposite directions to their parking spaces on the busy, wide-awake, after-midnight Quarter streets.

By the time Leo got home, any calmness, any shred of confidence he had gained from that last hug with Lake in the Quarter had worn off completely. He found himself alone once again with the visceral wound delivered by the election results. Despite Lake's advice, he was again taking the repeal of the ordinance personally. Taking shame and guilt into his body with no filter to stop it, enduring a transfusion of self-doubt.

How could this repeal have happened? He was back on the seesaw where he had first been accused of being different. Then he was behind the louver door hearing his mother vent her worries about his sexuality and later overhearing the queer joke told by Blaine Carter, his father's obnoxious law partner. These incidents had held sway over him then. He thought they had loosened their grip with the passage of time. But they were back, swiping at him mercilessly.

An avalanche of cringe-worthy incidents resurfaced. The "regular guys" in P.E. thought he threw a baseball like a girl; he had spent his high school years pretending to be someone he was not; and it had caught up with him when he had become the school heartthrob, the ultimate mirage. Had he wrecked Rebecca Bentley's life by leading her on? Had he been too deeply locked in the closet to do more with his fledgling friendship with Greg? Had that really been what had sent him off to Kenya?

He began to entertain the notion that the defeat of this ordinance was even some sort of punishment for not truly belonging in the world, for not fitting in. Was there a place for him? Or was the message from Miami-Dade that there was not such a place, nor for people like him?

He walked past the piano and into the outdated kitchen. He looked around. It was a small, windowless space with a worn linoleum floor and one door leading into the living room. It would be easy enough, once the door was shut. He could turn on the gas from one of the burners, lie down and just go to sleep. He hadn't figured out what would happen after that. Others claimed to know. Some were downright arrogant about it, condemning those who didn't believe as they did. Maybe there would be a place for him in death, but he could hardly know that now.

127

He sat at the small kitchen table for a while and thought about it further.

Seventy percent.

That many people in Miami-Dade believed that people like Lake Campbell were a threat to their children in school. That he and Lake and Terrence and Pauly and Mara and Greg and Yaro and every other gay man or woman in his life and all over the world were predators on the prowl and had to be stopped. Although he knew that to be completely false, apparently most of the world thought otherwise. Some Kenyans thought so. Apparently, a huge contingent of Floridians agreed with Anita Bryant and her accusations. Did he want to go on living in such a world? Would things only get worse, not better?

He got up and moved to one of the front burners, his hand inches away from turning on the doorway to the unknown. He took a deep breath for courage.

And then, something remarkable happened.

He thought of his piano which he had passed on the way in. It was nearly his. Just two more payments. If he owned nothing else in this world, he owned that snappy little spinet. It was his constant ticket to music and song. He recalled fondly that moment when his voice had appeared out of nowhere, and he had started singing along with Steve Lawrence on the car radio. Finally, he returned to the song he had performed for Lake and the other teachers on the selection committee at his *Carousel* audition.

"You'll Never Walk Alone."

He immediately knew he had to go to the piano and sing it as well as he had sung it so long ago. That was the rebuttal to turning on the gas and breathing no more.

So he did just that. His lungs rose to the occasion as the first words began to lift him up, his diaphragm reverberating with joy. *"When you walk through a storm, hold your head up high…"*

When he came to the end, he felt centered again, like he had just been administered a dose of powerful medicine. The crisis had been averted. Then he got up from the piano bench and headed toward his bedroom with his head indeed held up high.

On the way and with a hitch to his step, he even managed a chuckle under his breath. "You, Leo Marble, are way too dramatic for your own good," he said out loud. "Get a grip."

It was in the middle of the night that Leo got up from his bed, the infusion he had received from "You'll Never Walk Alone" having long ago worn off. He wondered why he didn't head right away to the bathroom to pee because he usually did so once as part of his nightly routine. Instead, something beyond his control directed him into the kitchen once again. He seemed helpless this time to ward off his earlier dark intent. All he had to do again was to close the door and turn on the gas, then lie down and await whatever transition the universe had in store for him. So he dutifully did just that.

This time, there was no urge to break away and rush to the spinet for help. This time, it was for real. There was no turning back.

He thought he heard piano music. Had someone broken into his apartment to sing and play? How was that possible? Was this the first thing you heard when you died? He realized he was hearing a show tune. What was it?

Ah, he had it now. It was "All The Things You Are" from *Very Warm For May.* What a lovely melody to accompany death! Whoever or whatever had chosen it for him had done well. True, it wasn't a Rodgers & Hammerstein work, but it had always been one of his favorites from other composers.

Finally, as "All The Things You Are" reached its climax, Leo took the deepest breath he had ever taken.

And then, he woke up, startled and with his heart pounding.

He sat bolt upright in bed, blinked at the shaft of light the moon was throwing on the far wall of his bedroom and managed a soft chuckle. Even his dreams were too dramatic for his own good.

Chapter 16

"The old adage is that revenge is a dish best served cold," Terrence was saying at another Coalition social meeting about a month after the repeal of the Miami-Dade ordinance. There was record attendance, and Terrence had to rent extra folding chairs to accommodate everyone. "But we are going to warm it up and light a fire under Anita Bryant's feet at the same time."

He waited for the ripple of laughter around the room to subside. "Some of you may not know that she is scheduled to be one of the performing artists at this year's Summer Pops Festival in June at Municipal Auditorium. This was obviously booked before she began her Save Our Children Campaign, or she would have thought twice about coming to a city like New Orleans with its long-time gay subculture after accusing us of everything dastardly and predatory under the sun."

Mara's hand shot up, and she got a word in edgewise. "I still can't believe she got away with it."

A buzz broke out across the room, and there were even cries of, "Boooo!" and "Amen!"

Leo, who was sitting between Mara and Lake, elbowed her gently and said out of the corner of his mouth, "I was absolutely convinced she would fail. What did I know?"

Terrence continued more forcefully. "Anyway, we are going to get a parade permit from the city to stage a march through the Quarter to Louis Armstrong Park and the auditorium to protest her appearance there. The police will work with us, and we will

not interfere with her concert. We will not be harassing people
who have paid their money to hear her sing or blocking entrances
or anything like that. This will be a peaceful protest to let her
know—to let the world know—that we will not let her depiction
of us remain unchallenged. We will not let her think that she has
silenced us because she got one ordinance overturned by hook or
crook, but mostly by lying to the world about us."

Applause interrupted him briefly at that point.

"We have a lot of work ahead of us," Terrence added. "We'll
be coordinating with the Metropolitan Community Church and
the gay Mardi Gras Krewes to sign people up for our peaceful
march. That's the only kind of recruiting we'll do, despite what
Anita Bryant and her pious fellow travelers say about us. We are
also going to work with the bars and discos to begin a boycott
of Florida orange juice. If you can't live without your OJ, be sure
you buy a brand that clearly indicates it's from California or
Brazil. Or take Vitamin C pills."

Again, Mara waved her hand. "I don't like orange juice anyway. It gives me gas."

"Anita Bryant gives me gas," Mara's fellow hairdresser, the
gold caftan-wearing George Kinsey, added. She had finally worn
him down enough to join the Coalition, and he had been making
his presence known all evening with his witty remarks. "She's
turned oranges, lemons and grapefruit into lethal weapons."

After the laughter subsided, Terrence added, "I'm glad we
can have a sense of humor about this, but it's a deadly serious
business. For those who can express themselves easily, we encourage a letter-writing campaign to the Florida Citrus Commission.
We have a handout over there for you on my dining room table
with the address and some guidelines. Be civil and straightforward in your language. Be business-like. Say nothing insulting
about them or Anita Bryant, but be frank about your boycott of
the Commission's products because of the Save Our Children
Campaign and the lies it promoted. I've already discussed this
with Leo Marble and Lake Campbell, who make their living

with the English language. They're working on a form letter of sorts which we'd like for you to modify with your individual touches if that makes you more comfortable."

"Yeah, I've never been a letter writer," Pauly Dixon said. "I communicate with jiggers and swizzle sticks. So what we bartenders have to keep in mind now is to screw screwdrivers, right?"

"Push Bloody Marys instead," Terrence said. "Or beer or wine or bourbon or whatever."

"I've heard tee-totaling is good for the complexion," George Kinsey said, pointing to his high cheekbones.

"We make this a pocketbook issue for the Citrus Commission," Leo added. "By the next time we meet, Lake and I will have drafted that letter for all of you to use if you want. But by all means, feel free to strike out on your own according to the guidelines."

"This is so exciting," George Kinsey added, clasping his perfectly manicured hands together, his curled eyelashes fluttering. "I've always wondered what it would be like to be part of a protest. I've always minded my own business and whipped up masterpieces with my styles and cuts. My mission in life is to make other people look good, and that's a great service to perform. But suddenly, I feel like an honest-to-goodness warrior. I'm so glad my friend, Mara, finally got me to come to one of your meetings."

She leaned to the left, catching his gaze a few chairs away and smiled. "It had to happen. Your energy belongs here."

"What can I say? She's the warrior princess, and I'm the prince. Or is it the other way around?"

"Well-put," Terrence said as a wave of giggles broke out. "But this is a different kind of war. It's insidious because it relies on fear and folktales. These Save Our Children people only think they know who we are, the many professions we actually embrace, what clubs and churches we belong to and attend, trying to blend in the best we can in a hostile world. But they are mistaken, of course, and we have the right to defend ourselves against this

latest onslaught of misconceptions. So as Leo Marble said, we
have to hit them in the pocketbook and make them pay attention to the truth. And one other thing: encourage your friends,
whether they be gay or straight, to join us in this fight. Spread
the word, write those letters, and give up Florida orange juice for
breakfast or at any other time. There are more of us than people
could ever imagine, and it's time we lifted the veil to reveal that to
everyone. We have exactly two more months to fine-tune all this,
so all of you, get out there and do your best. Troops dismissed."

It was George Kinsey who shot up and saluted Terrence in
military fashion. "Sir, yessir!" Others imitated the salute as the
meeting ended amid laughter and genuine camaraderie.

Leo and Lake were huddling at his dining room table, drinking coffee and munching on the last of the Napoleons Susie
Landry had baked and brought up the day before in honor of
Leo's evening recital consisting of "Some Enchanted Evening",
"A Cockeyed Optimist" and "Dites-Moi" from *South Pacific*.
They were nearly through streamlining the form letter they had
promised Terrence they would create for the Coalition, and Lake
was reading the paragraph with the real meat on it out loud one
final time:

*Please understand that I have no quarrel with Miss Bryant's
right to her opinion, misguided though it may be. I believe in
freedom of speech as much as the next American. This letter
is not about that. But the Commission has hired Miss Bryant
to promote Florida citrus products, a job she has performed
admirably for a number of years now. She has rightly become
identified with wholesome products that are good for one's
health. However, she has now embroiled you in religious
and political controversy which I am sure you would agree
is, as the saying goes, bad for business. Almost no one would*

disagree with her ability to achieve your objective of increased consumption of your products. Will that ability continue in the future now that she has become the center of controversy?

Along those lines, this letter is to inform you that I will no longer be purchasing any Florida citrus products for the fore-seeable future. Obviously, it is your decision to continue using Miss Bryant as your spokesperson. Just understand that it will come at an economic price for you. I wish it were otherwise. I bear no ill will against the Florida Citrus Commission, itself, because I am very certain that you could not foresee something like this developing in your wildest scenarios when you put Miss Bryant under contract.

Lake shot Leo a quizzical glance. "Sounds very polished to me. Do you think we missed anything of importance?"

"Nope. I think we've summed it up perfectly," Leo said. "It couldn't be more professional. We just need to remind every-one to use *respectfully yours* as their signoff. And not to include any P.S.'s or impromptu phrases containing vulgarity or temper tantrums of any kind. That would likely get their letter thrown in the trash can."

"Check."

"So I'll get busy running off copies for our next meeting, and we're good to go. I predict the corporate bigwigs at the Citrus Commission will sit up and take notice."

Chapter 17

In the coming weeks the task of approaching the two gay Mardi Gras Krewes to join the protest march against Anita Bryant's Summer Pops Appearance fell to Leo and Terrence after work hours, and they had formulated what they thought was a winning strategy.

"Their turf or ours?" Terrence had proposed.

"Theirs, I think," Leo answered. "They'll feel more comfortable that way. We don't want to do anything to put them on the defensive."

The first meeting with the Krewe of Sparkling Champagne took place on a Saturday evening at the French Quarter courtyard apartment of a man who went by the name of Julius DeSiard in his ordinary business life as a wholesale food broker. In Krewe life and in the gay subculture, he was the Grand Duke of Sparkling Champagne, and the founder of the organization. When their first parade had hit the streets decades earlier, it had solicited a chorus of "oohs" and "aahs" the likes of which jaded Carnival goers rarely offered up. This had been achieved by the dazzling touch of having all the participants on the floats waving lit sparklers throughout their route, even as they multi-tasked by throwing trinkets and beads to the noisy, "throw-me-something-mister" throngs lining the streets.

Never mind that the Krewe members went through hundreds of sparklers as they moved through the city; and since their parades were always staged at night, the fireworks effect was all

135

that more effective. They had quickly become a crowd favorite, especially with children perched on their parents' shoulders to get the full, magical effect.

As Julius offered sofa seats and glasses of champagne to his guests in his lavishly decorated living room full of oversized paintings with enormous splotches of color, Leo noted how small in stature the Grand Duke actually was. Both he and Terrence towered over the man; but what a booming voice he had to compensate for that genetic disparity. He was also the possessor of a smile that never left his face for a second. It was as if his muscles were incapable of any other expression.

"So," Julius began, drawing himself up, "what can we do to help you out with this Anita Bryant protest?"

It was Leo who answered after taking a generous sip of the bubbly in his hand. "As I said over the phone, it's unspeakable what she got away with down there in Miami. At this point, she's still holding onto her contract with the Florida Citrus Commission, but we want to do something about it if we possibly can. Justice has to be served somehow, and the Gay Coalition has come up with a strategy."

Julius nodded graciously. "And what do you really think we can do about it here?"

Leo pointed to Terrence, who handed over a copy of the form letter that the both of them had conjured up, and said, "We hope you'll be willing to distribute this to your members so they can send off these sentiments or something like them to the Commission. There's strength in numbers when it comes to a boycott, and don't think the bean counters in Florida won't notice. We'll be encouraging all the gay bars in the Quarter to stop serving Florida orange juice as well."

Julius's smile quivered slightly. "And you think that'll make a difference?"

"Over time, yes," Leo said. "The Commission hadn't bargained for Anita Bryant getting them into religion and politics when the only goal was to sell citrus products. She was, in fact, doing that quite well until she interjected all this bible-quoting while making things up about gay teachers."

"And then, of course," Terrence added, "we wanted to make sure you knew about her concert appearance here at the Summer Pops. She probably had booked this before she got into that controversy down in Miami, but we want her to know that she's in for a fight. We're thinking that if we're successful with this protest, perhaps others will follow suit and also follow her wherever she goes."

"Do you intend to disrupt her performance?"

"Absolutely not."

Julius paused, still maintaining the better part of his smile. "Do you see us leading the way with our sparklers lit?"

There was a hint of doubt now in Leo's tone. "The march will be in daylight. The sparklers won't be nearly as effective."

"Is that a no I'm hearing from you?"

"Definitely not."

Finally, Julius's smile vanished. "Then let me try this. Do you think we're... well, let's just say inappropriate?"

"If we thought that, we wouldn't be sitting here right now," Leo said. "As I said before, there is strength in numbers, and we earnestly solicit your participation."

Julius downed most of his champagne and said, "But on your terms."

Leo's tone was authoritative now. "If it is your wish to have your members march along with their lit sparklers held high above their head, then so be it. Done. And here's a bit of reassurance for you that you are indeed taken seriously. When Terrence and I applied for the parade permit, and we mentioned that the Krewe of Sparkling Champagne might be participating, the officer we dealt with beamed. He said, 'Is that the group with the lit sparklers?' And when I told him that it was, he said that his kids absolutely loved you and looked forward to your floats more than any other during Carnival. So, if the police department takes you seriously and their children think you're the bomb, you can bet everyone else does."

Julius poured himself another glass of champagne from the nearby magnum on ice and puffed himself up to his maximum height. "That's nice to hear. I'm still wondering what good this will all do, though. After all, none of us in the Krewe are teachers. And this thing Anita Bryant has done only applies to Miami, doesn't it? It has no effect on things here in New Orleans."

Terrence spoke up. "You might think that's true, but while she attacked gay teachers down there, Mr. DeSiard, there are significant underlying implications. As you well know, we gay people hold down every type of job there is, but we're largely hidden from view because many of us don't always enjoy the employment security we deserve by revealing who we are. Leo and I and the Gay Coalition feel that if this result is allowed to stand unchallenged, it will cast a shadow on all gay people trying to make a living from hereon. We are not demons to be feared, as Anita Bryant suggests, and we need to be respected, or everything is lost."

After sipping more of his champagne, Julius said, "But, to play the devil's advocate and shifting the subject a bit, it seems to me that by asking bartenders in the Quarter to boycott orange juice, their means of supporting themselves might be affected."

"Just Florida orange juice. They can buy California brands, or even brands from Brazil."

"Won't that be a lot of trouble? Especially if they have contracts with certain companies? I know how food and beverage contracts work, being a broker, myself."

Leo's brow furrowed for the first time. "I'm getting the impression you don't want to go along with this, Mr. DeSiard. I'm a bit surprised, or am I not reading you right?"

Julius scooted forward a bit in his floral-upholstered easy chair. "Let me make myself clear, Mr. Marble. The Krewe of Sparkling Champagne is not a political organization. I founded it so that our members could have some fun and participate fully in Carnival. Some had been denied membership in straight clubs over the years. Now they could never prove that their being gay was the reason, but it's easy to read between the lines. I finally got tired of the exclusionary bullshit and decided that we'd get our very own club going if certain types were going to object to us for various reasons, including some you wouldn't believe. In addition, the hypocrisy is galling because there are more than a few so-called scions of society that are in the closet, and I know what I'm talking about."

Leo was quick to answer and with some authority. "I don't doubt you for a second, believe me. All the more reason you should join us in this protest. Anita Bryant and her minions believe that we shouldn't even have the right to exist, much less hold meaningful jobs. You just pointed out that her attitude is not unique and has existed among certain people for a long time. Even in a so-called liberated city like New Orleans. Sometimes, things are not as they appear."

"We just want to be left alone and live our lives."

"That's what everyone wants. But some people don't want to leave us alone, and one of them with a high profile is coming to New Orleans to sing pop tunes like 'Paper Roses' as if everything is right with the world and nothing is at stake for anyone but her. We believe that with our boycott and letter-writing campaign, we can make her pay a price."

"Do you want my answer right away? I must discuss it with our members and see what everyone thinks."

Feeling a slight sense of relief, Leo said, "Within a week would be nice. And please present the form letter Terrence gave you so everyone can get the bigger picture."

At the door to the courtyard, Julius returned to a previous discussion. "But can't you just picture us leading the march with our sparklers lit, even in daylight? I mean, don't you think we'll need a little extra space like the trombones do in a marching band? We wouldn't want to sparkle anyone's behind, whereas out in front, everyone is safe from harm, so to speak."

All three men laughed, and Leo said, "I hadn't thought about it that way, but now that you mention it, it would surely be quite the amusing, fairy tale touch."

"That's the Krewe of Sparkling Champagne in a nutshell."

139

"We look forward to hearing from you soon," Leo said, and then he and Terrence turned to walk across the brick patio with its overhanging banana stalks toward the courtyard gate.

The second gay Mardi Gras Krewe had only been around for a couple of years and had not yet carved out a noticeable place for itself in the Carnival pantheon. Going only by the name of Sprites, it placed a heavy emphasis on elaborate costuming, due to the fact that its founder, one Ira Claxton, made his living designing costumes for theater groups, Mardi Gras Krewes and weddings. He lived in an Uptown apartment complex near live oak-filled Audubon Park, and that was where Leo had arranged to meet with him all by himself to make his pitch, as Terrence had other pressing duties that particular morning.

The fourth-floor flat, itself, seemed somewhat spartan to Leo, however, not only compared to Julius DeSiard's study in every shade of the rainbow, but considering the fact that Ira Claxton was constantly involved with stitching colorful fabrics together for out-of-the-ordinary clothing. His choices on the spectrum were predominately black and white on both the walls and the furniture; the place was screaming for a pop of color—anywhere. Even on the man himself. Alas, he was a large specimen whose girth rivaled that of Terrence but who had chosen to drench himself in black, thinking perhaps it would minimize his size. Instead, it made him look like an enormous lump of coal. He also appeared to be wearing mascara, perhaps a touch of rouge on his cheeks, and his fingernails were painted black.

After the two men had settled with Bloody Marys in hand out on the small balcony overlooking the sprawling park, Ira came right to the point. "I'm extremely interested in the Sprites participating in your protest march against that horrible woman who doesn't know what she's talking about. I would dearly love for the ground beneath her to open and swallow her up. But I do have my concerns."

"And what would those be?"

"As you probably know," Claxton began, "when we parade, we do so in drag. In costumes of various sorts."

"And?"

"Would we be hurting our cause?"

Leo stared down at the toothpick sporting three olives and sticking straight up out of his tomato-ey drink, but it gave him no counsel. "How so, Mr. Claxton?"

"Don't people expect us to show up in drag all the time? Wouldn't we be reinforcing Anita Bryant's accusations? Of course, we could show up in plain clothes, but that's not the Sprites' way."

Leo took a sip of his cocktail, feeling the cayenne pepper at the back of his throat. "Not every gay man does drag, you know. I don't. I've never had the slightest inclination to do so, and I don't think I'd be very good at it, either. My opinion is that whoever wants to show up should show up and march. If you and your Sprites want to do so in drag, I see no reason to object. The last thing the Gay Coalition believes is that all gay people are alike. That we are some monolithic demographic that crowds into gay bars late at night because we have no place else to go or nothing else to do. Our cause is that we believe all gay people should have the same rights as any other citizens. Which is obviously something that Anita Bryant and her Save Our Children campaign does not believe."

"I thought I should run this past you, though."

"Glad I was able to put your mind at ease." Leo paused to pluck off one of the olives and down it quickly. "I trust I've done that."

"Yes, you have."

Then Leo presented the final hurdle. "I presume you would have no problem marching with members of the Krewe of Sparkling Champagne? Not alongside them actually, but they'd be in the procession."

Claxton's big eyes bulged, and he puffed out his cheeks like a blowfish. "You mean that's a requirement?"

"No. It's just that we've met with them and invited them to participate. The more the merrier."

"Have they accepted?"

"Not yet, but my instincts tell me they will."

Claxton took a generous gulp of his drink and said, "Those walking arsonists. They're so stuck up, you know. They look down on us because we're newcomers."

"I'm sure that's not true," Leo said. "I got no inkling of that when we met with Julius DeSiard recently."

"Oh, he wouldn't say anything about us publicly. But privately, behind the scenes, he thinks we're a joke."

Leo finished off the two remaining olives and said, "Then prove him wrong. Prove you're serious about standing up for gay people here in New Orleans and everywhere. Join us in whatever costumes you like. Mary, Queen of Scots, Lucretia Borgia, Liz Taylor, Dinah Shore, whoever strikes your fancy. Or just the drag version of yourselves. I think it'll be a hoot and a half."

Claxton brought his hands together in a prayerful gesture. "I assure you, no one will be off limits. Why, I may even dress down and go as Eleanor Roosevelt in glasses and sensible shoes. You know, my parents adored FDR and how he held the country together during the War."

"And my father did his part by getting the Distinguished Flying Cross in the Pacific Theater," Leo added. "He didn't do it to have people like Anita Bryant a generation later threaten the employment rights of anyone who didn't fit her religious definition of an American."

"My goodness," Claxton said, his broad face beaming, "I feel like we should be leaning over the balcony waving the American flag at everyone over there in the park right this very second."

"Bring the flags with you when we march. I think that's a great idea. We're a part of America just like everyone else."

"Then it's a done deal?"

Leo finished off his drink, stood up and offered his hand. "Let's shake on it, Ira Claxton. And we'll let you and the Sprites bring up the rear so there'll be plenty of distance between you and those lit sparklers, that is, if they agree to march, too."

"Sounds like a plan. You should always save the best for last."

A couple of days later in the Coalition office, Terrence was bringing Leo up to speed on Renaldo Plaisance, the owner of La Draperie, one of the most successful antique and interior design businesses in the Quarter on Burgundy Street.

"I don't know all that much about him, except that he's swimming in money and also very piss-elegant."

Leo drew back in utter puzzlement. "What's that last term mean?"

"It means he thinks unless you can afford to buy his upper end acquisitions from around the world, you lack gravitas, a word he trots out all the time. If you come back from this appointment with him and tell me he used it less than a dozen times, I'll faint dead away. I've also been in his home once in the Garden District for one of his soirees. Good heavens, it's like a showroom, stuffed to the rafters with the most ostentatious pieces you'll ever see anywhere. Even in a castle or palace. If you ask me, I think his goal is to outdo Buckingham Palace."

"Then, why does he want to talk to us if he's that much of a snob?"

"I'm not sure. He just called to say he had some important business to discuss with the Coalition. He's not currently a member, so maybe he wants to join."

"And you think I'm the best person to handle this?"

Terrence offered up a wry smile. "You've been handling the gay Mardi Gras Krewes and coming away without a scratch on you. I think that's been the perfect training for someone like Renaldo Plaisance."

"If you say so."

A half-hour later when Leo walked into the brick and lacework building that was La Draperie at precisely ten-thirty that morning, he was genuinely surprised to see that the very fit and mustached Renaldo Plaisance approached him dressed in a tuxedo. Immediately, Terrence's term—*piss elegant*—did indeed resonate with him. Who came to work in a tux? Unless they were a model in a high-end fashion show. There was also a hint of incense in the air.

"Bonjour," said Renaldo, executing a quick little nod of the head. "You are Mr. Marble, I presume? I greet you with sincere gravitas."

"Yes, I am." Leo gestured broadly at the showroom full of plantation desks, secretaries, Belter sofas, crystal chandeliers, scroll chairs, room dividers, and oil paintings, among a myriad of other items. "This is quite an impressive display you have here, Mr. Plaisance."

Again there was a quick nod of the head. "No other shop in New Orleans approaches my inventory. We have things others can only dream of selling. Our depression glass collection is beyond compare in both cameo and American Sweetheart patterns. We have decoys galore by both Crowell and Lincoln. We have, if you'll pardon the conceit, our ducks in a row. And for the truly discriminating whose home is just dripping with gravitas, we have such things as Hubley doorstops, Art Deco clocks and Chinese cloisonne sideboards that will take your breath away."

"I wouldn't doubt it for a moment," Leo said, finding himself straightening his posture as some sort of reflex action to the formality he could almost reach out and touch.

"Shall we have a seat then and discuss this matter for which I summoned you? No one will disturb us, I can assure you. I only see my clients by appointment. I do not recognize the concept of a walk-in. That's for the pedestrian shops, and I don't mean that as a pun, either."

Renaldo chuckled richly and then led the way through the inventory to his small office in the middle of the store, where the two men were seated on opposite sides of his desk.

"First," Renaldo began, "do review for me again the Coalition's plan for this protest of that Bryant woman. I pride myself on keeping up with the news, and so, I am aware of what she's been up to down there in Miami."

Leo quickly summarized the organization's plans, and then there was an awkward silence.

"You realize, of course," Renaldo said finally, "that I cannot possibly participate in your street antics. It would not be helpful to my business. The utmost in decorum is always expected of me. I have a reputation to uphold."

"I can understand that."

Then Renaldo exhaled noisily and leaned in. "You have a trusting face and manner about you. Perhaps it's those freckles and that red hair of yours. So, I'm going to reveal something to you that I've never told anyone before, and I know you will keep my confidence. Not another soul must know the truth of my story. When I first opened up Ronnie's Antiques, as I called it back then, I wore my naivete on my sleeve as Ronnie Pleasant. I thought I could compete with the scores of well-established shops and interior designers that this city is famous for. I came down here from Columbia, Mississippi, however, and was pretty rough around the edges. The locals couldn't seem to relate to my thick accent and straightforward lack of finesse until I struck upon a gimmick that transformed me and ultimately my business."

Renaldo paused and narrowed his eyes. "Are you ready for this?"

Intrigued as he never thought he could be with someone he had just met, Leo said, "I can't wait to hear what you have to say."

And then it happened. Renaldo's vocal register and accent suddenly changed to something decidedly less refined. "I had the devil in me to do this, but I decided to live up to a gay stereotype to my advantage."

Leo's head jerked back, almost as if he had been slapped in the face. "What?"

"I'm not particularly proud of that, but the fact is that I'm pretty sure I was perceived as a redneck in those early days. My business had been so paltry with such a small clientele that I decided I needed a makeover. So, I went full in. I changed the name of the business from Ronnie's to La Draperie, and I became Renaldo Plaisance. Sounds very French, you will admit. Perfect for a city like New Orleans. I started dressing in a tux, using pretentious phrases and even some French words for good measure, and it began to work like a charm. People started thinking I must know my stuff if I were that elegant and prissy. In fact, I do know the antique business backward and forward—I learned it from my mother—and I can design the hell out of a room. I was just trying to do it in the wrong package. Like with a great gourmet meal, presentation is everything. So I went as high in the gay pantheon of behaviors as I could go."

Both men chuckled, and Leo said, "So when Terrence described you as *piss-elegant*, he was right about everything except your sincerity."

"Believe me, I sincerely wanted to make money."

"And that you've done." Leo hesitated for a second but then decided to press further. "And you're okay with it all?"

"A part of me is—the part that appreciates survival."

"I can appreciate that. At a very early age, I found out that being who I was might be dangerous for me."

"Ditto. When you're gay, the smaller the town, the greater the dangers."

Leo took a few moments to let everything settle and then found the right words. "I must admit I'm perfectly comfortable with our true confessions, but what is your business with the Coalition, if I may ask?"

"Ah," Renaldo said, pointing his bejeweled index finger in the air and then opening one of his desk drawers with aplomb. He then retrieved a check and handed it over. "This is my business."

Leo's eyes widened at first glance. "This is a substantial amount of money."

"Yes, it is. But I think it's time I paid up."

"Beg pardon?" Leo said, cocking his head.

"I've hammed it up to earn a living, and on some level, my performances gnaw at the edges of my soul. When that Bryant woman stirred the pot last year with that obnoxious campaign of hers, I began to feel a twinge of guilt about the act I've been putting on. So, to make amends in a manner of speaking, I offer it to the Coalition to do with as it pleases in lieu of actually joining. I'll be frank with you again and tell you that I have some very opinionated and obnoxious straight clients who would not approve of my becoming visibly militant about my orientation. They expect me to fit their preconceived notions which I willingly allow them to indulge. I am now trapped by the persona I have created, successful as it may be."

Leo allowed the pent-up air in his chest to escape all at once. "Wow! I thought I knew everything there was to know about being gay, but apparently, I was mistaken."

"What we both know is that there is way too much misinformation out there about the reality of it all."

"Agreed. And that's the purpose of our Coalition and why we are undertaking this protest march."

Renaldo then rose and offered his hand while the very next words he spoke once again assumed the panache of his earlier, carefully cultivated persona. "Voila! I wish all of you the very best in your endeavor. I am happy to do what I can and still maintain my gravitas and my equilibrium."

As Leo shook the man's hand, he could not help but flash back to his earlier conversation with Terrence at the Coalition office, and the biggest smile broke across his face. The gay subculture was indeed full of surprises.

A few days after Leo's meeting with Renaldo Plaisance, he and Terrence were sitting in the Coalition office around noon going over the organization's finances—which were now in excellent shape for the foreseeable future, thanks to the contribution from La Draperie—when there was a polite knock on their door.

"Were you expecting someone?" Leo said, looking up from his paperwork.

Terrence shook his head and called out, "Come in."

A tall, rugged young man in a gray three-piece suit and sporting a suave, pompadour haircut entered with a smile. "I hope I'm not disturbing you."

"Not at all," Terrence said. "The Coalition always has time for any and everyone. Our door is always open."

"Thanks. I'm Phil Junkin," he answered, walking over to shake hands. "I won't take up too much of your time."

"Pull up that chair over there in the corner," Terrence continued with a gesture after further introductions were made.

Phil ended up sitting right next to Leo and then said, "I'm on my lunch hour. You see, I'm a stockbroker at Kohlmeyer's, and I just wanted to drop by and thank you for what you've done for me."

Terrence exchanged furtive glances with Leo and said, "Please. Tell us what we've done for you."

"You've helped me make an important decision. I'm going to come out of the closet, and I'm even going to participate in your protest march against Anita Bryant. I want to be one of your foot soldiers, and I don't care who knows it."

Leo reached over and patted him on the shoulder. "Well, congratulations. We can use all the help we can get."

"Well, there's more I wanted to say to you. Sometimes after work, I go to the Moonglow Bar in the Quarter for happy hour where Pauly Dixon works as the bartender."

"Ah yes, Pauly's a good man," Leo added. "We know him well."

"That he is," Phil said. "I've wondered if I ought to turn him into my mentor. People do that to bartenders all the time."

Leo smiled. "He'd give you pretty good advice, I think."

"I need all the help I can get. You have to realize just coming to see both of you took all the courage I could muster. But Pauly's the reason I found out about your Anita Bryant protest in the first place. My favorite cocktail is a screwdriver, and Pauly mentioned that the Moonglow was no longer serving Florida orange juice when he mixed up my drink last time I went in. 'California all the way, now,' he told me. Then he filled me in on the march through the Quarter coming up."

"Are you concerned about coming out?" Terrence said. "What if someone from your office spots you in the march? Are you prepared for any consequences?"

"If it happens, it happens. Meanwhile, regarding the coming out part—I'm going to do it in stages. To my close friends first and see how that goes. Those are people I've known for quite a while now, so I'm thinking that unless I've misjudged them, they'll be cool with it. The workplace might be a little different. I might take it a little slower there. There are a couple of guys in the office that are, to put it nicely, horse's asses when it comes to the way they talk about women, and I've even heard one of them use the word queer once."

Terrence nodded his head enthusiastically. "Job security can be a real issue for some gay people."

Phil shrugged his broad shoulders. "Well, I certainly don't intend to lead with the information, no matter what. My sexuality has nothing to do with managing portfolios. It's not a need-to-know item. I'd just like to reach the point where I'm not afraid to ever mention it appropriately should the circumstances arise. These guys with girlfriends and wives can say whatever they want in everyday conversation, even if it's in bad taste. I can't believe I'd ever want to talk about any guy I was with the way they talk about their women."

"I'm sure we'd all like to reach that point," Terrence added. "Unfortunately, we're nowhere near that right now. As you just said, a straight man can talk about his wife or girlfriend with impunity in the lunchroom or men's room or wherever. It's something he takes for granted. Straight people take a lot for granted when you come right down to it—getting married, inheriting things from each other, being there for each other in the hospital, the list goes on and on."

Phil offered up a wry chuckle. "Tell me about it. Some guys are always in the TMI category when it comes to that. They act as if everywhere is a locker room."

"I know the type," Leo said. "I remember them as boys in my P.E. class in high school. There were a few queer jokes to bite your tongue over as well."

Phil glanced at his watch and then rose from his chair. "Well, I need to get going if I want a bite to eat before getting back. I just wanted to drop by quickly and give you the skinny on myself."

"Which we very much appreciate," Terrence said, as he and Leo both stood up and again offered a handshake. "We certainly hope to see you at our next Coalition meeting so you can get to know some very nice gay men and women." Terrence grabbed a slip of paper from his desktop and handed it over. "Here's the address, phone number, day and time. Hey, you might even run into someone you already know. It happens more often than you think."

At the door, Phil turned and said, "I feel like my life has really just begun now."

"Welcome aboard," Leo said. "We both know exactly how you feel."

After Phil had left, Terrence pointed to the empty chair where he had been sitting. "That is an example of the ripple effect, my friend."

Leo shot him a quizzical glance. "Details, please."

"Not particularly complicated. Just the old concept of a pebble skipping the surface of a pond or a lake. It sets in motion a wake of sorts. Ripples, if you will. You never know how far those ripples will travel. Phil came here because some ripples reached him, whether they were the result of Anita Bryant's campaign or our reaction to it. The hope is that they will change his life for the better."

At the next Coalition meeting in Terrence's house, Leo was reminded very much of Terrence's ripple commentary when Phil showed up for the first time and introduced clusters of the group to a prospective new member.

"Meet Yolanda Delery," he was saying to the threesome of Terrence, Leo and Mara. "She's the receptionist where I work, and a bang-up job she does for all us stockbrokers."

Yolanda flashed an ingratiating smile. "Phil, I just put people on hold a lot and point them in different directions when they show up."

"Nonsense," Phil continued. "You're also very good at getting my important messages to me in a timely manner. Someone has to direct traffic and keep things running smoothly."

Yolanda raised her hand and nodded her head quickly. "Guilty." Then she made a sweeping gesture to all the others. "But I'm very excited about joining your group, thanks to Phil."

It suddenly occurred to Leo that this pleasant and petite woman with skin the color of cafe au lait and whose hair was extraordinarily straight would be the first Black person of either gender to become a part of the Coalition. How had this fact escaped him, and why was it so in the first place? Being gay was not the only challenge in the world.

These ruminations were put into perspective when Yolanda took the floor once the meeting had begun in earnest, after Phil's effusive introduction.

"I'm very excited about being here tonight. But I feel I must warn you. What I'm going to say to all of you might not be easy to hear," she began, surveying the room quickly. "But it's the truth, and I'm not afraid to share it with you. This culture of ours has a pecking order when it comes to sexual orientation. It goes like this: at the top is the white, straight man; then comes the white straight woman; much further down the list is the white gay man; then the Black gay man a good distance below that. But at the very bottom is the Black gay woman. She gets the crumbs and bears all the weight of those above her. I've worked hard to even get the receptionist job I have at Kohlmeyer's, and while I appreciate what my friend Phil has said about me, I can't make any mistakes, believe me. When I was hired, I was told I had to 'do something about my hair,' since I wore it in an Afro."

Yolanda then paused and removed what was indeed her short wig to reveal the modest Afro she had been growing for some time. "This is who I am, but I don't think all that many people are ready to accept it. I find being a Black lesbian to be rough going, even in a laid-back city like New Orleans. I need all the help I can get, which is why I'm here tonight. Maybe there's something I can learn by being with people of like mind and just talking and listening."

She caught Phil's gaze and pointed in his general direction. "But it was meant to be. I overheard Phil talking to one of the secretaries in the lunchroom about this very meeting tonight, and I took it from there. I came out to Phil privately later on, and here I am."

A polite peppering of applause erupted, after which Mara said, "You've made the right decision, Yolanda. It makes all the difference to compare notes and experiences and know that you are not in this alone, even though it seems that way most of the time."

"I appreciate that," Yolanda said. "And if no one minds, I'd like to stuff my wig in my purse and wear this Afro of mine the rest of the evening."

"By all means," Terrence added. "This coalition is nothing if it's not about being who you are. Proudly."

Yolanda lost no time in popping the wig into her purse, beaming as if she had won the lottery, and then Terrence took the floor with more of the evening's agenda. But not before Mara made a motion that a robust effort be made to actively seek out more Black people for membership.

"After all," she concluded, "we come in all shapes, sizes and colors."

The motion was seconded and then adopted unanimously.

Later, as Leo gave Terrence a hug at the door when the meeting was over, he pulled back and said with a gleam in his eye: "Viva, la ripple effect."

Chapter 18

The protest march was just a few weeks away when Leo decided it was time to tie up a big loose end in his career with Arthur LeBlanc—coming out to his supervisor and mentor at long last. He had proven himself as a journalist many times over, so he believed this official revelation would be nothing more than a formality.

"I wanted to share this with you because of my upcoming participation in the protest march regarding Anita Bryant's Summer Pops appearance," Leo was explaining further while seated in his editor's pleasantly scented office. "I just felt this was the right time."

Arthur set his pipe down on the edge of a nearby ashtray and stared ahead silently for a few seconds. "You know the City Desk will be covering that, I suppose. Features will be doing an interview with Anita Bryant the day before as well. The focus will be on her life as an entertainer, not this recent political controversy. We've decided not to get into that and make it all about Summer Pops."

"I was aware."

"Were you worried that you might show up in the pictures during the protest march?"

Leo frowned. "I hadn't thought about it, no."

Arthur leaned back in his comfortable leather armchair and made a temple of his fingers. "For the record, I make it a policy never to get involved in or worry about the private lives of my employees. All that counts with me is the quality of someone's work. That's all that should matter to anyone, as far as I'm concerned. Of course, you might be interested to hear that I suspected you might be gay."

"Why is that?" Leo said, turning his head to the side.

"You never mentioned a girlfriend or a wife to me or anyone else. People speculate in any workplace once you're there long enough. It's human nature, although some would say it's just everyday gossip at the lunch table or in the restrooms."

Leo's smirk was accompanied by the relaxation of certain muscles throughout his body, and he said, "My involvement with the New Orleans Gay Resources Coalition has been significant over the past several years. We think we're providing a valuable service to gay men and women in need of help. Our director, Terrence Dennery, has suggested to me more than once that I propose a piece to you in *Sunday* on our organization. What do you think? This would be the perfect time for it."

"Not on my watch," Arthur said, putting the stem of his pipe back in his mouth and taking a puff.

Stunned by the response, Leo's muscles tensed up again. "Wait... what?"

The next thing Arthur did was laugh heartily. "You should see the expression on your face."

"Excuse me, but respectfully, I don't think this is funny."

Arthur put his pipe down again and said, "Relax. You misunderstood me."

"How? You nixed my idea without even giving it a second thought."

Arthur leaned forward with a devilish glint in his eye. "When I said 'not on my watch,' I meant that my watch will be over in thirty days. I've given notice that I am retiring after twenty-one years at this position. I'll be sixty-two this summer, and the wife and I want to do some traveling while we're still young enough to fully enjoy it. We want to see Maui, Iceland, places off the beaten path. So, it's kinda serendipitous that you came in to talk to me today. I intended to talk to you as well. I'm offering you the position of *Sunday* editor right here and now. I think you are fully qualified to take over and begin your own watch. So, if you accept, the Coalition story you're proposing will be all yours. I'd like for you to take full credit for it."

"Wow," Leo said, his eyes widening in pleasant astonishment. "I didn't see that coming."

"I'm sure. But more to the point, do you accept my offer?"

Leo stood up and extended his hand. "I sure do. And thank you very much, Arthur."

"My pleasure." He puffed on his pipe a time or two, releasing more rum essence into the room. Then he put it down once again and leaned in. "I'd like to clear the air about one thing, though. Because of his seniority, I wanted to be fair, and I did offer the job to Three-H first, but he turned me down."

Leo drew back slightly and frowned. "Why would he do that? As you say, he has seniority over me, and he's probably even more qualified than I am. In fact, I know he is."

"He said it was for personal reasons and wouldn't go into it any further. You'd have to ask him if you want to know more." There was a pregnant pause. "Oh, and one more thing. I've been informed by the higher-ups that *Sunday's* budget has been cut by one staff writer. Another good reason for me to leave. You'll be running things soon with just two writers, counting yourself. And Chase, of course."

After profusely thanking Arthur again for the unexpected promotion, Leo walked out into the sea of cubicles, genuinely puzzled. He decided that he and Three-H would have to have a talk.

Leo swallowed a bite of his fried oyster po-boy and caught Three-H's gaze again. They were sitting in the lunchroom together at a table isolated in one corner, out of earshot of other employees. Still, they kept their voices low during the conversation that ensued.

"To answer your question, I turned Arthur down because I'm getting a divorce."

The surprise registered in Leo's voice. "Did your wife find you out?"

Three-H put down his big gumbo spoon and said, "The opposite. I found her out."

"What?"

There was a snickering response as Three-H wagged his brows. "Lydia's naive phase is officially over."

"Elaborate, please."

"She actually came to me and confessed she was having an affair with an available member of our social circle, whose name I shall not mention at this point. Her exact words were, "I have discovered sex, and what I've been missing these past eight years with you. All these years, you made me think it was just about your pleasure, not mine. Because I can't recall too much, if you want the God's honest truth.'"

Leo took a sip of his iced tea to mull that over. "That would certainly get my attention."

"The other thing you don't know about our marriage is that she has all the money. The Henninghams have the name, but the Duvals are mega-rich with the name. Old money, you know. A sugar cane fortune. That's her house we live in on State Street."

"You never mentioned all that to me, no."

"Anyhow, I admit that I married her for her money. I figured that as long as I was gonna live a lie, I might as well live it in comfort." He winked and made a clicking noise at the same time. "As for her comment about sex, she was pretty much on target about that. I avoided it as much as possible, hoping hugs and kisses would do. Every once in a while, I would get drunk enough to do a passable imitation, including the time it led to her being pregnant with our daughter."

Leo winced slightly. "You don't have to go into further detail. I get the picture. I know all about faking interest in the opposite sex, though certainly not to that extent."

Three-H pointed to his gumbo and said, "I don't want this to get cold. Let's have some more of our lunch, and then we can talk a little more about my situation."

After a few more minutes of enjoying their food had passed,

Leo said, "I understand you have a lot on your plate with the divorce coming up, but I'm still not quite sure why you didn't say yes to Arthur."

Three-H tapped an index finger to his temple a couple of times. "It's a matter of perception. I don't even want her or my lawyer to know I was offered the job or that I'm gay. Accepting the position would mean a substantial raise in salary, and since Lydia's so all-fired set on sampling the joys of sex, I want her to pay the price and consider my economic status. I realize that doesn't make me a saint exactly, but I gave up trying to be one when I settled for an illusion just to fit in. I didn't see any other way."

Leo furrowed his brow and said, "Oh, what a tangled web, right?"

Three-H nodded and finished off his gumbo. "I want to thank you, though."

"For what?"

"For rejecting my advances and showing me that I don't have to hide anymore. Legally, Lydia and I have to live apart for a year because we have a minor child together. But after that, assuming we can settle things amicably, I intend to start over and get out of that damned closet. I'll still see my daughter, Hannah, of course. I'm sure Lydia won't have a problem with joint custody. But eventually if I'm lucky, I'll find a man to share a life with. This divorce will actually give me a second chance to be myself."

Leo extended his hand, and they shook on it. "I hope it all goes your way. Sincerely."

"If it does, I'll be free to join your Coalition. I can't give anything away right now. Maybe I'll meet someone that way."

"Just remember, please," Leo added with a chuckle, "that we're not a dating service."

"Duly noted. I'll settle for understanding friendships like yours."

Chapter 19

A police estimate of three-thousand protesters had assembled in front of St Louis Cathedral and all around Jackson Square as the day and its zero hour had finally arrived. The *Times-Picayune's* ongoing coverage of both Summer Pops and the Coalition's planned activities had also attracted hundreds of curious gawkers along the predetermined route from the Square to adjacent Decatur Street, north along narrow Dumaine and finally to Louis Armstrong Park on North Rampart Street. There, the police had a generous space cordoned off for what would be a silent protest. No chanting had been planned, although anything spontaneous but civil and within reason would not be stopped. The Coalition believed that their peaceful sheer numbers would deliver the strongest message and give them the most favorable coverage possible.

All of the Coalition members were in the throng, including newcomer Phil Junkin, with one notable exception: Lake Campbell. As a result of all the publicity Anita Bryant's appearance at Summer Pops was generating and the interest from parents at St. Michael's and other parochial schools regarding the teaching profession from the Miami-Dade election results, the Archdiocese of New Orleans had issued the following statement that was distributed internally, but not publicly, one week before the march:

The Archdiocese wishes to state that while it takes no position regarding the recent Miami-Dade County ordinance repeal and believes that that was a local issue decided by the voters of that area, it wishes to also remind its parishioners and all of its employees that the church's official position on homosexual activity of any kind is that it is a sin and should be viewed accordingly.

Incensed, Lake had thrust a copy of the memo into Leo's hands that very evening as they sat together in the camelback living room. Then with passion in his voice, he said, "They have no business getting into this. This can of worms Anita Bryant opened up has everybody wriggling around without a clue. It makes me want to march into Father Babineaux's office tomorrow, tell him who I am and dare him to fire me."

Leo inched closer on the sofa and patted Lake's arm. "Now it's my turn to calm *you* down. Yes, it would have been better if they had stayed out of it, but the truth is, coming out might cost you your job. You have no idea how Father Babineaux really stands on all this, but you can't take the chance that he'll be all in on the party line. He might not want to protect you. He's Catholic, after all."

"Yes, of course he is."

"And you're not. But you are an employee of his... of theirs. They're paying you to play by their rules. I think it would be a mistake to tell them about yourself and bring your relationship with Ignacio into this. Were you considering that, too?"

Lowering his voice only slightly, Lake said, "Why should I hold anything back? They didn't hold anything back in this pontificating memo. I was also considering making up a sign for the march which would read: GAY TEACHER MARCHING."

Leo exhaled and took his time coming up with the right words. "You and I are so much alike. We want to change things and make them better. I've been able to come out at work as a journalist, and I haven't had to pay a price for it. But your situation is completely different. Your profession is suddenly under attack. Granted, it's unwarranted, unjust, and, frankly, off the wall. But you could lose your job as the good teacher you are. I can honestly say that you were the best teacher I ever had. I know a lot of my classmates felt the same way. But you just can't go around advertising something that has to remain private in order to survive in today's world. No, it shouldn't be that way, but I care too much about you to let you do that. You've got your heat up way too high. Turn it down to simmer and live to fight another day."

Lake remained quiet for several minutes, doing reflexive things like cracking his knuckles and twitching his lips. Leo thought it best to let him work things out in his head, saying nothing more to him.

Finally, Lake spoke up, sounding somewhat calmer. "I've always been an all or nothing person. I'm either in on something one-hundred percent, or I don't do it at all."

"And?"

"And I'm going to take your advice. Maybe all I needed was to get this outrage of mine off my chest. I hope you didn't mind being my sounding board."

"You know the answer to that," Leo said, chucking Lake's arm gently with his fist.

"So, no, I certainly won't be barging into Father's office, and I think it might be best for me not to be in the march, either."

"Not carrying that sign, of course. But you don't have to drop out altogether."

Lake shot him a sideways glance. "Maybe I do. This town is predominantly Catholic, of course. I might be spotted by someone in the crowd whose child goes to St. Michael's, or someone might take a picture of me and set off a chain reaction that leads me to Father Babineaux's office anyway. I do treasure my teaching and can't put it on the chopping block. What was I thinking? I let my emotions get the better of me."

Leo managed to pull off a strange expression that combined a frown with a smile. It came off looking like he was straining or smelling something unpleasant. "Talk about your rollercoaster rides. You've gone from willingly sacrificing your career to paranoia about it in a matter of minutes."

"That, my friend, is a summary of what it's like to be gay in this world," Lake said, bringing their exchange to a close.

Lake was as good as his word and was therefore missing from the restless throng around Jackson Square. No amount of pleading could turn him around once he'd made up his mind, and Leo had finally resigned himself and had to let it go.

Nonetheless, Leo was proud of all the meetings taken and proselytizing that he and Terrence, Lake, Pauly and the others had done over the past several months. Terrence had worked closely with the New Orleans Police Department, and they had agreed to provide a single car escort leading the way with flashing blue lights, as well as one bringing up the rear. There would also be a few officers walking alongside the protesters in case there were any unpleasant surprises from onlookers. Law enforcement was used to every kind of elaborate event from jazz funerals to Mardi Gras parades, and this seemed little more to them than business as usual.

On a given signal, the throng with its lit sparklers at the front and colorful female impersonators bringing up the rear—including Ira Claxton impersonating Eleanor Roosevelt—*I'm sure she would have approved*, he told Leo and Terrence when he first arrived— began to move in an orderly fashion to Decatur Street with no incident. Most of the marchers carried whistles in case of physical confrontation. Halfway up Dumaine, there were a couple of signs on the perimeter that read FAGS ON DISPLAY; but Terrence had used a megaphone several times over while everyone was assembling to instruct everyone to ignore any signs, catcalls and threats they might encounter, use their whistles if necessary, and to let the police handle anyone who tried to get out of hand.

Every once in a while, the procession would slow down enough for sidewalk onlookers to verbally engage marchers on the edges where Leo was, but he steeled himself, looked straight ahead and took them in stride.

"Looks like she brought all a' you queers outta the woodwork today," a heavy-set man wearing a Saints cap said to him with a sneer at one point. "I knew this town was fulla the likes a' you, but not quite this many."

Leo remained calm and said nothing, which produced another insult.

"Red-headed, freckle-faced fag! You're an insult to Howdy Doody!"

Leo moved ahead but not before the man pushed his way in and tackled him from behind, bringing him to the ground. There had to be a difference of at least sixty or seventy pounds between the two, and Leo found himself with his face pressed against the dirty asphalt. The shrill sound of whistles erupted around him, and soon two police officers came to his rescue and pried the man off his back, quickly hauling him away. For all that, Leo sustained a minor abrasion on his left cheekbone, dusted himself off and urged everyone to resume their protests with a renewed sense of purpose. Soon enough, the march proceeded in orderly fashion.

Further along during another lull, a nun leaned in toward Leo and said, "I'll pray for you." But the deadpan expression on her face and the lack of emotion in her tone made Leo wonder if she meant she would be piously praying for his redemption or for the success of the protest. Either way, he did not care what she thought, any more than he cared to linger on what kind of twisted agenda the man with the Saints cap was carrying out with his sudden attack. Neither of them were marching with him nor were they in his shoes. It had been his long-held observation that while many people preached about putting themselves in other people's shoes, very few actually did it.

Finally, the protesters had reached their destination on North Rampart across from Louis Armstrong Park and Municipal Auditorium, all of them remaining behind the ropes that the police had set up for them. At one point, there was another police escort approaching from a different direction and leading the way for a limousine with darkened windows. As it passed by, speculation spread throughout the buzzing crowd:

"You suppose that's her?"

"I just checked my watch. Her concert is in forty-five minutes. That must be her."

"Should we boo in case that's her?"

"I hope that was her so she could see that not everybody agrees with all those lies she's been spreading."

"You think if we threw water on her, she'd melt?"

"We got an escort, so I guess she gets one, too. Wish things were that equal all-around."

In fact, some people did boo, and some who didn't carry lit sparklers even raised their fists, but there was nothing more than that of an activist nature to observe. The Coalition had stressed over and over again to its participants that the protest was to be peaceful, and everyone lived up to that directive. And then, without further incident, the time allotted to the protest finally elapsed, and the crowd began to disperse into their normal haunts. Leo took note of the TV and newspaper reporters that had covered everything before, during and after, with Terrence being the focus of most of their interviews. He knew there was nothing Terrence couldn't handle, and the results would be professional.

"Do you think Anita Bryant got the message today?" one female reporter was asking, as Leo lingered nearby.

"Whether she does or not," Terrence began, "we want the public to see that we are here, and we will not take what she's said about us lying down. Particularly the gay teachers in this country. They go to work every day only with the intent of educating our children, helping them to learn about the world we live in, and all this mischief that this Save Our Children Campaign is accusing them of is pure and simple poppycock without a shred of evidence to back it up. All teachers realize the importance of separating their private lives from their duties as educators. They all realize that any inappropriate conduct is grounds for dismissal."

"Were you surprised when her campaign was successful in overturning the Miami-Dade County ordinance?" the reporter continued.

Terrence allowed himself a smirk. "There's so much misinformation out there about those of us who are gay. Old wives' tales, shall we say? Let's also admit that Anita Bryant pulled every one of them outta the closet, if you'll allow the pun. When people get better educated on the subject, they'll realize that gay teachers and every other gay man or woman in every profession are just trying to do their job and do it well. All this hysteria won't stand the test of time."

Leo stayed a bit longer, as Terrence continued to handle everything thrown at him. In the end, the story would likely be picked up by the Associated Press, and their main goal of publicizing their opposition to the results of the Save Our Children Campaign would get a fair hearing nationwide. All the while, the letter-writing campaign to the Florida Citrus Commission would continue, as the coffers of Californian and Brazilian citrus growers grew fatter.

Leo's plan was that Lake was to come to the camelback after the protest was over, and the two of them would celebrate with his homemade dinner of baked spaghetti, Greek salad and garlic bread. Leo didn't consider himself the greatest of chefs or anything close to that, but over the years he had mastered that particular menu and had served it before to others with compliments received all-around.

He had pulled a tightly wedged stack of mail out of the little brass box with the lid to the right of his door and headed up the stairs without sorting through it. Once inside, he dropped it on the living room sofa and made a beeline to the kitchen to warm up his spaghetti. He opened the oven and inhaled the delicious odor. Soon his dish would be bubbling up nicely, and all that remained to bring it to perfection would be to sprinkle on a layer of Parmesan cheese for the final crusting.

He poured himself a glass of cold club soda and returned to the mail: a utility bill, three pieces of junk mail, a couple of grocery fliers, the water bill, the latest copy of *Time* magazine. And then, a letter with a last name on the return address that mattered: Lightman.

He was always excited to get letters from Greg, but particularly on this occasion since it had been two months since he'd heard anything.

Then, Leo frowned. He'd almost missed it. Yes, the name was Lightman, but the rest of the address consisted of a P. O. Box and Lexington, Ky.

Not Nairobi, Kenya.

Was Greg back in the States at last? Did this mean he had returned with Yaro in tow? Would he be seeing them both soon? What a joyous reunion and introduction that would be!

Leo couldn't tear open the letter fast enough. Unfortunately, an adrenaline flash felt like it was melting his sternum when he finished reading the first sentence and continued burning through flesh and bone as he struggled through the rest:

Dear Leo,

I know you're probably asking yourself, 'Why is Preston writing to me?' As Greg's next of kin, the Peace Corps has informed me through Kenya's Country and Outreach Unit that he has gone missing. The Country Director over there in Nairobi says he did not report for work over two weeks ago, and they have been searching for him ever since to no avail. According to Greg's letters, the Peace Corps considers him one of their very best volunteers, so I know they will spare nothing in an effort to return him to the fold. When Greg commits to anything, he goes all-in, as I don't have to tell you.

I know this is hard for you to hear, as it has been for me and my wife, Sherrie. We know that Greg kept in touch with you, as he did regularly with us. We are very distressed and

165

hoping that he will turn up soon. I know no more than this.
There was nothing else in their letter. But if you would like
to call me anytime to ask for updates, my number is enclosed
in the P.S.

Sherrie and I send our best to you in this time of uncertainty.
Warmest regards,
Preston

Leo dropped the letter into his lap, and painful, worst-case scenarios began to fill his brain. He tried his best to push them out, push them away, but they kept gnawing at him. He picked up the letter and read it again. There was no mention of Yaro. But then, Yaro was not a member of the Peace Corps. He was employed by the government of Kenya in the National Education system at the primary level. All Leo could think of was to call Preston long-distance immediately, so he hurried into the kitchen, gathered his thoughts for a minute or so, picked up the phone on the counter and made the call.

On the third ring, Preston answered.

Leo felt another spurt of adrenaline and sensed his quickening pulse. "Preston, I just got your letter. This is Leo."

Preston's empathy poured through the phone line. "Yes, I thought I'd be hearing from you soon, buddy. I'm so sorry to be the bearer of such terrible news."

"Gosh, I thought you were Greg at first. You sound so much like him, it's uncanny."

"Yes, people do say we sound alike. We just don't look alike. He's the redhead, and I'm the brunette. But let me say that I understand you calling me right away. Sherrie and I haven't been the same since we got this news. We know what you must be feeling right now, so if there's anything we can do for you, go right ahead and ask."

Leo had it all lined up in his head. "Could you get that letter they sent you and give me their address and any other contact info that's on there? That Country Outreach bunch, or whatever you said they were."

"Sure. Hold on. Give me a sec."

After about a minute or so, Preston returned, and Leo wrote everything down on his kitchen counter notepad.

"Thanks," Leo said. "I'd like them to put me in touch with the National Educational system in Nairobi. I'm sure you know about Yaro Pala, don't you?"

"We do. The love of Greg's life."

Leo exhaled noisily. "I was thinking that maybe he knows something about Greg's disappearance. It's worth a shot, don't you think?"

"I do. I don't know why we didn't think of that, but we've been so upset, we haven't been able to think straight. Other than Sherrie, Greg's the only family I've got left."

"The way I figure it, if anyone would know what happened to him, Yaro certainly would."

The rest of the conversation was spent mostly on further commiserating with one another and a vow to keep in touch. It was only after Leo had hung up that the burned smell permeating the kitchen brought him back to reality. He spun around and opened the oven to the sight of a layer of scorched pasta atop his beautiful dish. He cursed under his breath, but everything was salvageable. He put on his oven mitts and brought it out to perform minor surgery which consisted of scraping off the top and sprinkling on that layer of Parmesan for a quick fix. It actually helped him to wait patiently for it to melt, a calming effect he desperately needed. Anything to keep his mind from drifting into the unwelcome news about Greg.

At the dinner table after Lake arrived, it was all Leo could do to down a few mouthfuls of his spaghetti and salad. He kept returning to speculation about Greg and his plan to try and get in touch with Yaro if he possibly could.

"I must have told Greg a thousand times to be careful."

"I know I'd feel the same way you do. I'd make every effort to reach out to him and the powers that be over there," Lake said at one point. "Meanwhile, you've got your life over here to manage, too. You're the new editor of *Sunday*, and you have a lot on your plate. You've got to stay focused and hope for the best."

Leo kept on indulging his worst instincts. "I just have a bad feeling about this. I can't shake it. Greg would never have quit the Peace Corps and wandered off somewhere on his own without telling me. Unless…"

For a while, it appeared that he wasn't going to finish the sentence, but finally did. "… he couldn't."

"Try not to go to such a dark place," Lake said. "It won't help things. Be gentle with yourself."

"I'm wondering if there's anything that can help."

Lake conjured up a smile. "How about after I help you clear the dishes, you sit down at the piano and entertain us with one of your famous recitals? One of your rousing R & H spectaculars. You know—your voice and their songs."

"I appreciate the suggestion," Leo said. "But I don't think show tunes will help right now."

The next morning at his desk at the newspaper, Leo received a surprise visit from Julius DeSiard, himself, the Grand Duke of Sparkling Champagne.

"Mr. Leo Marble, sir, I come to you untouched, unharmed, with not so much as a scratch on me," he said with a sweep of his hand. Then, he took a whistle out of his pocket and blew it once.

Startled, Leo's head jerked back. "Wow. You certainly got my attention with that."

Julius lowered his tone, his radiant smile diminishing slightly and then pointed to the whistle in his hand. "It could have been otherwise without this. I feel I must report something important to you in the spirit of what your Coalition is trying to accomplish."

"Please, go right ahead."

Julius returned the whistle to his pocket and began. "Well, after the Krewe broke up and a few of us stopped by a Quarter watering hole for a celebratory drink, we all went our separate ways. I headed home to my apartment by myself. I had only walked a block or two when I started getting this feeling. Have you ever gotten the sensation that you were being followed?"

Leo shook his head.

"I did, yesterday afternoon. It seems I have this recurring dream in which that happens to me. Only this time, I got the distinct impression it was happening to me in waking life. So, at one point, I managed a sort of a half-turn and craned my neck, and I was able to see that there were definitely two burly men some distance behind me in T-shirts. I thought, 'Maybe it's just nothing. Just a part of the parade throng breaking up.' I picked up my pace a bit, the closer I got to my courtyard gate. I happened to notice that there weren't any people around on the opposite side of the street, so I began to get more and more alarmed, should something actually be about to happen. Finally, I was about half-a-block from home when one of the men called out from behind, 'Hey, we saw you with your sissy sparklers prissing around out there today, you little fairy! You're gonna get what's comin' to ya!'"

"Damn," Leo said, shaking his head.

"Well, I'm proud to say I thought on my feet, brought out my whistle, blew it as loud as I could and shouted, 'Police! Help! Police!'"

"And what did they do?"

"They turned on their heels and ran like the cowards they were. I halfway expected to see skidmarks on the sidewalk." Julius allowed himself a self-satisfied chuckle.

"Good job," Leo said.

"Yes, I thought so, too. What I also wanted to say to you was that I now definitely see that I can't just go about my food broker and Krewe business as I did before without acknowledging that there are those out there who mean me and others harm just for being who we are. I used to feel safe in my routine life, but I see how Anita Bryant has stirred up something dangerous and made it easier for people to act out their prejudices. I know those men weren't bluffing. They intended to hurt me."

THE MAJESTIC LEO MARBLE

"They surely did, just as one man actually tackled me and brought me to the ground at one point yesterday. You were in front leading the way, so you weren't privy to that." Leo pointed to the bandage on his cheek. "But this is not much worse than cutting myself shaving."

Julius sighed and sat back in his chair. "Just one question. Whose idea was it for us to bring whistles?"

"Ah," Leo said with an expression of great satisfaction. "That was the brainstorm of one Sgt. Andy Ferrell, Terrence told me. Apparently, the sergeant's children are crazy about your floats and sparklers in the parades, and he suggested the whistles to Terrence as a safety measure. So rest assured, we had the New Orleans Police Department on our side, and most people think your Krewe is a lot of fun."

"I know that now," Julius said. "And I also wanted to tell you that I have decided as a broker not to do business anymore with Florida orange juice brands. At least for the time being."

Leo quickly offered his hand across the desk. "Glad to hear it. The one thing we can't do as gay people is to sit idly by and let people believe all these misconceptions about us. When we first talked about this, you expressed some doubt as to whether or not this would have any effect. I assure you that it will. It just may take a little time. I've always thought that patience belongs on the side of the angels. Maybe a handful of us can't get the job done but think of the difference that hundreds of thousands of us will make across the country with the sort of decision you've made."

His dazzling smile fully restored, Julius said, "I look upon that whistle as my wake-up call."

Chapter 20

Leo was a quick study at assuming his editorial responsibilities at the paper. Arthur had chosen well. With Three-H and Chase still aboard, Leo thought of his staff as an invincible trio. No assignment, no topic was out of reach and undoable; and one of the first Leo undertook on his watch, as Arthur had put it, was a piece on the Coalition, connecting it with the protest march through the Quarter. Three-H had a particular gleam in his eye during his interviews with Terrence and was careful to close the door to Leo's office behind him when the two of them huddled to review the copy he was in the process of creating. Three-H was still observing the required year of separation from Lydia and could not afford any slip-ups or leaks from company snitches after possibly overhearing random but revealing comments.

As for Chase, Leo decided to clear the air about his own sexuality with his excellent photographer, while not revealing to him that he knew what was going on behind the scenes with a certain married woman.

"It's totally cool with me," Chase said, sitting on the other side of Leo's desk. The room still smelled of Arthur's pipe tobacco after decades of saturation. "I've always said what people do away from work is their own business."

A devilish little elf perched itself on Leo's shoulder, causing him to consider just for a microsecond saying something cryptic like, "Especially in your case." But of course, the elf was mentally banished, and Leo's better, professional nature prevailed. "I

171

totally agree with you. All that counts with me is the quality of your work, Chase."

"Thank you," he said, beaming. "I did enjoy working with Arthur, but I think I'm gonna like working with you as my boss even more. Sometimes, Arthur was a bit of a stick-in-the-mud about things, but he always meant well."

While his *Sunday* work continued to go off without a hitch, Leo waited patiently to hear from either the Peace Corps' Country and Outreach Unit or the National Educational system in Nairobi. It took a couple of weeks for him to get a response from the Country Director informing him that Greg's status had not changed, even though they were doing everything they could to track him down. Calls to Preston revealed nothing new received at that end, either. A call to Peace Corps Headquarters in Washington, D. C., though taken seriously, led Leo right back to the Country and Outreach Unit in Kenya and its "no-change in status" mantra. Though he felt caught in a loop of desperation, he held out hope that his National Education contacts in Nairobi would come through for him.

Three more months passed. Then nearly six. The end of the year was nearing. Leo and Preston kept in touch, but there was never anything new to report. It all seemed like a lost cause. Preston even hired a private detective, but it turned out to be a great deal of money spent on dead end after dead end in a foreign country that was not nearly as open to such things as the USA was. Finally, a letter arrived from National Education in Nairobi, waiting in Leo's mailbox after work one evening.

With great trepidation, Leo sat on his sofa and opened it, feeling like he had been stabbed through the heart by the following words:

> *... and we regret to inform you that the primary teacher you inquired about, Mr. Yaro Pala, of Nairobi, was reported to us some time ago as missing and is officially regarded as a missing person. Nairobi law enforcement was brought in to try and locate him, but they have been unsuccessful to this point...*

There was more polite verbiage, but it didn't register in Leo's brain, which seemed about to explode. The speculation was over now. He knew what it all meant, no matter who might try to tell him otherwise. Not after all this time. He knew then that neither Greg nor Yaro would ever be found, that if they had somehow gone off somewhere together to live a different kind of life, he would have heard from them by now. He was certain they would have made the effort. It was all he could do to keep from screaming the primal scream of someone in deep, visceral pain.

Instead, he moved quickly to his precious spinet and took his rage out on the keys, both black and white. He banged away over and over while tears welled up. The cacophony continued for a minute or more. He did not care if it might do further damage to his already-compromised ear. He did not feel better when he finally stopped; he felt helpless and up against a wall of hurt that kept rebuilding itself every time he thought he'd managed to tear down a few bricks. The march through the Quarter back in the summer suddenly seemed like a futile gesture, a scene that could easily have been deleted from an ever-changing libretto that was mocking him.

That night, he went to bed without calling either Lake or Preston. They would know about his interpretation of the situation soon enough. He wanted to be alone to mourn. This time, he knew he was not being overly dramatic and theatrical as he had in the past just for show and his own amusement. He had held it all in long enough. The harsh reality of being who he was, of Greg and Yaro being who they were, spoke to him through his tears.

On some level that he had tried to ignore, he had known it would turn out this way, once Greg had described his clandestine meetings with Yaro; once Greg had told him about Kenya's "cultural" climate and that it was hostile to those who were attracted to the same sex. His warnings to them to be careful had apparently fallen on deaf ears; or perhaps they hadn't, but someone, or even more than one person who had had it in for them, had been far too clever by half, had stalked them and then covered everything up efficiently.

This was not some play whose script could be rewritten or reimagined because the critics didn't like it in an out-of-town preview. For the first time in his life, Leo felt cynicism creeping into his brain and bones, replacing the resiliency he had tried to preserve at all costs.

Leo chose to deal with the disappearance of Greg and Yaro by talking Terrence into holding a memorial service for them a couple of months later at the Metropolitan Community Church on South Claiborne Avenue. It wasn't a highly structured event and consisted mostly of people from the Coalition standing up and giving their own testimony regarding how much they missed loved ones and how important it was to have some sort of closure in life when they departed.

For Leo, it didn't seem like it was enough, but he didn't know what else to do. There were no bodies, no caskets, no urns. He invited Preston and Sherrie to come down for it, but they had already arranged a more traditional service in Lexington and instead just sent a spray of flowers. Closure was certainly something Leo longed to have, but it just wasn't available. Instead, there was just a hole, a leak in his well-being that would never be patched.

He also started diving deeper into his work and keeping longer hours than he needed to. He became friends with the security guard, a tall, sturdy Black man named Raymond Sylvester, Jr., who roamed the second floor and other areas of the building after the daytime employees in the classified department had left. Typesetters, proofreaders and news and sports reporters with late deadlines were usually the only other ones around.

"I know this paper gets a decent day's work outta you, Mr, Marble," Raymond said to him one particular evening, popping his head into the doorframe when he saw that the light was still on. "I hope you take a good, long vacation the way you're here practically around the clock. And I don't mind sayin' to you that

I don't mind keepin' an eye on you when you leave the building real late at night."

"I appreciate you saying that, Raymond. Sometimes, a job is the only thing you have to keep you going."

That wasn't quite true for Leo. The Coalition continued its boycott of Florida orange juice and its letter-writing campaign to the Citrus Commission. But they were all disappointed when the Commission made it quite clear publicly that they were not going to cancel Anita Bryant's contract. She would remain as their spokesperson for the time being.

Then, one afternoon in late spring, Lake called Leo up at the newspaper and said, "Tonight, I want to take you out to dinner, if you don't have other plans. But we don't go Dutch. It's my treat."

"I don't have any plans, but why can't we go Dutch as usual?"

Sounding rather mysterious, Lake said, "There's something very important I need to talk to you about, and I won't take no for an answer on my picking up the tab. Is Commander's okay with you?"

"Always."

Later that evening, as they walked into the famous Garden District restaurant with its signature blue-and-white turret above and awning encircling it below, Leo was far more concerned with what Lake had to tell him than the dinner menu; although he fully intended to stick with his favorites—turtle soup with sherry, followed by the always-dependable crab cakes.

"So, tell me what this is all about?" Leo said, after they had been seated in the tropical courtyard, ordered and been served their drinks.

Lake took a swig of his Manhattan and said, "First, I wanted to celebrate our friendship and assure you that it means a great deal to me, no matter what happens. I don't think I need to prove that, but something has come up that I can't ignore."

Leo sipped his club soda and shot him a skeptical glance. "Wait... you aren't dying, are you?"

"No, nothing like that," Lake said, throwing his head back and laughing. "But I am shaking up my life."

"Surely, you're not quitting your teaching job, and please tell me you didn't march into Father Babineaux's office and spill the beans. I thought we'd settled that a while back."

"I'll quit beating around the bush and get to it." Lake took another swallow of his Manhattan and said, "Yes, I am giving up my teaching job. I let Father know I would not be returning this fall, and I lied to him about the reason. I told him it was because I was burned out and needed to step back, but as I said, that was a lie."

"What is the reason, then? You've already shocked me all the way down to my socks."

Lake averted his eyes briefly but kept a smile on his face. "I love Ignacio very much, and I'm tired of living most of the year without him and settling for summers and other bits and pieces of time. The Delgado family is a very proud one, and I could not convince him to move up here to be with me. So I'm going to move to Mexico City so we can be together year-round. The Mexican Standoff is over, and I wanted you to be the first of my friends to know."

Leo was doing his best to process what he'd just heard, but there it was again: that old, familiar hurt inside. Perhaps not as weighty as some that had come before, however, so he forged ahead. "Why did you make this decision now?"

"I'll be fifty this fall, Leo. I thought I'd be settled in life by that age, but the way things are, I'm not. You know how the gay world is with its emphasis on youth, and everything else be damned. Both my parents are gone now, so there's no family here in America to hold me back. And, then, to be honest with you, what happened with Greg and Yaro made me think long and hard. Not that we know their fate for sure, but after all this time, it doesn't look hopeful. I get sick to my stomach just thinking about it. Besides, no matter who we are or where we live, we don't have forever. We ought to try and make the most of what we have. As I said, your friendship means a lot to me. Being a teacher means a lot to me, and Ignacio even says he might be able to find a position for me teaching English down there. I hope all of this explains my decision to you."

"I have to admit it does," Leo said with warmth in his voice, deferring to his better nature. He could not possibly begrudge his best friend a chance to be with the love of his life, even though he himself still had no one of his own. As Raymond Sylvester, Jr. had pointed out recently somewhat off-the-cuff, he was all about his job at the newspaper.

"So when will you start this new version of your life?" Leo added.

"After this semester is over, of course. I'll be leaving early in June. And once I'm settled in, you'll have an open invitation to visit us anytime. Ignacio's home is something to see, and he's well-fixed. In fact, I want you to promise me right now that you'll take a big chunk of time off from the newspaper and come down to be with us for a while. It'll make things easier all-around."

"Actually, I have a month's worth of vacation coming to me," Leo said. "Even the security guard got onto me recently about taking a break. He probably thinks I'm a workaholic, and I probably am. So, yes, I'll make you that promise. And I've always wanted to visit Mexico."

Lake extended his hand. "Then let's shake on it right here and now."

The timing was perfect as their tuxedoed waiter was approaching with their turtle soup, even though Leo enjoyed it and the rest of his meal with mixed emotions. Once again, it appeared he was fated to endure a never-ending succession of life-changing events that required him to fall back on his inner strength.

Chapter 21

Lake's letters to Leo took the place of those he had received over the years from Greg. The gist of them was that he and Ignacio were living out their dream for the most part. There was only one glitch that kept it from being perfect. They wanted to get married but couldn't. It wasn't just a matter of Ignacio being Catholic and his church being firmly opposed to approving any such ritual for the foreseeable future. There was no other denomination in Mexico City or in the surrounding states that offered such a ceremony. At least Ignacio's father and mother, Luis and Concepcion Delgado, were very fond of Lake, particularly because he spoke fluent Spanish, was respectful of their culture and was studying for Mexican citizenship. More than anything else, they wanted their son to be happy and did not care what anyone else thought, going against what they had been brought up to believe by their church.

Meanwhile, 1979 moved along with Three-H's divorce going through with an exceptionally amicable financial settlement, after which he handed in his resignation. Leo now had a position to fill and what amounted to hundreds of resumes to sift through in response to ads placed in certain markets across the country.

"I thought after you took that long vacation to Mexico, you'd cut back on staying up in here half the night," his favorite security guard said to him one evening, again poking his head in.

"I've got to hire someone to replace Mr. Henningham, Raymond. I've never hired anyone before, so I'm a little nervous," Leo told him, staring at the stack on his desk in front of him.

"I bet you'll do just fine."

"I'm not so sure."

However, once Leo began winnowing the pile down seriously, he discovered that a huge percentage of the resumes were borderline illiterate, unprofessional or lacked the necessary credentials to be hired. Many were form letters with TO WHOM IT MAY CONCERN greetings, followed by the always impersonal colon. Such a lazy approach was easy to dismiss. The ad that had been placed clearly read: SEND RESUME TO: LEO MARBLE, *Sunday* editor, c/o *Times-Picayune,* along with the P.O. Box and the zip code.

"If you don't take the time to even use my name, I don't have the time to give you a shot," Leo would think to himself and then drop such resumes into the trash basket beside his desk with great delight.

Eventually, after what he considered to be a perfectly fair filtering procedure, he had it narrowed down to three entries.

One was an experienced reporter named Lance Arceneaux with the Baton Rouge *Advocate,* who might understand the nuances of assignments in a state like Louisiana with its Huey Long history and the problems of a large, quirky city like New Orleans. Later, Mr. Arceneaux did nothing to spoil his chances of nailing down the job during his interview.

Another, Grant Varnado, had worked for the Mobile *Press-Register,* and here Leo couldn't help but be amused when their conversation strayed to the storied rivalry between New Orleans and Mobile regarding the origins of Mardi Gras. Mobile claimed to have started it all, while New Orleans pushed back heavily on the notion. Perhaps Grant would understand how unique the Gulf South was because of unresolved tiffs like that, and he was still in the running when his interview concluded.

The third candidate, Angelle Wilkinson, hailed from Boston and had worked for the *Boston Globe Spotlight* team for six years. It was a very prestigious outfit that had won major awards while probing current political and cultural issues without blinking, and Leo wondered quite frankly why she wanted to leave it and head down to the Crescent City to dig into its problems. The fact that the *Sunday* staff had never employed a woman gave Leo pause. Mostly, women at the newspaper were assigned to deal with recipe columns, wedding announcements, bridal and baby showers or to take classified orders from people who wanted to place ads to sell or rent everything under the sun. That was, after all, the lifeblood of the newspaper.

"I appreciate your coming all this way for the job, but I'm curious as to why you want to leave the *Spotlight* staff," Leo was saying as his interview with Angelle got underway in his office. "*Sunday* would like to be half as effective as *Spotlight* is."

Angelle, a tall, comely brunette with hair parted down the middle and hanging nearly to her waist, took her time, looking slightly surprised by the question. "I think you underestimate your reputation, Mr. Marble. There was an AP story that the *Globe* ran a while back about a Gay Coalition here in New Orleans that staged a protest against Anita Bryant's Summer Pops appearance. You were mentioned in the piece by the founder, Mr. Terrence Dennery."

"Yes, I was involved with it then and still am. I'm impressed that you remember our names."

"That whole anti-gay teacher campaign was outrageous and so unfair. As for Boston itself, it has its own charms, such as the Back Bay, but there's no Mardi Gras up there. I guess I've always been fascinated by your city and thought I would like to take a stab at working down here. I do think I have the credentials, as you've pointed out."

Leo, who had been slightly slumping in his chair at the beginning of the interview, was now sitting up and taking notes. "You sound like you're chomping at the bit to get started."

She leaned forward in her chair with an easy smile. "Yes. And just in case you're wondering, I'm not gay. I have a brother who is, though, and I've always supported him since he came out ten years ago. I espouse many liberal causes, and I'm proud of it."

Now it was Leo's turn to be surprised by her directness, but he found the right words. "I guess we both know that the personal information you just shared with me rarely comes up in a job interview. I'm not supposed to ask you about your religious or political beliefs...or your private life, of course."

"Pardon the pun, but I'm a straight shooter," she said without a hint of looking or sounding ill-at-ease.

"Very clever," Leo said, briefly pursing his lips.

Sounding quite pleased with herself, Angelle said, "You might as well know that I took a little vacation to come down for the interview, and I intend to take in as much of the city as I can. So even if I don't get the job, I consider that this will be time well-spent. I win either way."

"I must admit I do like people who know how to combine work and fun. How long will you be here?"

"A week. I'm staying at the Monteleone, by the way."

"Excellent, old-line choice. Go by the Tourist and Convention Commission in the Quarter and get some brochures on various things to see and places to eat. Although I do recommend you take the St. Charles Avenue streetcar to Commander's Palace for a real treat. I always have the turtle soup and crab cakes, but anything you order will be memorable, I assure you." He paused and then rose to extend his hand. "I've truly enjoyed meeting you, Miss Wilkinson, and I can tell you that you are still in the running."

Over their handshake, she said "All you need to know about me is that I'm the best there is at squeezing twenty-five hours out of every twenty-four."

Leo and Lake had discussed on more than one occasion during their extraordinary friendship the importance of recognizing themes, strains and patterns in life. There was also the question of signs. That sometimes they appeared to impart information from sources unknown, if only one were on the lookout for them. Over the next few days, as Leo pondered the resumes of his three fully qualified candidates for *Sunday*, he wondered if he was being fair to Lance Arceneaux and Grant Varnado because they had not volunteered their political views nor indicated any affinity one way or another for cutting-edge, social issues. They had played it safe, while Angelle Wilkinson had not.

Was he being influenced by the fact she had mentioned her support for her gay sibling and contempt for the Save Our Children Campaign? Was that a sign?

Then, *the* sign fell into his lap. The story came over the AP wire three days after his interview with Angelle Wilkinson. The Florida Citrus Commission would not be renewing Anita Bryant's contract. It had taken longer than the Coalition and other organizations across the country had thought it would. But the continued orange juice boycott and letter-writing campaign had finally paid off. Anita Bryant had won the battle but lost the war.

That did it for Leo. He knew then that he should hire Angelle, and he phoned her at the Monteleone to let her know. She thanked him profusely.

"So when do you want me to start?" she added, switching to a matter-of-fact tone, as if she had known all along she would get the job.

"Whenever you can manage after you give notice."

Within a month, she was on the staff, settled in and overflowing with ideas. In her first weekly meeting with Leo and Chase, she proposed the following:

FEMALE ENTREPRENEURS IN NEW ORLEANS
INSIDE GAY MARDI GRAS KREWES
NEW ORLEANS' UPCOMING JAZZ MUSICIANS
THE HOMELESS IN THE FRENCH QUARTER

Chase seemed to be onboard with all of them, but Leo had second thoughts about the "homeless" concept. Was it that much of a problem yet?

"I don't ever want to shy away from controversy, but I think we should tackle the other three first, in no particular order. Later on, we could look into the homeless issue."

"I love going into the clubs and listening to the jazz sessions. I can guarantee you some great, moody shots with the smoke rising to the ceiling," Chase said.

"Is that alright with you, Angelle? Do you want to do that piece first?" Leo said.

"Suits me. I'm pleased you liked my list and my input."

"Keep up the great ideas."

The piece Angelle and Chase put together on the new generation of jazz musicians was well-received, and it was Leo's perception that Chase had never done better work. Angelle's copy was incisive, never rambling, and the quotes she coaxed from the striving young artists were humorous and inspiring.

Leo paired them again on the Gay Mardi Gras story, sending them to interview both Julius DeSiard and Ira Claxton, intending to save the Female Entrepreneur assignment for himself. The kaleidoscope of people behind these colorful krewes came to life in print and photo, and Leo took note of the fact that *Sunday* had never received so many complimentary letters since he'd been working on the staff. He had a winning team in Angelle Wilkinson and Chase Knowles, and they were making his job that much easier. His *Sunday* staff was truly making its mark under his guidance.

As the months passed, Leo began to notice that Angelle and Chase were becoming more than just cohorts. Little things like intense, tell-tale gazes at the lunch table in the cafeteria, a stolen smooch here and there when they thought no one was looking. Leo saw no reason to become alarmed as long as what appeared to be a burgeoning romance did not affect their work.

Then one morning, Chase knocked on the doorframe. "Got a minute?"

Leo waved him in and nodded pleasantly. "Sure, what's up?"

Chase took a seat and launched right into it. "I have a problem. I think Angelle and I are falling in love."

"I'm a pretty observant person. This comes as no surprise to me. Why should you and Angelle falling in love be a problem? I have no objections. Don't worry about the fraternization thing. You're both consummate professionals in my eyes."

"Thanks," Chase said, flashing a smile. "I wasn't worried about you, though. It's Angelle I'm worried about."

"Okay. Explain."

Leo observed that Chase had never sounded so unsure of himself as he continued. "Well... it's just that... there's this long-term relationship I've been involved in. I'd rather not go into detail about it, if you don't mind."

Leo waved him off. "No need. Three-H gave me the bare bones of it when I first joined the staff. And, no, he did not mention her name."

"Why that sonofabitch! How did he find out?"

"He didn't say. I didn't ask. Please, go on with what you were explaining to me."

"I'm breaking it off with this woman," Chase added, exhaling. "It's way past time I did. I was never in love with her, but I am in love with Angelle. My problem is... or my question to you is... should I tell Angelle about it and take a chance that it might turn her off and ruin what we have going? I guess you could say I feel guilty about my so-called arrangement. Now, I look back on it and say to myself, 'What the hell was I thinking? Was the money worth it? Or was I just lazy as all get-out?'"

"Then by all means, don't tell her about it. Angelle may have episodes in her past that she's not particularly proud of. I suppose we all do when you come right down to it. It's my opinion that there are far more mismatches in love than there are the real thing."

Chase cocked his head and drew back slightly. "Maybe I don't have the right to say this, but isn't that a bit cynical?"

"Maybe it is. Don't pay attention to my last statement."

Despite his last-second retraction to Chase, Leo was aware of the cynicism that had crept into his persona lately. He did not like it, but mismatches in love were all he had ever known.

Angelle breezed into Leo's office one afternoon six months later, sat herself down and said, "I'd like to share something with you, if you don't mind."

"Shoot."

"My brother, Jay, has found out through the grapevine that WDSU here in New Orleans is going to be creating a new slot on the meteorology staff next year. As I believe I've told you, he's had a job as weather anchor for a UHF station in Boston for a while now, but he thinks it may be time to move on."

Leo knew just what to say. "I don't suppose you living here has anything to do with that."

She held up her right hand and batted her eyelashes. "I can't fool you. Jay says my letters to him about living and working in New Orleans lit a fire under him, and he became determined to get down here one way or another. It's not that Boston doesn't have an active gay community, you understand; and then there's Provincetown out on the Cape which is a hoot. But he thinks it's so cool that I'm working for someone like you and that we're tackling all these issues the way we are. He wants to make that kind of contribution eventually."

Leo allowed himself a strange, little hiccup of a chuckle. "He does realize by now that he can't choose and control the weather, doesn't he?"

"Touche. But he truly loves meteorology. He pours over data for hours and not just because he has to to make forecasts. He's the most left-brained person I know. For relaxation, he trots out his college calculus textbook and solves equations. Can you imagine?"

Leo raised his eyebrows, more in amusement than surprise. "To be honest, I can't. I'm pretty right-brained with all my writing, and then there's the singing and acting I've done. I'm a huge fan of show tunes and singing them at the piano."

"So you've said. But you've yet to treat me or Chase to one of your little concerts."

"We'll have to remedy that soon."

"Anyhow, Jay isn't completely left-brained. Do you by any chance like oldies-but-goodies?"

"As a matter of fact, I do. I'm particularly partial to the late 60s when I was in college." Innocent but bittersweet memories of Greg and "I'd Like To Get To Know You" flashed into his head.

Angelle leaned in smartly. "You should see the vinyl record collection Jay has. Mostly 50s, 60s and this last decade, but even a few from the 40s as well, none of which he was old enough to remember." Then came what Leo instantly recognized as the payoff pause. "If he gets the job, he'll want to get involved with the Coalition, of course."

"Yes, he will," Leo said, going along with it all as if it had been perfectly rehearsed. "We can't have too many new members, and new blood coming from Boston sounds like a great addition."

After she'd left, he sat back and reflected on the observation Chase had recently made to him on the subject of cynicism. Then, his discussions with Lake about major themes, recurring patterns and signs in life bubbled up once again. He came to the intriguing conclusion that maybe he didn't have to go as far as believing he had a guardian angel somewhere up there. That had yet to be proven, despite all the declarations from pulpits everywhere. But he might possibly have a guardian Angelle in the neighborhood.

THE THIRD ACT

THE THIRD ACT

Chapter 22

It was mid-May of 1981, and Leo had just treated Terrence, Angelle and Chase to a lineup of classic Jerome Kern songs at his spinet: his dream song—"All The Things You Are" from *Very Warm For May;* "Smoke Gets In Your Eyes" from *Roberta;* and "The Song Is You" from *Music In The Air*. He was in rare form vocally, hitting the high note at the end of "All The Things You Are" without a hitch. He had disdained his usual R & H tendencies, and the results were spectacular, judging from the applause he received from his utterly relaxed friends seated around his living room sipping on their wine.

He took a couple of bows, bending from the waist in exaggerated fashion and said, "Please, no more. You'll give me the bighead."

"Your head is just the right size for all the talent it contains," Angelle said. "And thanks again for finally staging this mini concert for us. We've been looking forward to it for a long time."

Leo moved across the room to join Terrence on the sofa and said, "Sometimes I don't multitask as well as I should, but tonight, Terrence and I are doing a bit of it. We have some very important information to impart, and we're going to give you a sneak preview of our next Coalition meeting subject before we tackle the muffalettas I picked up at Central Grocery after work. In this case, we will have dinner after the concert."

"Sounds like we're plotting something," Angelle said.

"No, but what we have to tell you is deadly serious." He

189

gestured toward Terrence. "I turn things over to our head honcho."

Terrence dug down into his pants pocket, pulled out a piece of paper, scanned it quickly and began. "What I'm about to reveal is cutting-edge info from the Bay Area and one of my contacts out there who runs a gay organization in San Francisco similar to ours. A new disease has been identified that seems to be affecting some gay men particularly but other demographics as well, and it attacks the immune system. Or, as my friend says, compromises it so as to make it vulnerable to other opportunistic diseases. There's some research being done, and it appears one of the main ways it's spreading is through sexual contact."

"Is it an STD?" Chase said. "God knows, we certainly don't need another one of those."

Terrence frowned and shook his head. "It appears to be more serious than that. At least two dozen men have died so far, and they were all gay. The first cases were reported several months ago in June, and since then, it's been given a name: Acquired Immune Deficiency Syndrome. I've been informed by my friend that the CDC is getting involved and that some of the networks and newsmagazines will be doing stories on it quite frequently from here on out. I think the Coalition has an obligation to make all our members aware of this new development as soon as possible and take it out of the realm of rumor and hearsay. Word is people who have traveled out to the Coast have been buzzing about it here and there in some of the clubs and discos. There appears to be a lot of denial out there."

The alarm clearly registered in Angelle's voice. "I have to admit I've heard nothing about it, since I live in a very different world. What you've said makes me very nervous."

"That's the thing," Terrence continued. "There's reason to believe that this new disease has already spread to other demographics by other means. My friend has made mention of needle-sharing and even blood transfusions spreading the virus. The CDC certainly doesn't want it to become a pandemic, and they want to get to the bottom of it as soon as they can."

"As they should," Angelle said.

"Right. So, this is what I'll be communicating to all of you next week at the meeting:

Those of us who are part of the gay subculture don't have much margin for error. We are widely misunderstood, often persecuted, sometimes prosecuted and for many more years than we care to count relegated to existing underground and after midnight. We are criticized for sneaking around and socializing in bars when in most cases that is the only possible way we can meet and try to carve out some kind of life for ourselves. For some, however, that's problematic or even dangerous, so they choose to lead double lives with elaborately arranged camouflage schemes to fit in and avoid social ostracization. Let's face it: we aren't introduced to each other at church socials, and there are those who think we either don't exist or shouldn't exist. Organizations like ours are comparatively new. There are enough risks as it is, so we cannot afford to have a deadly disease yapping at our heels as well. I believe the Coalition has a duty to keep our community up to date on this situation because our very lives may well depend upon it.

Terrence paused, looked up from the page and said, "Well? What do y'all think?"

"Beautifully expressed, even though you paint a very bleak picture. Is it too soon to consider all this as a possible *Sunday* piece down the road?" Angelle said, nodding in Leo's direction.

"Good call. I can certainly see it happening," he told her. "And you and Chase are getting in on the ground floor. So, we've had the music and the message, now let's have the muffalettas, shall we?" He gestured toward the kitchen. "Any volunteers to help me? I'm not territorial at all about these things."

Everyone pitched in, and in no time, they were all savoring the monstrous Italian meat, cheese and chopped olive sandwiches that had sustained many a New Orleanian for centuries. It was an evening that satisfied both the brain and the stomach.

One week later, Leo was having his usual trim at Long May She Wave, and Mara was holding forth with an anecdote about her cousin Diane, who was trying to lose weight by drinking water and chewing bubble game all day. "Of course, she hasn't lost much weight because she keeps backsliding. She has goodies hidden all over her apartment, so she isn't fooling anyone but herself. But her jaw muscles are growing by leaps and bounds. I think she could rival the bite of a gator or a great white shark."

Everyone within earshot laughed, including George Kinsey one chair to the right—dressed in a flowing yellow and white caftan—tending to his client, a muscular young man named Eddie with a blond ponytail. In George's case, his laughter eventually morphed into a prodigious cough.

"There you go, coughing again," Mara said. "You should take something for that."

"Just my eternal allergies," George explained. "They always lie in wait for me this time of year, like a snake in the grass. I bow down to no man, but I'm afraid pollen has my number. I earnestly wish I could refuse its many invitations to take me out on the town for a good hacking. The truth is, I can be had for a good sneeze."

Mara nodded as she worked diligently on Leo's sideburns. "You're so good with funny images. If you weren't a stylist, I think you'd make a wonderful stand-up comedian."

"Funny you should say that," George continued. "Before I moved here from San Francisco, I briefly considered that. There are so many clubs in the city out there to try."

"There are clubs here, you know," Mara pointed out. "You could pursue it in your spare time, if you still wanted to."

"And what spare time is that, pray tell?"

Mara cocked her head in his general direction. "Good point. You're my most popular stylist."

"No way would I trust my ponytail to anyone but the man in the caftan, as I call him," Eddie added. "No way, no how."

George puffed himself up. "My friend, Eddie here, speaks the truth. When I went out to spend last Christmas with my friends in San Francisco, we worked your appointment around my trip, didn't we, dude?"

Eddie was practically beaming. "Righteously so." Then he leaned over toward Leo and added, "My parents didn't like it when I started wearing my hair in a ponytail. They said they thought it made me look like a queer. Their words, not mine, of course. Seems to be a word that people aren't afraid to use no matter what, no matter when, no matter who it hurts. I happen to have a girlfriend, and she likes my hair the way it is just fine. I found Long May She Wave and George here just in time because my Dad's barber kept trying to talk me into cutting my hair short. I could tell my Dad had been talking to him because the word *buzzcut* kept popping up. But, hey, George didn't care, didja?"

"All that matters to me is pleasing my clients and making them look their best," George said. "It's their hair, and they have to wear it."

"You do a bang-up job of that, too," Mara added.

"At any rate," George continued, "I can certainly empathize with your cousin, Mara. I've been fighting the battle of the bulge most of my life, and that's why I prefer to wear these caftans of mine. They're so forgiving of my dietary indiscretions. New Orleans is maybe the worst city in the country to try and count calories. Not that it was any easier out in San Francisco. Because the truth is, the last thing you're expected to be when you're gay is fat. Sounds brutal, I know, but that's the way it goes down."

The rest of Leo's haircut time was spent exchanging pleasantries, occasionally punctuated by more of George's coughing.

"You can get a good antihistamine to get that under control," Leo said to George as he headed out. "I get allergies from time to time, too."

"Yeah," George called out. "I have a doctor's appointment tomorrow."

At the Coalition office a couple of days later, Terrence was reading out loud to Leo with great interest a new article he'd found in a medical journal:

> *... and the disease has officially been labeled AIDS at this juncture, according to the CDC. The term HIV-Positive has been officially designated as an identifying marker and is beginning to generate the sort of dread that polio and the cumbersome, restrictive iron lung accomplished earlier in the century before the Salk Vaccine became a reality. There is one theory that suggests AIDS may have originated in Africa among the general population and migrated by various means to America. There has even been the theory circulating that the virus somehow moved from monkeys into humans, though that remains completely unsubstantiated. Moreover, deaths among gay men continue to mount mostly in metropolitan areas, presenting itself through what has been informally called 'the gay cancer,' but is more scientifically referred to as Kaposi's sarcoma, characterized by large, purple splotches on the skin of those affected.*
>
> *It has yet to be conclusively established, however, whether AIDS can be transmitted through the air or whether it exclusively requires the exchange of bodily fluids. Physicians, nurses and hospital workers alike have all expressed concern that they might be exposing themselves to the disease just by being in the same room with patients or handling their soiled linens. At the same time, the CDC has made research into the disease one of its top priorities.*

Terrence paused for a well-earned breath and looked up. "Pretty scary stuff, huh?"

Leo looked wide-eyed. "Understatement of the year."

"I'll bring all this up at our next Coalition meeting, of course."

"That's the least we can do," Leo said, shrugging.

Leo headed home after the sobering exchange with Terrence, fixed himself a club soda and then collapsed in front of the TV, starting to surf around for something that would either soothe his spirits or be nothing short of mindless entertainment. He was simply not in the mood to think.

He happened to land for a second on one of those stations specializing in evangelical pitches—the sort that made it quite clear that the viewer's credit card number was the only sure way to "salvation." All that "God" required was a valid expiration date. Revulsed, he was about to change channels when an obnoxious snippet caught his attention and froze him in place.

"... and for the homosexual, AIDS is the wages of sin," the televangelist, an older man whose gray hair sprayed ferociously into place and nearly resembling a serving of Dairy Queen soft-serve atop his head, was proclaiming.

Leo wanted to move on but found himself strangely mesmerized. It was as if some part of him needed to hear the very worst being said about people like himself. After all, there was some wisdom in knowing the enemy well enough to anticipate and fend him off.

"God has had enough of the homosexual's crimes against nature," the televangelist continued, all the while keeping an obsequious smile plastered on his wrinkled face. "So, He has sent AIDS to punish all who cling to such behavior. God is saying to them, 'Enough. I will not allow you to continue these evil ways. If you continue, you will surely die, and there will be no redemption for you. You will reside in Hell, among all other sinners, even though you will surely be the worst of them all.' For there is no worse sin in the world than for a man to lie with another man as with a woman, the Bible tells us. And as we all know, the Bible is the true word of God and must be obeyed by all or suffer eternal consequences. Let no man deny this great truth. There is only one way to obtain the salvation we all desperately need, and the existence of AIDS now conclusively proves that God has reached his limits of tolerance with us. It was hard enough on him when we disobeyed him and got cast out of the Garden of Eden that he so graciously prepared for us so that we would never have a care in the world. We cannot vex God this way and expect him to reward us in Heaven..."

Leo had reached his limit and shut the TV off, closing his eyes and shaking his head. Instinctively he knew that the worst was yet to come, and he had better get psyched up for it. For there were people who took such televangelism seriously, throwing their hard-earned money and credit card numbers after these sermons, such as they were. Furthermore, people around the country were starting to die, and the televangelists and certain other members of the cloth were having a field day rejoicing and pointing fingers, while raking in the "prayer contributions" without batting an eyelash.

Mara paid a surprise visit to Leo and Terrence at the Coalition office late one afternoon a couple of weeks later. The moment she walked through the door, Leo could see she was stressed out. Her makeup, usually the picture of perfection, was a mess. Her mascara was running, her eyes were red and puffy, as she appeared to have been crying.

"What on earth's wrong?" Leo said, standing up and offering his chair.

Once she had settled in, she said, "I've just come from driving George to the airport. He had to catch a flight to San Francisco."

"Judging by the expression on your face, that must have been quite a tearful goodbye," Terrence said. "Tell us what's going on."

Mara tried to keep the emotion out of her voice but was unsuccessful. "George has... he has full-blown AIDS. That cough he'd had for so long, it was just the first stage. He went to the doctor not long after, and they ran some tests. This thing has gotten far along real fast, and the doctor explained to him how opportunistic AIDS really is. He already has Stage 3 lung cancer."

Beyond stunned, Leo felt the same way he had when he'd received the news about Greg and Yaro—he was a bottomless pit of dark emotion clawing for the relief of daylight. It took him a few seconds to gather himself, while Terrence could only shake his head. "Oh, God. So why is he going to San Francisco?"

Mara steadied herself with a deep breath. "As George explained it to me, the doctors out there know a little more than they do anywhere else. When George said that he was from there originally, his doctor told him upfront that there wasn't much they could do for him here. Might as well try what treatment they have out there."

"We would have liked to have said goodbye," Leo added. "Seen him off, just as you did."

"Time is of the essence. And then, George said he was embarrassed to have come down with it in the first place. He said he felt like he had done something wrong."

Leo practically spat out his words. "Oh, hell no! That's what those preachers on the air and Anita Bryant want you to believe. That AIDS is something gay people deserve because they are evil. I wish George had given us a chance to console him at least."

Then Mara broke down completely, the tears streaming down her face. "I don't think any of us could do that for him. He's been carrying the weight of the world on his shoulder for a long time now. He puts on a brave, funny front, but his parents kicked him out of the house when he told them about himself years ago. They're unrelenting about it still. I asked him if he thought he should try and call them and let them know about his condition, but he said it would be useless and that he didn't want to have to deal with a final rejection."

Leo continued to hold onto Mara tightly, and Terrence said, "Then... the prognosis is... hopeless?"

After taking the time to gather herself, Mara said, "It would probably take a miracle."

The three of them sat with her last statement for a while, but the silence only seemed to make things worse. AIDS had finally hit home. It was no longer just a series of words in a magazine or newspaper article. It was a flesh and blood reality with seemingly no upside.

A week or so later, Angelle popped into Leo's office early one morning with a smug look on her face.

"I wanted you to be the second to know that my brother Jay just got the weekend weather gig at WDSU he's had his heart set on. He'll be starting next month, and I'm already tracking down some apartment possibilities for him. There are even a few near me. It'll be nice living in the same city with him again. We sorta looked after each other up in Boston."

Leo felt a faint stirring of hope within and smiled. "You say I'm the second to know. Who was the first?"

"Chase, of course."

"Right. By the way, any change in the status of your relationship?"

"Such as?"

"Marriage on the horizon?"

"We've discussed our long-term goals and that sort of thing," she said. "Pillow talk and all that, but we like things the way they are right now."

"Whatever works. Anyway, congrats to your brother. I know how important he is to you."

Leo noticed that Angelle had started tapping her finger on the edge of his desk as her eyes nervously moved from side-to-side. "Was there something else you wanted to tell me?"

She stilled her finger and caught his gaze. "Yes, it's about me and my brother. We actually don't have a biological connection. Mom and Dad adopted us both, but it's amazing how much alike we are in so many areas. Not that I solve calculus problems to pass the time. I mean, who does that? Or that I'm all that crazy about the weather. I mostly just don't want it to keep me from getting to work on time. No, what I mean is that Jay and I see the world the same way as an endless series of possibilities. We never see the glass as half-empty. I think we both have an optimism gene, if there is such a thing."

Leo laughed. "Mostly, I think you have a 'fits-right-in' gene. It was apparent to me when I interviewed you for this job."

"I'd like to think so."

Leo shook his head dramatically. "I know so. The quotes you wheedle out of people blow me away. You make them feel at ease, and they tell you things they wouldn't tell anyone else. Like that young jazz musician, Littleman Morgan, who said he'd had a dream when he was twelve about becoming the next Louis Armstrong. Then when Chase got that shot of him doing his imitation of Satchmo's trademark smile, that piece went platinum. The work you two did together went through the roof."

"So maybe Chase and I are married to *Sunday*, then," Angelle said, tilting her head with a saucy grin.

"I'll settle for that."

After she'd left, Leo couldn't help but review his boatload of memories about not fitting in at all from the very beginning and how they still dominated his thinking more than they should. Maybe it was time for a massive infusion of something different that put those feelings in their place once and for all.

Chapter 23

Leo appreciated the fact that Jay Wilkinson was starting out so straightforward with him, but the words were still hard to hear.

"I think we would both agree that this AIDS Crisis has made it that much harder to reach out to people," he was saying as the two of them were sitting together on Leo's sofa in the camelback. They were not holding hands. "I don't necessarily agree with the sentiment, but there are those out there who are starting to say that dating is a death sentence. Who knows what's safe anymore? They say it's not airborne, and you have to exchange bodily fluids to get it, but you hear something different every day. The photos they show of people who are sick are frightening."

"But we aren't dating, Jay. We're just meeting for the first time, and from what your sister has told me about you, I was expecting more of an optimistic outlook."

Jay looked surprised, then amused. "Ah, I see. So does cautious optimism count?"

Leo was relieved by the humorous retort. This lean, dark-haired young man with the delicate features and darting eyes was capable of more than one note after all. That might be a beginning.

"My usual procedure when I have people over is to treat them to dinner and a concert, but the order is strictly up to you," Leo said, pointing to his spinet across the way.

"Would it be rude of me to ask what we're having?"

"Not at all. My famous baked spaghetti. But be forewarned—my menu is limited, and I'm no gourmet chef."

"I'm sure you underestimate yourself. Wine me up again and serenade me," Jay said, his mood lifting noticeably.

This time around, Leo had chosen Paul Francis Webster and Sammy Fain's score for their adaptation of the film, *Calamity Jane*, which starred Doris Day. First he sang "Higher Than A Hawk", worked in "The Deadwood Stage" and finished with "My Secret Love".

After a hearty round of applause, Jay said, "You must have had professional training with that beautiful voice."

Leo turned around on the piano bench and beamed. "Just my Granny Marble's music school back in Beau Pre. Actually, my voice just appeared one day while I was listening to Steve Lawrence on the radio. It just needed a little fine-tuning after that."

"Steve Lawrence as in Steve Lawrence and Eydie Gorme?"

"The very same. He was singing 'Go Away Little Girl,' and suddenly it turned into a duet."

"I have that 45 at home. I used to sing along with it, too. Such a teenage infatuation love song."

"Your sister said you had quite the collection." Leo moved quickly to join him on the sofa again as the pace of their exchange accelerated and the enthusiasm in their voices grew more evident.

"All my favorites starting with just before puberty in 1958. My first slow dance was with a girl named Audrey to the Platters' version of 'Smoke Gets In Your Eyes.' I had far more interest in the music than I did the girl. She never knew that, of course. I was always polite."

"That's such familiar territory," Leo said. "Did you do a lot of camouflage dating?"

"Of course. It was a chore. But I didn't do it all that long. I sat down one evening and told Angelle about myself, and she's been supporting me ever since. She wouldn't let me go on with the facade and even helped me come out to our parents. I guess they were upset at first, but they eventually came around. I don't think parents are ever prepared to hear something like that."

201

"Same with mine. I've since found out that some people aren't so lucky. They can get disowned and kicked out of the house, but that didn't happen to either one of us. So we should be thankful for that, plus we're nearly the same age," Leo said, Angelle having already filled him in on such details.

"I like to think of it as the same point of origin. We don't need footnotes to have a conversation."

"Interesting way of putting it." Then Leo didn't see why they couldn't start playing the game. "What are some of your other pop favorites?"

"From high school?"

"Sure, why not?"

"'Any Day Now' by Chuck Jackson. 1962."

"Love it. Let's take turns," Leo said. "I'll go."

"'Hold Me, Thrill Me, Kiss Me' by Mel Carter. 1964."

Jay gasped. "I think I want that played at my funeral. I can even see myself jumping up out of the coffin to sing it."

Leo laughed, and it felt like something tangible was floating up out of his body, off his shoulders and up to the ceiling where he looked up and banished it with his eyes.

"Did you like the Fifth Dimension as much as I did?" he said, his emotions soaring now. "From the first time I heard them, I felt like they really had taken me up in their beautiful balloon."

Jay seemed equally transformed. "Yes, they blew me away, too. But not just with the obvious ones like 'Up, Up And Away.' I kept on listening to album after album and became more partial to 'Workin' On A Groovy Thing,' 'Wedding Bell Blues,' 'Stoned Soul Picnic,' 'The Girl's Song' and numbers like that."

"Ditto."

"Marilyn McCoo was the soul of that group."

They were both hooked now, and Jay said, "How about the Bacharach, David, and Dionne Warwick collaboration? Those were my college years at Boston College."

"Mine, too, but at Sewanee. I had to resist the urge to tell my choirmaster, Mr. Markham, that all the Bacharach, David, and Warwick hits were what we should have been singing at All Saints instead of all those stuffy hymns," Leo added. "I felt like saying, 'There's more than one way of praising the universe. Why not "I Say A Little Prayer For You"?'"

"Perfect. I had a college friend who described Dionne's voice as the 'one that keeps on singing and never stops,'" Jay added. Then he started mouthing the lyrics along with the melody to "You'll Never Get To Heaven If You Break My Heart," and Leo joined him.

They sounded good together as they settled into a rhythm complete with hand gestures, and at the end of the song, Leo said, "I could do this all day and then stay up all night for much more."

"You're just gonna have to come over to my apartment sometime and listen to your heart's content," Jay said. "Music was meant for more than one."

"And I just can't quit this game," Leo said. "What about the Carpenters? 'Rainy Days and Mondays' still does it for me."

"Karen's contralto voice gives me the shivers. The good way, of course."

"And Chicago?"

"'Beginnings,' of course. The long album version. Best brass section ever."

Leo snapped his fingers. "Herb Alpert. 'This Guy's In Love With You.' 1968. Almost forgot that one among my musical treasures."

"Best slow-dance record ever. I was starting up with a guy by then. His name was Barrett, but everybody called him Bingo. We had a secret thing going in the dorm at BC," Jay said. "I must say, no one ever knew because we always locked the doors when we slow-danced together. That's actually all we did. I always thought Herb Alpert was singing just to the two of us."

Leo had to make an effort to push memories of Greg and graduation at Sewanee out of the way by changing subjects quickly. "Well, I think it's time to put my baked spaghetti to the test."

203

"Listen," Jay said, "I can forgive anything except bad taste in music. I'm sure I'll be a big fan."

There came a time after dinner when comparing musical favorites came to an end, but the silence had a poignancy of its own. The two were content to just sit there on the sofa, reflecting on all that they had shared in such a short time. This time they were holding hands and looking into each other's eyes.

Finally, Jay spoke up. "I just wanted to say that I never for one minute thought of this as a fix-up."

"Me neither."

"My sister generally knows her way around most everything," Jay continued. "She's a woman of many talents."

Leo nodded enthusiastically. "She's the best hire I ever made. Not only that, she's helped Chase become the best photographer he could possibly be. In this case, there is a great woman behind the man."

"I like Chase," Jay said. "I think he'd make a fine brother-in-law. He's cool with everything he needs to be cool with. He's been around."

Leo couldn't help himself. "Are you saying that marriage is in the works? I can't seem to get anything out of your sister."

"Maybe. She'll probably wake up one morning and decide that that's what she wants, and Chase doesn't know it yet, but he'll have to go along with it. On some level, he probably already knows that." Jay paused and conjured up his best smile. "So, about my record collection. Would you like to come over and listen to it sometime? Maybe next week even?"

"I think that can be arranged." Then Leo laughed. There was something strange and surprising about it, and he elaborated. "You can also explain to me your fascination with calculus, or so your sister says. I got a D at Sewanee. Absolutely hated the class. To this day, I have no idea what that little squiggly thing is, but since I'm told you solve calculus problems for entertainment purposes, maybe you can help me finally understand it. Those equations are hardly what I'd call relaxing."

Jay suddenly assumed a professorial demeanor. "All I can say is that the two of them make sense to me in the same way. Music and math, I mean. They're part of the same universal language. I find nothing inconsistent about the fact that I crave certain types of music and certain types of math. They make me feel complete, like I belong in the universe."

"My grandmother got a double-major in music and math at Randolph-Macon," Leo said, searching for common ground. "I seem to have inherited the music part, but not the math."

"Ah, well," Jay added, "we're all different. I've never embraced the virtue of sameness. I think it's rather lazy."

There was another brief period of silence, after which Leo leaned in and said, "Do you think we might kiss each other gently on the cheek? I'm a little skittish because of all the uncertainty out there about AIDS and how you can get it. I guess I've become paranoid to some extent."

Jay did not answer. Instead, the two men drew closer, ever closer, until they had met the challenge in as soft and tender a manner as possible. Then they pulled back slowly and smiled. A first step. A baby step.

More exploratory questions followed after several more exploratory kisses, while they maintained constant contact with an arm here and a leg there. Eventually, they looked more like a pretzel than two men getting to know each other better on a sofa.

"When did *you* know for sure?" Leo said, locking onto Jay's eyes. "I've already told you about my so-called affair with Charles Atlas."

Jay didn't answer right away, almost looking like a little boy trying to solve a riddle. "Not as young as you were, but maybe around ten or eleven."

Leo smiled, nodding enthusiastically. "Did anything or anyone trigger it?"

"James Dean."

"Wow!"

Jay's expression now conveyed a hint of mischief. "Angelle and I had gone to the movies to see *Rebel Without A Cause,* and afterward, we compared notes. Turned out, we both said we had a crush on James Dean."

"I guess you know the skinny on him is that he was supposedly gay."

"So I've read. Do you think there's actually something operational out there like *gaydar* that helps us identify one another?"

"Maybe. I think more often we rely upon ordinary introductions; however we can get them. Like this one your sister arranged for us."

Jay's face was serene as he exhaled gently. "Yep. As I said, she always knows what she's doing, believe me. Anyhoo, that was the beginning of my sister becoming my biggest advocate, especially when the two of us told my parents when we got into our teens. Any time they had some prickly point to make—and the worst was, 'What did we do wrong?'—she had a soothing answer ready. She was like aloe vera for the wounds they were carrying around and got us all over the hump. I'll forever be indebted to her for that."

One month later, Leo and Jay, Mara, Terrence, Pauly and the rest of the Coalition were packed into the Metropolitan Community Church, numbed by George Kinsey's death but paying tribute to him the only way they could now. His friends had buried him out there, and now there was nothing left for his New Orleans friends than the many testimonials to how one George Thomas Kinsey had touched people's lives. Coalition members were far from the only ones who showed up for the memorial service. There were many of his long-time clients, other hairdressers, and everyday friends he had made through daily life in a diverse and welcoming city.

Among those, the most touching were the comments of Mrs. Agnes Underwood, a petite woman pushing seventy, who stood before the group and touted his skills in making her comfortable throughout the most difficult period of her life.

"I had started to undergo chemo for breast cancer a while back and had lost all my hair, including my eyebrows," she began. "Then, George transformed me." She pointed to her head. "Yes, this mass of blonde curls is a wig, but George made me feel that it had put down roots and started a family. To be honest with you, I had never looked better, even though I'd never felt worse." She paused and traced her brows with her index fingers. "Then, he told me that no one could draw on eyebrows like he could. So he taught me how to do it right. 'Too many people end up looking like clowns or Snow White's Wicked Stepmother, Miz Underwood,' he would say to me. 'Too much Mirror-Mirror-On-The-Wall going on out there. Subtlety is the key. Less is more.' Although I have to say that there was nothing subtle about George. He always got to the point quickly with a zinger that you'd never forget. I'd always walk out of Long May She Wave feeling like I'd just received an extra Social Security check, or at least had gotten a kick-up-your-heels, free floor show."

"That was our George," Mara said, as the polite applause started up. "His very own Ed Sullivan act."

Later, Mara took Leo aside during the reception which followed and said, "I'm happy that George didn't die alone out there and that we can do this little bit for him here. I know he'd want us to have some sorta closure."

Leo gave Mara a heart-felt hug and said, "Thank you for helping him to belong. He had a lot to give."

"Yes, he did. People would come into the salon on their first visit, get hooked and ask for him all the time."

Leo began to form a word with his lips but then backed down, making a grim slash instead.

"Were you going to say something?" Mara said.

"I was... it was just that George never talked about having anyone in his life. Was there ever anyone?"

Mara sighed plaintively. "George and I were a lot alike. We

207

both got badly burned early on in relationships. I know I've been skittish ever since. The woman I was involved with left me not for another woman, but for a man. That was really hard to take. George didn't give me many details about his man that got away, the one Judy Garland sang about so eloquently, but I don't think he ever recovered from it. Yet, somehow he came down with AIDS. Go figure. Maybe we're better off not knowing how that happened."

Leo's expression was distant, as if he were not even in the room. "I think that's true of a lot of things."

When Leo and Jay returned to the camelback to console each other further, they both remained largely silent, trying to make sense of things as they sat on the sofa.

Finally, Leo came to life. "I'm gonna write a letter to Lake about all this. He always gave me such good advice. It's been a while since I've heard from him anyway."

After Leo had finished the letter at his desk, he returned to Jay and said, "We just can't be ruled by fear this way, sweetheart. We aren't promiscuous. We're practically celibate by some accounts, but this is no way to live. We're too cautious."

"I know," Jay told him. "It's just that George was a grim reminder of what could happen if you're not careful."

"But we are."

Then they gently kissed each other on the lips. There was in the gesture a measure of both affection and defiance, and there was an innocence to it that nothing could spoil.

Leo had begun to worry when Lake didn't reply to his letter right away. His former teacher was usually so prompt. He did not want to entertain his darkest thoughts, and a long-distance phone call might expose him to an immediate shock from which it would be difficult to recover. Instead, he plunged himself into his work at the magazine with Chase and Angelle and tried to stay on an even keel emotionally with Jay.

Meanwhile, there was no breakthrough to report on the AIDS

epidemic front, except that Terrence confirmed that more cases had appeared throughout the New Orleans area over the last few months. Bars and discos were taking a big hit as regulars made it clear to owners here and there that they didn't want to take chances. Some people began to feel stalked by an invisible enemy.

It was with great relief, therefore, when Leo came home from work one evening to find a letter with Lake's return address waiting for him in the mailbox. He trudged up the stairs with it, caught between the twin urges of wanting to tear it open immediately and hold it at arm's length indefinitely. But finally, he summoned his courage and began reading:

My Dear Leo,

Forgive my tardiness in replying to your long, thoughtful letter. Ignacio's mother has been extremely ill with pneumonia, and we have been intensely involved with seeing that she gets the utmost care while visiting her in the hospital. The prognosis looks good, however, and Ignacio is greatly relieved. Mama Delgado is one of a kind, and we don't want to lose her.

Here in Mexico, the incidence of AIDS is lower than in the US, but it has arrived nonetheless in certain populations. Needless to say, Ignacio and I are not at risk because we have always been faithful to each other, which I'm sure is the case with you and Jay. However, I have a delightful suggestion for the two of you, courtesy of Ignacio. You make an event of it, a big splash, as you will see. It is guaranteed to take your mind off AIDS and HIV and all the rest of it while keeping you perfectly safe. There are actually two versions of it that you and Jay can try. The first is la ducha segura *and the second is* la espuma de jabon segura.

The first is translated as the safe shower. *The second is:* the safe soap suds *or a roundabout way of saying bubble bath.*

Let me explain further. In the first, the two of you take a shower together, just in case you haven't already done so.

I can't imagine that you haven't. If not, though, what are you waiting for? Warm water falling down upon your heads and warm flesh against warm flesh. The constant friction, of course, does the trick, and you are perfectly safe. In the second, you can immerse yourselves in a bubble bath or indulge a good soaping up underwater, and all is well. You are fresh and clean, and you have been intimate without taking any risk. I highly recommend either of these measures, and I believe you and Jay will start to feel better about your lot in life. By all means, do not get down in the dumps, and don't let fear of AIDS keep you up at night. Above all, don't abandon each other because of all the grim news. True, it's yet another challenge that you and I have to face, but we are survivors.

Now, tell me honestly: who can take issue with a good, old-fashioned bubble bath? Hasn't it been a symbol of wholesome sex since forever?

Love always, Lake (y Ignacio)

Indeed, who could take issue? Soapsuds in the sink. Louisa Marble bathing her little Buddha there. The warmth, the wetness. One of his earliest memories returning to the fold of awareness.

Leo let Jay read the letter the following evening, and when he finished, he started laughing. "Are we the dullest gay couple ever? I think maybe we are. Why didn't we think of this? It sounds great. So relaxing."

"Doesn't it?"

Jay pointed quickly to the bathroom. "Do you have any bubble bath crystals in there?"

"Bought some at K & B's on the way home from work today. I had the distinct feeling it might come in handy."

"Then let's get to it. Let's take an honest-to-goodness bubble bath in honor of Lake, Ignacio, ourselves and the dear, departed George, shall we?"

They lost no time in disrobing, after which Leo poured the

crystals into the warm water rushing out of the spout and wedged the stopper into the drain. Soon, the bathtub had a head on it like an enormous vat of beer, and the two of them had settled in carefully at either end, tickling each other's feet for good measure.

Sounding like two little boys immersed in their own little world of horseplay, they began to engage in the submarine activity Lake had described, and their laughter eventually turned into great sighs of relief. The aftermath of soaking in silence seemed heaven-sent.

"That does it. I've made a momentous decision. We ought to move in together," Leo said out of nowhere.

Jay pushed aside a frothy cluster of bubbles and said, "Really? In my place or yours?"

"Mine. The spinet's too much trouble. It took Werlein's forever to get it up the stairs years ago. I was a nervous wreck the whole time. I don't even want to contemplate the trip down for my precious baby."

"Are you sure we're ready for this?"

"We've been *too* cautious. I told you Lake would give me some great advice. I say you move in with me, and we start really living."

Jay sat up a bit, his head now completely out of the water. "What about your landlords and your lease? You'd have to add me on, wouldn't you? And, to be blunt about it, who would I be? Just your roommate or more?"

The question nearly destroyed Leo's afterglow. "I hadn't thought of that. Damn!"

"What kind of people are they?"

"Quiet, retired, sweet-natured. The wife, Susie, treats me almost like I'm her son."

"Is she ready for a gay son?"

Leo looked annoyed. "I wish we didn't have to take these things into consideration. I pride myself on being out and proud and all that, but does Susie Landry have to know everything?"

"Then just tell her I'm your roommate. Or better yet, your

cousin or brother or some other kind of relative. That usually goes over well. Nothing controversial about that."

"I guess that's the best way to go," Leo said, sighing. "I like living here, and the Landrys really are great landlords. When things need fixing, they get fixed right away. And I've treated them to many a recital at the spinet, which they love. I guess I should keep things the way they are and not regard this as an opportunity to make a political statement."

"Everything doesn't have to be. The upside is that you and I can go to bed together every night, and with your spinet and my records, we can have a sing-along around the clock."

"And if you get tired of that at any time, you can trot out your calculus textbook and solve more of those squiggly problems of yours."

"Infinity," Jay said authoritatively. "I told you that squiggly thing represents infinity. The mathematical term is lemniscate. If you'd like for me to explain further…"

"Spare me, sweetheart. I'll never get to where you're going in a million years. Trust me."

Leo and Jay decided on cousin status for the lease, rather than brother, because of the drastic difference in hair color, and fortunately, the Landrys gave Leo no trouble in adding on another person. In fact, Susie Landy was effusive in her praise when she was introduced.

"Imagine. Susie and Gabe Landry having the weekend weatherman living right above us," she said, clasping her hands together. "You look just like you look on TV, only much taller. We swear by what you say. We call you our Umbrella Man, don't we, Gabe?"

He nodded dutifully with a smile and said, "Yes we do, honey. We never leave the house without your forecasts."

"Jay also sings," Leo added. "He'll add a lot to my recitals."

And thus, while the Landrys suspected nothing, Leo Marble and Jay Wilkinson officially became a cohabiting couple.

Chapter 24

Leo thought his father would never shut up about including Granny Marble in his upcoming May visit to Beau Pre to introduce Jay to the family as the love of his life. He could hardly get a word in edgewise during the contentious phone call.

"Yes, she's your grandmother, but she's also my mother, son," Joseph was saying. "I've known her longer than you have. Why go out of our way to upset her at her age? She'll be 90 in six months. All these years, she's had this particular pristine impression of you. Maybe it's best we don't disturb it. At least we've agreed that your uncle Brady doesn't need to be brought in on this just yet."

"Yes, I gave in to you on that one. But I'll soon be 36, Daddy. Jay is going to be a part of the rest of my life, and I'm proud of us. I want to share the love we have for each other with everyone closest to me. I don't think that's too much to ask for. You sound like you're still looking at it as something to cover up and hide, and we don't see it that way. So, for the record, is Granny Marble in good health? She wouldn't just keel over from weakness if I told her the truth, would she? She's never been a 'case-of-the-vapors' type, you know."

"Of course she's well. I don't think she's ever been sick a day in her life. She'll live to be 120 and receive some sort of proclamation from the White House which she'll put in a gold frame."

"I think you underestimate her all-around, Daddy," Leo said, chuckling. "Strong of body, strong of mind."

But Joseph would not quit. "Yes, that's true. But there's this

213

AIDS thing going around, too. Don't you think your grand-mother will worry herself to death about that? I have to be honest with you and say that your mother and I worry about it quite a bit ourselves, despite your reassuring letters to the contrary. They're painting such a drastic picture on the news, I sometimes have to turn it off to get some peace of mind. Your mother feels the same way."

Leo continued, determined not to give up. "I grant you that AIDS is not a walk in the park for anyone. But Jay and I take precautions, and we are monogamous, the same way you and Mama are. I have every reason to believe that we will continue to be safe, and you have to trust us on this. My being gay is not something abstract that you can just brush off semantically. It's who I am and will always be. Now, I'm in love at last, and I never thought I would get there with all the missteps and mismatches I've had in my life. I was always on the outside looking in."

Joseph was silent for a while. When he finally spoke, he sounded less anxious. "You do have a way with words, son. But then, that's how you're making your living down there. We're awfully proud of you for that. We look forward so much to read-ing your magazine."

"Then just stretch that a little to include the person I love and want to spend the rest of my life with. You're gonna love Jay, and he's gonna love you, no two ways around it."

"I have no doubts that we will, but I still have reservations about telling your grandmother. I guess we can't stop you from telling her about Jay and that aspect of your life, but I'd like for you to think it over carefully. You don't have to tell her everything."

"I have a plan in mind, Daddy," Leo said, sounding myste-rious. "Jay and I will play our parts, and I think we'll be a hit."

"You and your theatrical flair. It's been there inside of you from the very beginning. Why you aren't an actor, I'm sure I don't know."

"I have been at times, and I'm still a singer, and I can't very well let go of any of it now. By the way, how was your latest checkup?"

Joseph's joy oozed through the phone line. "All clear again. Still cancer-free, and the smoking patches are working fine for me, too. I guess some people do get second chances in life."

"Some get more than that," Leo said. "I'm always keeping an eye out for the signs."

As the result of last-minute negotiations, Joseph and Louisa had agreed to meet Leo and Jay at Granny Marble's school, which she had finally closed down six months ago after twenty-five, successful years of teaching the people of Beau Pre piano, voice, organ and violin. She had sold off all her pianos except for one of the grands that remained in the spacious recital room; and it was on that last one that Leo planned to play and sing a selection of his favorite R&H numbers, after introducing Jay to his three family members as his new roommate down in New Orleans. Everyone had dressed for the occasion, and Granny Marble had once again chosen her favorite lavender outfit.

All the formalities went off with polite efficiency, Joseph offering a vigorous handshake, and Louisa and Granny Marble their genuine hugs.

"I see you changed your mind," Joseph whispered to his son, taking him aside at one point. "I think it's best."

Leo managed a smile and headed toward the piano where he took his seat. Then he turned to his audience of four and said, "Granny, I remember so well how you had us introduce our pieces at our recitals, so I'm going to do just that right now in tried and true fashion."

"Excellent."

He took a deep breath. "I shall now play and sing 'If I Loved You' from *Carousel*; 'You Are Beautiful' from *Flower Drum Song* and 'This Nearly Was Mine' from *South Pacific*. This is my way of thanking you, Granny, for introducing me to the world of music at the tender age of five. Ever since, it has sustained me through thick and thin. I will be forever grateful for that."

"Thank you, dear grandson. It was my pleasure," she said, bowing her head graciously.

As Leo began his performance, he was careful to maintain eye contact with his audience, landing more often than not on Jay's adoring face. He missed not a note in any of the three pieces and thought he had never sounded so relaxed, his voice so nuanced.

After the applause and cries of, "Bravo!" and "Beautiful!" had faded away, Leo got up, moved to Jay's side and said, "This book Jay brought in with him that he's holding now is a calculus textbook. He's almost never without it. He's so enamored of math, particularly higher math, that he solves equations in his spare time to relax."

He turned to face Granny Marble. "When Jay found out you had taken a double major in math and music at Randolph-Macon and then had used it to start up your own music school from scratch, he was most impressed. He also figured that your math training made you a very good businesswoman. About that, he was not mistaken."

That brought out Granny Marble's best smile, and she said, "Not everyone appreciates math the way I do—the way we do. What an interesting young man you are, Jay. I've always said, the higher the math, the higher the intellect."

He thanked her, and then Leo said, "The thing is, Granny, I only inherited half of your genetic components. The music part, obviously. But I'm missing your math gene. I've always struggled with it and even got a D in calculus at Sewanee. It was part of my two-semester math requirement to get my degree, even though I was majoring in Music. I just kept asking myself every time I went into that classroom, 'When on God's green earth am I going to use this? I'm not going to work for NASA.' I guess I'm just not as complete as you are."

"You're making way too much of this," she said, blushing. "I've always been a believer in celebrating differences."

"Exactly. But I wanted to take this opportunity to let you and my wonderful parents know that I'm no longer incomplete. Jay is my missing better half when it comes to math. With that infinity symbol of his, he goes where I dare not go. He solves where I dare not solve. Meanwhile, I run a few arpeggios on the piano and warble my way to happiness."

"How clever," Granny Marble said with warmth in her voice.

"Yes, it is," Louisa added, exchanging furtive glances with her husband, who looked slightly apprehensive.

"But even if Jay were lousy in math, he would still be my better half," Leo said, putting his arm around Jay's shoulder. "Family, please welcome into your hearts, the love of my life. My very special someone."

The moment had arrived. There were a few seconds of silence, but not long enough to generate any tension.

"Welcome to the family all over again, Jay," Louisa said, hugging him even more genuinely than she had before.

Joseph patted him on the shoulder and said, "Same here, young man. We couldn't be happier."

Then it was Granny Marble's turn, and she did not take long to express herself eloquently. "Your young man is charming, Leo. As for you, I've suspected this about you all these years but haven't let on, of course. Apart from that Rebecca Bentley back in high school, you never mentioned a girlfriend once you got out in the working world. Never once. No two people are alike, but I did have a point of comparison. Your father was the exact opposite. A girl in every port, as they say. Until he found our wonderful Louisa, of course, and then the sailor was home from the sea for good."

She nodded toward her daughter-in-law, who was beaming, and then continued. "Being a math major, I can put two and two together with the best of them. Which brings me to this: Leo, I've loved you since I laid eyes on you with all that red fuzz on your head, and you have done nothing but continue to sing your way into my heart ever since. That red fuzz runs in my family. You were one of mine. Still are, of course. Believe it or not, I can understand what it's like to be different, appearances to the

217

contrary. When I was a freshman at Randolph-Macon, I would get funny looks from all the boys in all my math classes. Their attitudes didn't change much all the way up to my senior year. It seemed the higher the math, the higher their resentment or suspicion, I don't know which. They wouldn't even date me, not that I would have had anything to do with most of them. Quite the conceited lot. Most of them are at that age. Women weren't supposed to be interested in subjects like that. We weren't even supposed to go to college back then, but your great-grandfather saved up all those years that he worked as a train conductor and put me through school. I made the most of it, and I'm thankful I had the good sense to realize the gift I'd been given. So now, it turns out that I have a grandson who doesn't fit the pattern, if there is one size that fits all anyway. That's nonsense, of course. I didn't exactly fit, either, and I've managed quite well in life. I have a strong feeling that you and Jay will manage quite well, too."

"I love you, Granny," Leo said, hugging her tightly. "I think we will, too. We plan to give it our best."

"Thanks for your good wishes, Mrs. Marble," Jay added. "That means a lot to us."

"Moms, you never told me and Brady all that about how you were treated in college," Joseph said. "You always painted such a rosy picture for us as a happy pioneer and trailblazer. You said you waltzed through it all. Never had a care in the world back then, and now we get this testimonial."

"My dear son, there are lots of things mothers don't tell their children for their own good," she said, with a wink. "But what I want to tell everyone right now is that I insist on taking all of you out to dinner. My treat. This news calls for a celebration. We would do no less if Leo were bringing the girl of his dreams home to meet us for the first time."

"Moms, that sounds delightful," Joseph said. "We appreciate it, of course, but that'll amount to quite a tab."

"Joseph," she said, her eyes trained on him like laser beams, "I just sold five pianos, including one of my baby grands. Plus, my savings account is quite healthy after all those years of teaching. I think I can afford to take my family out on the town now and then when the occasion arises."

"And we accept your offer graciously," he added, looking a bit sheepish. "Your treat, it is."

"Thank you. Everyone, order anything you want on the menu, and save plenty of room for dessert."

Chapter 25

The nonstop flight from Moisant in New Orleans to Boston had been mostly smooth with only a bit of turbulence encountered over Washington, D.C. Then, the rental car Leo had reserved for their trip to Biddeford Pool to meet Jay's parents was ready for them as promised. Now the two were speeding up the coast of New Hampshire toward Southern Maine and their final destination of Wilkinson Summer House. Toll stations popped up here and there which slowed things down a bit, particularly after they got onto the Maine Turnpike, but otherwise the trip remained uneventful. They were just a few miles from the Saco exit when Leo decided that a rehearsal of sorts was in order.

Keeping his eyes on the road, he said, "Okay, let me run it all by you again, and you buzz in if I get anything wrong. You call your father Dad, and he's a surgeon at Massachusetts General. His real name is Joshua James Wilkinson, and his friends call him Josh. You call your mother Mum, she dabbles in interior decorating, and her maiden name was Elizabeth Bostwick. She prefers to be called Beth by her friends. So far, so good?"

Jay suppressed a little giggle. "Perfect. I think you're ready for Alex Trebec and *Jeopardy*."

"I just want to make a good impression, that's all."

"You will. Just be you. That'll be enough."

Leo drove a couple of miles further and said, "Oh, and if politics should come up, your parents are rock-ribbed, Rockefeller Republicans who don't particularly trust Ronald Reagan and his background, but they also didn't care for the way Jimmy Carter handled the Iran hostage crisis. Except that I'm not supposed to bring any of that up, if possible. No need to go there if we don't absolutely need to."

"Right."

"And if AIDS comes up, we tell them what we know and that we are a monogamous couple."

"Just remember that my father is a doctor, so he's likely to be up on the latest. Something tells me that he's not going to go there, though. I'm sure he trusts me to be doing all the safe, careful things. There's something to be said about being a doctor's son."

Once Leo had exited the Turnpike, however, Jay turned into a tour guide deluxe, oozing with tidbits that spoke to his obvious fondness for every square inch of scenery they covered from tidal pool to sand dune.

"This stretch we're approaching now is Fortunes Rocks Beach, and as you can see, a lot of these houses aren't that fancy. Just a few rooms to get away from it all during the summer, and, of course, the beach is the main attraction. Lots of people from Boston have places up here."

Leo just smiled and took it all in as they drove along slowly. Seeing how Jay was transformed by every feature of the landscape was more than enough of a reward for him.

"Just up ahead where St. Martin's Lane opens up a bit is St. Martin's In the Field Episcopal Chapel, where we all went to church on our visits," Jay continued. "It's very small and plain, as you can see, but I remember many a service there over the years. Angelle and I weren't always on our best behavior because we couldn't sit still. We wanted to be outside on the water in the kayak or out on the deck playing card games like Go Fish or Crazy Eights. What can I say? We thought summer was for vacation, not for school or church."

Finally, their long journey by air and land came to an end. Leo parked the car in a gravel lot between a large barn and Wilkinson

Summer House, a modest, two-story affair whose outstanding feature was the large deck Jay had described overlooking the glistening blue waters of Wood Island Bay.

"Honk the horn and let them know we're here," Jay said.

In no time, Josh and Beth Wilkinson emerged, and Leo was meeting them at last. The good doctor was just as Jay had described him—tall, with a well-trimmed mustache, a booming voice, and still very much in shape due to his fondness for tennis and sailing at the nearby Abenakee Club. Jay's Mum, Beth, was the very epitome of conservative taste in clothes, wearing a colorful red sweater and pleated blue skirt with a close-cropped brunette hairstyle that framed her youthful face. They both could have stepped out of a catalog for sportswear and were most welcoming to Leo as the introductions were made.

"Get your luggage and let's all head inside to get you both settled," Josh said after the handshakes and hugs. "We want you to get good and relaxed. As a physician for all these many years, I can tell you that Biddeford Pool is good for what ails you."

"I can't believe how cool it is here," Leo said, as he took his suitcase out of the trunk. "When we left New Orleans, it was ninety-two degrees with humidity you wouldn't believe. Five minutes after you take a shower this time of year down there, you're sweating up a storm once you go outside."

"I told Leo to brace himself," Jay said, handling his own luggage. "We can even have fog up here some days. I told him to pack a couple of his best sweaters, but he doesn't have any. Meanwhile, it's been quite an adjustment for me getting used to the subtropical climate of New Orleans. I can predict the weather just fine down there, but I sure can't control it."

"Maine in June requires no air-conditioning," Mum said as they all walked toward the house. "Nature does that for us, and at night, we generally sleep under blankets."

After Leo and Jay had gotten reasonably settled in the very upstairs bedroom Jay had called his own as a boy, Mum served everyone a lunch of lobster rolls and green salad out on the deck.

Then she offered to give Leo the grand tour, not of the house, but of the outdoors, which was the main attraction of living in Biddeford Pool.

"As you can see, we don't have much of a beach," she began, standing with Leo and Jay at the edge of the manicured lawn which gave way to wooden steps and a railing leading down steeply to huge, misshapen rocks. "But we do have the best view in Biddeford Pool." She pointed straight ahead. "That little strip of green out there with the lighthouse at the southern tip is Wood Island. To the north is Saco Bay, and on the other side of the island is the Atlantic Ocean. At night, you'll hear the buoys clanging. They won't keep you up, though. Believe me, they'll put you right to sleep."

"I guarantee you the best night's sleep you've ever had," Jay added.

"When we bought this piece of property back in the 1950s, I thought this was the most majestic view in the entire world." She turned to focus briefly on her son. "I've never told you this before, but I wanted to call it Majestic Cove. But it already had a name—Philip Rock—so I deferred to history."

"I don't like Philip Rock nearly as much," Jay said. "It's not nearly as descriptive."

"Well, since you and Angelle will inherit the property after we're gone, you can change it to whatever you want and have note cards printed up to prove it. I doubt there's such a thing as the geography police, but I know for certain you can't be brought up on charges for your stationery."

"I don't like to think of you as gone, though. I'm nowhere near ready for that yet."

"Fact of life, son."

Although Jay looked decidedly uncomfortable at the turn the conversation had taken, Leo was smiling at the discussion of a name change. It was music to his ears, but he decided to keep it to himself. Some things did not translate well or defied explanation. But it all made sense to him. Here he was on the coast of Maine

223

in June, his love for Jay busting out all over. It made him want to sing loudly, embracing the tide coming in which was clashing with the rocks, the salt air beguiling his nostrils. He recalled what Margaret Markham had said back at Sewanee about all the chorus girls being taken with John Raitt during the original run of *Carousel* at the Majestic Theatre. He remembered how his mother had sped up his healing from a bad case of the flu by introducing him to the cast album of *Carousel* when he was only ten. He had listened to the voices of Gordon MacRae and Shirley Jones over and over, falling in love with every note. Eight years later, he had felt ten feet tall singing R&H's epic, "Soliloquy", believing during those seven minutes under the glare of a follow spot that his diaphragm could conquer the world, could overcome any adversity he might encounter, starting with being the closeted heartthrob of the school. It was energy that would actually serve him well once the real world began pressing in on him, pulling no punches.

Alas, there was no piano in Wilkinson Summer House to entertain Jay's parents as he so sincerely wanted to do; but their warmth and acceptance was more than enough when it came to interaction. He envisioned that there would be other opportunities to play and sing for the Wilkinson family, and he would take it from there.

After a dinner of clam chowder, fresh vegetables and homemade blueberry pie, everyone moved to the living room just off the deck to watch the sun go down through the wide windows. Although Leo had grown up with breathtaking sunsets on the Mississippi River at Beau Pre, the one he was experiencing now at Biddeford Pool gave him a sense of completion that he could not easily explain. The orange and crimson streaks across the sky behind the Wood Island Lighthouse were like strokes of a fragile painting that would not last long. It would soon disappear in trembling fashion, but it would leave behind in Leo's core a sense of finally belonging rather than always being on the outside looking in.

After the horizon had vacuumed up the last of the setting sun, Mum said, "You boys must be tired after your long trip. Dad and I will turn in, too, if you'll excuse us."

And though manners were made quickly, Leo and Jay weren't quite ready to jump into bed and wait for the buoys to start up with their clanging lullabies.

"Get it out of the suitcase," Jay said. "Come on, give. I saw you pack it."

With great fanfare, Leo produced the bubble bath crystals which were then poured into the clawfoot tub in their black-and-white tiled bathroom. They intended to wash away their travel weariness with the boyish horseplay they had perfected at Lake's suggestion, and it did not fail to achieve its relaxing aim once again.

Then they piled into bed, snuggling together under the blankets after kissing each other goodnight and waiting for the sounds of the salt water lapping at the shore outside and the buoys to bless them with a well-earned rest.

They slept in the next morning, and Mum did not disturb them, instead waiting for them to arise and fixing them a late breakfast of oatmeal with fresh blueberries and buttered toast with blueberry jam. That second full day was spent paddling the kayak to Wood Island and back, and then driving up to Portland for a tour of the busy waterfront and a gourmet dinner at Fore Street and its open, wood-fire grill.

At the end of the third half-day, Leo stood with Jay out on the deck, his arm around his sweetheart's shoulder and said, "Someday, if it ever becomes legal, I want us to get married here. I think everything in my life has been leading up to that."

Jay kissed him on the cheek and said, "Mine, too. We must do everything in our power to make it happen."

When it came time to leave and head back down to Boston for the flight home, Dr. Josh Wilkinson sounded just the right note. "Jay, your Mum and I are so happy you've found such an outstanding young man to spend your life with; and Leo, I hope we've made you feel welcome in our family. From Angelle's letters, it appears she's found that special someone, too, in your magazine photographer, Chase Knowles. That kind of happiness is all we've ever wanted for our children. Have a safe trip back and continue to use safe judgment in this crazy world of ours."

That, Leo noted, was the only reference, veiled as it was, to the AIDS crisis that the good doctor had made during the visit, and it came off in well-intentioned and appropriate fashion. The warm hugs and kisses on the cheek that Mum gave to both her son and Leo tied a neat little bow on everything.

Back on the Turnpike, Leo turned to Jay and said, "I wonder if things'll change enough for us to get legally married some-day. It seems a million years away to me with all the pushback from AIDS that's happening. Maybe it'll never be in the cards for people like us."

Jay managed to minimize the doubt in his voice. "I don't know. What I do know is we can love each other the best we can. That *is* under our control, if nothing else is."

On the flight home, Leo thought about that last statement several times, his head resting on Jay's shoulder. Maybe getting married was a pipe dream. Maybe it would never happen. But one thing was perfectly clear: it was time to settle down earnestly to life with Jay.

Chapter 26

By the end of another couple of years, Jay had begun to develop a flock of "groupies" as a result of his job as weekend weatherman. That was what Leo and Jay decided to call them because their letters to him with requests for signed pictures of him were mostly from females of varying ages, including a few who could be rightly termed elderly.

"This dear little lady named Maybeth Aucoin says she's proud to be eighty-eight and claims she cannot go to bed over the weekends unless she tunes in my forecasts," Jay was saying, handing over the woman's letter as the two of them sat at their small kitchen table wading through the latest bundle the station had collected for him. "She even included her own glamor shot, if you will."

Leo could not suppress a chuckle as he zeroed in on the wizened, smiling face before him. "She reminds me of Granny Marble a little bit. It's probably the gray hair and the attitude. I like the way she's got her head cocked. She knows some things."

To keep his fans satisfied, it was Jay's practice to answer the requests with signed, black-and-white glossies of himself at his own expense, but it was a time-consuming task once a week, usually undertaken after the fortification of a meal of baked spaghetti. Leo had volunteered to streamline the process by learning how to imitate Jay's signature perfectly. Over and over, he wrote his share of the magic words in cursive: BEST WISHES, JAY WILKINSON; and no one was the wiser.

The two of them had nearly completed their weekly task when Jay began reading out loud a neatly-typed letter which had 'professional businessman' written all over it:

Dear Mr. Wilkinson:

On my frequent visits to New Orleans, your performance as weekend weatherman on WDSU has impressed me very much. I'm Byron O'Malley, and I own a media company looking into starting up a new cable outlet which will compete with the highly-successful Weather Channel. I scout any number of markets in my work, and I would like to discuss a possible place for you in our forthcoming lineup which I would like to start up soon. I will be in New Orleans this coming Monday, the 21st, staying at the Royal Sonesta in the Quarter. Would you be available for a dinner meeting around eight that evening? My plans are flexible if this is not convenient for you...

After Jay had finished the rest of the letter, Leo could only manage the one word, "Wow!"

Jay had a look of disbelief on his face. Finally, he said, "What do you think?"

"About what? The dinner meeting?"

"No. The idea of my working for a cable channel. What if it required us to move away from New Orleans? What if you had to give up your job?"

Leo leaned back in his chair and briefly glanced up at the ceiling. "You're getting a bit ahead of yourself, aren't you? Maybe you wouldn't have to leave. Don't they have reporters that move around depending upon the weather? Maybe you'd just work on the hurricanes and the thunderstorms and the floods instead of just being in a studio somewhere."

Jay mulled it over for a decent length of time. "Suppose I had to be gone a lot. I don't think either one of us would like that too much. We've gotten into a routine. We've gotten used to each other. And then there are your little concerts at the piano. I like them very much."

"I do too, sweetheart. Why would you think they would come to an end?" Leo leaned in and gave his partner a sideways glance. "You know, this isn't like you. I've never seen you back down from anything. You got the job down here because you went after it full-bore. All these objections you're bringing up are before the fact." Leo reached out and gently put his hand atop Jay's. "Listen, kid, you have my support. At least check this thing out. If it doesn't seem right for you, just say thanks but no thanks."

Jay gave him a wink. "I think maybe that's what I was waiting for. Your approval. I'd never do anything without taking you into consideration. You're right. There's no harm in checking it out."

"Attaboy."

As Jay sipped on his glass of Chardonnay while sitting across from Byron O'Malley in his elaborate Royal Sonesta suite with the chandeliers and fussy window treatments, he thought that this tall man certainly fit the description of a media mogul. His clothes were expensive-looking, if a bit over the top. Burgundy suede was not a blue collar, working man's outfit, to be sure, making Jay's perfectly respectable three-piece suit seem completely drab. Nor were the several, ostentatious rings on both hands of the man's fingers business as usual. O'Malley, himself, wore a rather imperious air to accompany his overpowering cologne, and his full face and roving eyes completed the picture.

"I took the liberty of ordering for us," O'Malley was saying. "I hope you don't mind. I thought room service here in my suite would give us a bit more privacy for our discussions. I trust you like trout amandine. I absolutely adore it and get it every time I visit New Orleans."

Jay put his glass down on the table and said, "I was brought up in Boston, and my family has a summer house in Maine, so seafood came with the territory. I'll admit it was New England seafood, and lobster rolls are still my favorites. But since moving down here to New Orleans for my job, I would never turn down all these great Louisiana dishes. And that includes crawfish in all its forms—boiled with corn and potatoes, as a salad or as etouffee."

"Ah," O'Malley said. "Just as I thought."

Shortly after, the waiter rolled in their dinner, laid it out, and the two men started to dig in. Jay was a bit surprised that no business was actually discussed throughout the meal. Instead, it was small talk, consisting mostly of O'Malley's anecdotes concerning his visits to New Orleans and how well-traveled he was. It was almost like he was name-dropping expensive, trendy destinations. It was only after they had polished off the creme brulee that O'Malley ventured into the purpose of the evening.

"The first thing I noticed about you," he began, "was how telegenic you were. I'd be lying if I didn't admit that this business is full of faces. The truth is, if you don't have that certain look, whether you're a man or a woman, you could finish second or even third in the race. It's all about the ratings, you know, and that means advertising dollars. It may seem unfair, but I've found that life in general is unfair. You have to make of it what you can."

Jay blinked, slightly embarrassed, and said, "And you really think I have that look?"

"I'm certain of it."

"I'm flattered."

"You should be. Not every man or woman has it. I consider myself an expert on the market, and I think you underestimate yourself."

Jay decided to change the subject. "So, when do you see this new channel of yours starting up? And do you have a location in mind for it? I know the Weather Channel is out of Atlanta."

"I haven't decided on a location yet, though I'm thinking of something in the center of the country—perhaps St. Louis. As for the start date, that's up for grabs, too."

Frowning, Jay said, "I'm a little confused. I got the impression from your letter that things were a little further along than this and that you were ready to do a start-up."

O'Malley rose from his chair and moved to the marble wet bar where he turned and said, "I'm going to have a brandy. Won't you join me? The evening is young."

Afraid to refuse, Jay nodded, even though he had always found brandy too heavy, turning his eyelids to stone after only a few sips.

After a bit of swirling, sniffing and a couple of sips of his own, O'Malley said, "What you need to know about me, Jay Wilkinson, is that I am a man who always does his due diligence. I always vet those who interest me. I don't like surprises of any kind."

"That only makes good sense."

"For instance, I happen to know that you are one of the boys."

Temporarily frozen by the remark, Jay could think of nothing to say.

O'Malley smiled, leaning forward. "Don't be alarmed. You can relax. I'm one of the boys, too. I certainly wouldn't hold it against you, if that's what you're thinking. I can see the worry on your face. But the truth is quite the opposite." He dug into the lining of his suede jacket and handed over a check. "This should convince you that my interest in you is very real."

Jay's eyes widened as he viewed the amount. "A cashier's check for five-thousand dollars? What's this for?"

"For services rendered."

The adrenaline practically doing a dance throughout his body, Jay said, "What services?" Although some part of him in the back of his mind suddenly knew even as he asked the question.

"I think you must know, dear boy. I find you very attractive. Your ability to predict the weather successfully is secondary."

Unwilling to suppress his outrage, Jay said, "If you vetted me as you say you did, you must also know that I have a partner for the rest of my life. That must have turned up if you were doing that sort of investigating."

"I'm aware," O'Malley said, looking smug. "Don't you think that 'rest of your life' bit is unrealistic, though? We gay boys play around a lot, don't we? This town is full of us, isn't it? Surely you cheat on Mr. Leo Marble. Isn't that our way? I have a sailor in practically every port I visit, and I'm offering you the chance to become one of them. Chance of a lifetime, the way I see it. You'll be well-paid every time I visit."

Getting to his feet, Jay said, "That may be your way, but it's not mine. If Leo and I could get married, we would. But things aren't set up that way. We've already done what we could to protect each other. We've gone to a lawyer and drawn up our wills so what's ours is ours, no matter what happens and despite the laws on the books. We'd be practically invisible otherwise."

O'Malley's laugh seemed almost contemptuous. "You don't have to change a thing, my boy. Keep your precious little love affair burning brightly. All you have to do is make yourself available when I'm in town a few times a year. I am the King of Discretionland. No one has to know. Is that too much to ask?"

"Yes, it is." Jay tore up the check and watched the pieces flutter to the carpet below.

"A futile gesture. There are more checks where that came from. Think about it. I don't imagine what you get paid at the station is all that much," O'Malley continued. "Are you telling me you couldn't use the money?"

"I couldn't use the shame I'd feel," Jay said. "Besides, Leo and I do just fine together financially. We're not hurting."

"Well, well, a gay boy with morals. How quaint. I thought playing the field was in our DNA."

"We have nothing more to say to each other." At the door, Jay turned and managed an obsequious smile. "Thanks for the dinner."

On the way home, Jay struggled mightily with what he should tell Leo about the ordeal he had just endured. He had never thought of himself as particularly naive, but what Byron O'Malley had just put him through was evidence that he might be more trusting than was advisable in this day and age. His adult world had always been filled with equations, theorems, isobars and barometric pressure. It was neat and clean, and there was no moral code attached to any of it. He had rarely dated in Boston, so he was relatively inexperienced in the ways of the world; but his love for Leo had only deepened over the time they had spent together. That was cement made out of pure affection and devotion.

Nonetheless, he was experiencing a profound sense of embarrassment at this dinner meeting he had just taken. It came into his head that he had used poor judgment, although Leo had encouraged him not to back away from the promise of the letter. Maybe Leo would feel as bad as he did if he knew what had happened. Maybe sharing the guilt wasn't such a good idea.

He hadn't quite made up his mind which way to go until he had gotten home, collapsed on the couch and Leo had actually snuggled up to him and asked him the question.

"So, what's the verdict? How did it go?"

The answer fell into place with no further thought, however. "I had to turn it down, babe. He says he thinks he's going to run the thing from St. Louis, and I just don't want to move there. I didn't think you would want to, either. We've got a good thing going right here."

"So there was no runner or reporter deal where you could stay here? You'd have to move there for sure?"

"Yep."

"Are you terribly disappointed?"

It was a struggle to keep his true feelings completely submerged, but Jay managed. "The most important thing to me is our life together. Things are just fine the way they are. We have something a lot of gay couples and tons of singles don't have. We have good jobs with security to boot, and we're true to each other."

Leo drew back for a second or two but then leaned over and gave his partner a kiss on the cheek. "That was quite a speech, babe. But if you're sure you're doing the right thing with this job offer, then more power to you."

"Believe me," Jay added, "it was an offer I could easily refuse."

Chapter 27

Three more years of the status quo passed uneventfully. Leo's *Sunday* magazine was starting to win press association awards regularly, and Jay was next in line for the weekday weather slot as soon as Kirk Rodgers, a New Orleans icon with decades of experience, retired in six more months. The AIDS crisis was starting to ameliorate a bit, and those with HIV were no longer automatically viewed as the pariahs they once were, although they were hardly celebrated. The televangelists and other clergy members were still stirring things up, which hardly improved the overall picture. However, nothing made up for the death toll the country—indeed the world—had experienced, even if progress was being made on the glacial side. Fortunately, George Kinsey was the only member of the Coalition who had come down with AIDS and passed away. Both Leo and Terrence liked to think that all the articles and advisories issued by the CDC that were the subject of many a Coalition gathering were at least partly responsible for that happy statistic. Members had evidently listened and played it safe.

Through it all, Leo had never abandoned his impromptu concerts on the spinet for his Coalition friends. Nor for just Jay and Gabe and Susie Landry, coming up from downstairs as was their custom. In fact, he was at the end of a sparkling performance singing and playing an R&H medley of "Younger Than Springtime" from *South Pacific*, "That's For Me" from *State Fair* and "Do I Love You?" from *Cinderella* when Gabe and Susie motioned to him from their spots on the sofa next to Jay.

235

"We have a proposition for you," Gabe said, licking his fingers as he finished up the last of Susie's batch of Napoleons.

As Leo moved to join them, Jay switched to his favorite easy chair to make more room, and Gabe continued. "Here's the deal. Susie and I have an invitation to move in with our daughter Gabriella, now that all our grandchildren are grown, married or moved away. She's been a widow now for a while, and she thinks the house is just way too big for her to putter around in. We're thinking of taking her up on her invitation. We're not getting any younger, and we kinda like the idea of having someone around to keep an eye on us."

Susie picked up the story, oozing with her usual, unrestrained excitement. "So, we wondered if you two boys would be interested in buying this camelback from us. Believe me, it's easy as pie to make the note. All you do is rent the upstairs like we've been doing, and that pays it for you. Helps pay the taxes, too. Believe me, it's the best investment we ever made shortly after we got married. It's never let us down."

Leo and Jay exchanged surprised glances. "Wow," Leo said. "I know I didn't see that coming."

"I'm sure," Susie said. "You don't have to decide right away, of course. Now, we do have some friends that are interested as well, but we wanted to give you sweet, hard-working boys the first refusal. That only seemed right to us. You do such a good job with your articles and your weather forecasts."

"Fair enough," Leo managed. "Did you have a figure in mind?"

Gabe reached into his shirt pocket, unfolded a piece of paper and handed it over.

"This seems quite reasonable," Leo said, after a quick glance. "I would have thought you would ask much more."

"We went with our appraiser's figure. He said it was what the market would bear," Gabe added. "We're not looking to gouge anyone, especially fine young men like you two."

"Jay and I will give it serious consideration," Leo told them. "Thank you for thinking of us first."

Susie winked and then gave each of them a final hug before leaving. "Think nothing of it. We've gotten to where we think of the both of you as family."

In bed that night, with a full moon spilling through the window to give an extra dimension of drama to their conversation, Leo said, "Do you want to pay our mortgage or someone else's? Because that's what it boils down to. Susie Landry made some good points."

"You're assuming we would qualify for a loan," Jay said, propped up against his pillows and playing the devil's advocate.

"Why wouldn't we? We both have excellent credit, and we have a respectable amount in our savings accounts as collateral."

"True enough."

"Isn't owning a home part of the American Dream?"

Jay practically snorted. "Are gay people supposed to be included? Last time I looked, we weren't really a part of the equation."

"Yeah, I know. Sometimes it feels like we're not. But we don't have to accept that naysayer's vision of us. We do have the wherewithal to pull this off, if we both agree."

Jay went silent for a while. His tone was light-hearted when he finally spoke up. "You know there's a big full moon out. Perhaps we're under its influence even thinking about doing this."

"You mean you think we're crazy?"

"Maybe."

Leo's tone grew more serious. "There's only one thing I'd have to insist upon if we did this."

"What's that?"

"We'd stay upstairs and rent the downstairs." Leo could clearly see the frown on Jay's face in the moonlight.

"Why's that? The downstairs is bigger. We'd have more room."

"But we could charge more rent to our tenants for that very reason."

"Good point."

"But that's not the real reason I'd want to stay upstairs. I wouldn't want to disturb my baby."

Jay's forehead filled with even more creases. "What baby? Do you know something I don't know?"

"You should know by now what I mean. My spinet, of course. It practically took the National Guard to get it up here when I first moved in."

"You're exaggerating."

"Not by much. I was so worried about scratches or any kind of damage that I was a nervous wreck. I don't want to go through that again. I'm even thinking getting my baby downstairs will even be harder than it was getting it up. I have this vision of it being lowered on wires and something breaking and it being smashed into a zillion pieces. That would break my heart, and I don't think I could go on living without my black and white keys and my sharps and flats. That was the first piece of real furniture I ever owned."

Jay was laughing now. "I'm assuming you won't bring any of this up when we go to the bank. It's probably not the sort of thing a conservative banker wants to hear."

Leo chucked him lightly on the arm. "I beg to disagree. It will show him how seriously I take my ownership of very nice, material things. People like that generally pay their mortgages on time. So, are we agreed? Do we want to look into buying this house or not?"

Jay leaned over and kissed Leo gently on the lips. "Okay, let's go for it. Let's start paying our own mortgage and take part in the American Dream."

It did not hurt Leo and Jay one bit that Porter Kincaid, their by-the-rules banker, had long been an admirer of their writing and forecasting. Nor were their combined assets anything to ignore. They were therefore easily approved for the home loan, and the Landrys were delighted to accept their offer. True to his word, Leo insisted that he and Jay rent out the downstairs while keeping his "baby" safe and secure in its upstairs loft.

When the first Coalition meeting took place after the Landry's had moved out, Leo made the announcement to the group at Terrence's place.

"We wanted all of you to be the first to know that Jay and I are renting out the spacious downstairs of our camelback in the Carrollton neighborhood, and if any of you are looking for new digs or know of anyone who is, we are willing to negotiate on the rent. So, spread the word."

Phil Junkin raised his hand immediately. "I'm actually looking. I'm tired of Metairie and would like to move in closer to work downtown."

"Our place would fill the bill then. Plus, you can take the streetcar whenever you want. Jay and I both do when the spirit moves us."

"When can I get the grand tour?"

"How about right after this meeting breaks up?" Leo said.

Phil agreed, and soon Leo and Jay were showing him around the downstairs with its two bedrooms, two baths, living room, dining room, spacious kitchen and screened porch with a ceiling fan to ward off the New Orleans humidity.

"Well, what do you think?" Leo said when the tour was completed. "Is the rent to your liking? What about the damage deposit?"

Phil nodded enthusiastically. "It all seems reasonable to me. I've been saving up for a move, and this is not that much more than I'm paying now, but it has a lot more space for all my stuff. Sometimes, I feel like I'm living in a closet." He caught himself with a faint gasp and smirked. "I see I've made a pun. Of course that phase of my life is over in a very real sense."

"Then let's head on up, and you can sign the lease," Leo added, patting Phil on the back.

Upstairs, the three men topped things off with a toast—Jay and Phil with their glasses of Merlot and Leo with his usual club soda with lime—and then Phil said, "There's something I've been meaning to ask you fellas, if you don't mind. It doesn't have anything to do with my moving in, though."

When they had all settled in around the living room, Phil continued. "I need your advice on my... well, it's about my personal life. Things are fine at work. I don't know how everyone feels personally about my coming out a good while back, but no one's said anything to my face. Anyone can talk behind my back, I suppose, but life goes on, and I'm doing well in my career."

"That's good to hear," Leo said.

"But I need some advice about my private life. I think you guys are just the two to ask because... well, you happen to know the object of my affection. Only, he doesn't know."

Jay spoke up with a sly grin on his face. "Ah, the old secret crush. Who among us in Gay World has not had one?"

"You read me just perfectly."

"So who is it?" Jay added.

"It's... Terrence Dennery. He's completely oblivious to me at the meetings, and he's always talking to so many people before and after. I just can't seem to get a word in edgewise. Well, I suppose I could if I tried harder, but that's why I'm asking your advice."

Leo's face lit up. "So you fancy our Terrence, do you? I couldn't be happier to hear this."

"Yes, I do fancy him, and I've never felt this way about anyone. Do either of you know if he's seeing anyone?"

Leo gently shook his head. "That would be a big negative. I think I know Terrence pretty well, and he's under the impression that he's not particularly loveable because of his weight and his age. There's a slice of the gay world that puts a premium on that, of course. I think they need to grow up, but that's not for me to control. I know he comes off as forceful and determined because of the way he handles our meetings, but the truth is, he's rather shy and introverted when it comes to the dating scene. He's been hurt a time or two. Hey, we all have."

"Well, that's some information I didn't have before," Phil said. Then he took a deep breath and started rambling. "I can't exactly explain why I'm attracted to him. Maybe it's the red hair and the red beard. Sometimes I find myself thinking of him as a warm, fuzzy pirate. I keep wanting to go up to him and call him Redbeard and say something like, 'Arrggh, matey!' Is that ridiculous or what? Talk about your lame approaches. I clearly need some help."

Both Leo and Jay were laughing now with definite abandon, and Leo said, "Who can ever explain these attractions? With Jay and myself, it was a discussion of oldies-but-goodies that got us started, and we took it from there. So, let me understand this. You haven't said anything to Terrence ever about your interest in him?"

"Nope. I feel like such a buttoned-down, stockbroker wallflower. You'd think I could finally find a moment alone with him just to tell him I'd like to go out with him. But it looks like I'm as shy as he is."

Leo looked thoughtful for a brief span and said, "Well, I think maybe we can do something about that. Why don't Jay and I have you both over for dinner one night? We'll play matchmaker and tell Terrence you'd like to get to know him better. The rest will be up to the two of you. I think he'd be delighted to hear that. Of course, there will be no guarantees the two of you will click. We don't do this for a living, you know."

Phil looked like he was ready to take off and fly out the window up into the skies. "Would you really be willing to do that?"

"Sure we would," Leo added. "That is, if you're willing to put up with my one culinary specialty—"

"It's baked spaghetti, Greek salad and garlic bread," Jay interrupted out of the corner of his mouth.

"Sounds wonderful. But maybe you could leave off the garlic in case everything goes well?"

Leo pointed his index finger playfully in Phil's general direction. "Done. Fingers crossed for you, then."

*

The game was on. Leo could see it clearly in their eyes. Sitting next to each other and sampling their food here and there, Terrence and Phil were definitely making a connection. Occasionally, Leo would shoot Jay a furtive but approving glance at the growing rapport.

"It was highway robbery," Terrence was saying in between bites of Leo's spaghetti.

"They say she lost by seven votes," Phil responded emphatically.

Terrence put down his fork and exhaled noisily as the debate continued. "I've seen both films I don't know how many times. There is just no justification for giving Grace Kelly the Oscar that year over Judy. *A Star Is Born* will forever be her masterpiece, whereas I don't think *The Country Girl* was close to Grace's best work. I think she did a much better job in *Rear Window*. Of course, Jimmy Stewart makes everybody look good."

"*Rear Window* came out the same year, and so did *Dial M For Murder*," Phil added. "I really think the Academy gave Grace Kelly the award for her body of work that particular year. Two Hitchcock films put her over the top, even though she wasn't nominated for either one. Isn't that the way of the world?"

"You may be right, but all you have to do is watch Judy singing *The Man That Got Away* early in the film to realize that it was still highway robbery that she didn't win. What a classic it's become since then, whereas no one really remembers Grace Kelly dressing down and looking frumpy in a housecoat in *The Country Girl*."

Phil busied himself twirling spaghetti strands with his fork and said, "I wish somehow we could go back in time and correct that injustice. I think it would have made a huge difference in Judy's career. She mostly backed away from movies after that, but she did turn out some blockbuster concerts, including the one at Carnegie Hall."

Leo stepped in after a sip of his club soda. "Well, it looks like you two gentlemen are up on the subject of Hollywood injustices, particular when it comes to the Oscars."

"Oh, I guess we have been leaving you two out," Phil said. "So sorry."

"No, no, that wasn't what I meant at all. Jay and I have been enjoying the exchange. The old adage is that you can't be gay and not like Judy. So far, I haven't found anyone who doesn't fit that description. Plus, the woman had extraordinary talent that doesn't come along that often."

"That adage is harmless enough," Terrence added. "But I think we all have to admit that as a group, we are the victims of stereotypes galore. I mean, we're all supposed to be hairdressers and decorators and closeted actors and barflies and also incapable of long-term relationships."

"Jay and I are proving them all wrong," Leo said. "And so are you two. All of us are on the cutting edge, coming out the way we have and asking to be treated with respect."

Over a dessert of bakery-bought tiramisu, the conversation had somehow drifted onto the subject of the disco years, now well in the rearview mirror, and Phil was holding forth. "I am one of those white men without a sense of rhythm. I can wear business clothes well because I'm tall, but that's it. If I had been married to anyone back then—man or woman—seeing me on the dance floor would have been grounds for divorce. I had the incredible ability to send limbs going off in different directions at the same time. Like there was an invisible puppeteer above me on drugs."

Leo laughed and spoke up next. "I liked working out back then to the hot groups and solo artists—Earth, Wind and Fire, Donna Summer, Kool & The Gang, The Village People—"

"Ah, The Village People," Terrence interrupted, the picture of amusement. "Half the country didn't even get what was going on in songs like 'YMCA' and 'In The Navy.' I was no dancer, but I got a chuckle every time I heard those tunes on the radio. I think there was a conservative backlash of sorts when the gay sensibility finally got outed, so to speak."

"No matter what, it's still a big deal, though," Phil said.

Leo cocked his head. "What's a big deal?"

"Having to come out. Making the decision yea or nay. Whether to risk your job or your friendships or your church membership or a host of other things. It's something straight people never have to face. They have the luxury of testing out the dating waters and making mistakes and being supported when they do. Gay people are not even supposed to be out there trying."

"I'll go one step further. We're not even supposed to exist," Jay added, after finishing off the last of his wine. "A lot of people think of us as glitches in the scheme of things. That we're not a part of the universe which, by the way, we understand so very little about anyway."

"Well, we four are here to put our feet down and declare that we belong, no matter what obstacles we face," Leo said. "And correct me if I'm wrong, but I think the gay world just welcomed a new couple into the fold tonight."

Terrence pointed to himself and then to Phil with his best smile. "You talking about us?"

"Who else?"

Phil leaned over and gave Terrence a kiss on the cheek, which was immediately returned.

"And there," Leo added, puffing himself up, "is the irrefutable proof."

Chapter 28

The next summer, one week before his 43rd birthday, the call came through for Leo from Beau Pre just before he was headed out for work.

"Granny Marble died last night in her sleep," Joseph told his son, sounding very much in control. "It's the way she would have wanted to go after her long, productive 91 years. There was no warning. It just happened. I think we'd all like to go that way."

Having long ago decided that Granny Marble would live forever, Leo felt the shock throughout his body. His legs and feet felt hollow. In a world full of uncertainties, he thought Granny Marble would always be a constant he could depend upon. Now, she was gone to parts unknown.

"When are the services?" Leo said, making an effort to suppress the emotion brewing inside of him.

"Saturday," Joseph said. "Do you think you can come?"

"Of course I can come, Daddy. I wouldn't miss it. Jay can make it, too, since he's no longer doing weekends."

"He's more than welcome."

Leo caught his breath and pressed on. "How are you and Uncle Brady doing, Daddy? Tell me the truth now."

Joseph took his time. "As best as could be expected under the circumstances. I think everybody Moms knew thought she was going for a world record when it came to longevity."

"You can't see it right now, but I'm raising my free hand," Leo said. "Count me in that number."

After the two men had signed off with mutual expressions of love and concern, Leo sat down on the sofa and told Jay what had happened, unable to keep a hitch out of his voice.

"Are you going to be okay, babe?" Jay said, putting his arm around Leo's shoulder.

"It hasn't really gotten through to me yet deep down where I live. My brain knows it, but the rest of me seems to be vibrating wildly, looking for an explanation. I know there will be tears at some point, and I'll want you around when that happens."

Jay kissed him tenderly on the cheek. "You can count on that. I'll always be here for you."

"Would you like to go up for the services with me? You're more than welcome. Granny Marble was genuinely fond of you and your mathematical brain."

"I felt the same way about her. I'd be proud to pay my respects."

Leo momentarily felt the hollowness in his legs disappear. There was no substitute for being 'married in his heart' to the man sitting beside him.

It was during the busy reception in the church fellowship hall following the understated Saturday Beau Pre services—long on familiar hymns but short and to the point on the eulogy, as Granny Marble had requested—that Joseph took his son aside and handed him a letter.

"Granny Marble said I was to give this to you when the occasion finally arose. That was several years ago, but it was after you and Jay came up to introduce yourselves as a couple. It was then that she gave this to me for safekeeping. So, here it is at long last."

Leo and Joseph found adjoining seats on the perimeter of the large room full of chatting people, where Leo opened the envelope carefully and began reading:

My dear grandson,

If you are reading this, I am no longer walking amongst all of you in my lavender best. I cannot say what I am up to, but rest assured, I am not overly concerned about it one way or another. Perhaps I will be playing music. Or maybe solving a math problem. I sincerely hope to be involved in the universe in some constructive form or other. Isn't that what we all wish?

What I am concerned about, however, is you and your lovely friend, Jay. As someone who took chances that women were not supposed to take at the time of my coming of age, I applaud the fact that you and Jay are stepping up to claim your lives on your own terms. This world belongs to everyone. No one should be excluded.

I know that life is unfair at times. It requires patience and determination to achieve your goals. My wish for you and Jay is that you can do so out in the open and proudly. I realize that at this time it is not possible for you to participate in a sanctioned marriage, but change is inevitable.

When I was in college at Randolph-Macon, women could not even vote. There were a lot of other things we could not do, some quite obvious, and others hidden behind the doors of smoke-filled rooms, and even in the halls of Congress. I won't go into detail, but suffice it to say that I have not taken my life for granted; neither my marriage to your grandfather Sykes nor my successful Marble School of Music. Both required constant work, as all good things in life do.

I can't foresee the future, but perhaps things will change enough at some point to accommodate you and Jay. To that end, I have made arrangements in my will, for you, my grandson, to receive the sum of $25,000 to be set aside for use on the occasion of your marriage, no matter when and how that comes about. Call me intuitive, but I can see that happening somewhere down the road.

247

I want to wish you and Jay every happiness. May both of you live long and happy lives, as I have.
All my love,
Granny Marble

Leo handed the letter over to his father and waited for him to finish reading it.

"That's quite generous of her," Joseph said, handing it back. "It's almost like she's lighting a fire under your feet to get married, isn't it? Leave it to Moms."

Jay joined them after he had spent some time chatting with Louisa Marble across the room, and Leo gave him his turn looking over the good news.

"Your grandmother had a lot of faith in change, didn't she?" Jay said, as Leo tucked the letter into his pocket. "I wish I were as confident."

"She witnessed a lot of it in her lifetime. I think she knew what she was talking about." Then, Leo shrugged. "I suppose we could get married in New Orleans tomorrow if we wanted to at the Metropolitan Community Church. Outsiders would sneer and call it a gay joke church, of course, and it wouldn't be recognized by the state of Louisiana, either." He turned to his father. "We've done everything we could to protect ourselves, our income and our property legally, though."

"Very smart, son. I'd expect nothing less of you."

"When I visited with Jay's parents in Biddeford Pool, he and I kinda made up our minds that we really wanted to be married up there right off the Atlantic Ocean," Leo said. "You wouldn't believe the setting—the blue water, the rocks, the lighthouse on Wood Island, the clanging buoys at night. It was made for romance."

"Then that's what you both should shoot for," Joseph said. "And now you have a $25,000 incentive to find a way to work something out."

"You have to like her cutting-edge optimism," Leo added. "I think that sums up life for me and Jay right now."

*

Seven months later at the Coalition office, Terrence shoved a Xeroxed article under Leo's nose. "It's about the Unitarian-Universalist Church. They've only been around for a few years, but they perform gay marriages all over the country now. Almost all the older established churches have been standoffish, as you know. I did a bit of research at the library, and it turns out the UU has a congregation in Southern Maine in Portland. That's not all that far from Biddeford Pool, I believe."

Leo finished reading the article with great interest. "Yeah, Portland's just a short drive north on the Turnpike. How did you find out about this church anyway?"

"You know me. I keep up with everything going on in the country about our cause with my contacts. Jim Stuart at the Boston Coalition called me up and told me about it. So I haven't forgotten that you and Jay would like very much to be married at his family home there in Biddeford Pool. Preferably legally, but that might not be possible for a while yet. I just thought you'd like to be aware of what's new on the horizon. I've already told Phil about it, and we're keeping it in our to-do-someday-maybe files."

"Can I take this home to Jay?"

"That's why I copied it for you." Terrence handed it over and continued. "By the way, I have some news for you. I'm moving in with Phil next week, that is, if you guys don't mind. I'm not officially on his lease, but we want to live together as a couple before taking the next step the way you guys want to do."

"Of course we don't mind. Two gay couples in one camel-back. Our very own version of *Upstairs, Downstairs.*"

"Without the servants," Terrence added, laughing. "We gay guys like to do everything for ourselves."

"Hey, nobody's going to do it for us. History's not on our side there."

"Still," Terrence said, "it gives me a good feeling to know that with our Coalition and what it stands for, we might be changing history."

Leo and Jay were taking a warm, soothing bubble bath in the tub together, one at either end, while discussing the pros and cons of a wedding at Biddeford Pool in the near future.

"I just don't want it to appear like we're doing this suddenly because of the money Granny Marble set aside for me," Leo was saying, playfully making a beard of lavender-scented soap bubbles.

"Who's going to think that?" Jay said. "Only your immediate family will even know about that provision in your grandmother's will. You don't intend to go around announcing it to people, do you?"

Leo wiped off his beard with one swoop of his hand. "Of course not."

"You're not afraid of the commitment, right?"

"Do you even have to ask?"

"Then what's to stop us?"

"Nothing. But you and I are going to have to sit down and come up with a guest list that doesn't hurt anyone's feelings."

Jay blew some bubbles in Leo's general direction. "I'm not blowing you off, but if we're gonna do this, we have to do it right. And just because we invite a lot of people, doesn't necessarily mean they can afford to travel all the way to Maine and stay for a day or two."

"Good point."

Jay narrowed his eyes. "You can't possibly feel guilty about the money your grandmother left you, can you?"

"I wouldn't say guilt is the right word. I certainly wouldn't want to disappoint her, either. I'm just wondering if we should wait until we can have a marriage ceremony that's actually legal and spend the money then. There's a part of me that feels like we'd be throwing her money away otherwise."

"Here's a thought, babe. Your grandmother may be right that

things may change somewhere down the line, but right now, we can't count on it. We could always return to Biddeford Pool and repeat our vows if the laws change."

Leo's tone seemed to soften. "That's true enough."

"Meanwhile, I don't want to darken the mood here, but our parents aren't going to live forever. Maybe we should go ahead and do this while they're all still healthy and alive and able to bear witness to our joy. I mean, your precious grandmother is gone now, and no one is getting any younger."

Leo maneuvered his toes underwater and managed to pinch a small piece of skin near Jay's waist.

"Ouch! What'd you do that for?"

"Just my playful way of telling you that you've finally vanquished any misgivings I've been having. You've convinced me. Let's start planning this extravaganza. After you get your parent's permission, of course."

"Playful way? Painful way is more like it. You'll see. You'll be sorry when I learn how to pinch using my big toe and my second little piggie the way you do."

"Hey, it's just a love pinch, but I'll never teach you the technique."

Jay managed a good—natured chuckle. "I'll find a manual somewhere. Anyway, are you kidding about getting my parents' permission? They've been after both Angelle and me to tie the knot for some time now. With separate partners, of course."

Leo splashed some sudsy water toward Jay's end. "So it looks like you and I may just order up the 'I do's' before Angelle and Chase get to it."

Jay lifted both hands out of the water and gestured, palms up. "I have to say that I never in a million years growing up believed that I'd get married before she did. At least, not to a man. Maybe this will spur a proposal from one of those two."

"They've been dating long enough. Why don't we consider making Chase my best man, and Angelle maid of honor? Maybe that'll do the trick."

"Our fathers each should be our best men," Jay said. "Why not? There's really no precedent for ceremonies like ours. My sister could be maid of honor, yes, but our mothers could be matrons of honor. Hellfire, we can do this any way we want. We can make the rules on our own, since most of the world hasn't bothered to include us in theirs."

"So we can."

"And we don't have to figure everything out right this second," Jay said, straightening up and leaning in for a kiss.

The two men spent some time in a liplock as they rubbed their slick bodies together. It was the perfect ending for a serious discussion about the bright future they envisioned for themselves.

Chapter 29

As their wedding in Biddeford Pool drew nearer and nearer after months of planning, Leo and Jay savored a small victory in the battle for acceptance of who they were and what they wanted out of life. When it was time to go shopping for matching gold bands at a mall jewelry store in New Orleans, the attractive young female salesclerk who introduced herself as Penny greeted them with a smile and did not blink when Leo told her that they wanted to buy wedding rings for their upcoming ceremony.

"Are you looking for gold, silver or diamonds?" Penny said, gesturing toward the extensive display case.

When they told her gold would do nicely, she brought out a selection, and they tried some of them on. "We can size them for you for free, of course," she added, when they had found a pair that almost fit.

The gold bands were ready on time as promised, and neither Leo nor Jay cared whether the young woman had been motivated by her commission or genuine acceptance of their upcoming marriage, such as it was. The salient point was that they were treated like anyone else who went shopping for jewelry; and that counted for something in a country that was still somewhat paranoid about AIDS, with some even being resentful of the militant activities of certain gay people and organizations around the country. There was, in fact, an ongoing "queer backlash" to deal with.

As a result, Leo and Jay did realize there were plenty of people in an assortment of churches that were not now and

253

probably would never be supportive of their goals. Thus, they carefully sought out through word of mouth the Rev. Annette Bailey of the Unitarian-Universalist Church of Portland, Maine, on a preliminary planning trip to Maine. She was a handsome, middle-aged woman whose voice had a soothing quality that was the first thing anyone noticed about her, and Leo and Jay knew they had found the right person when she began speaking.

"Our church has performed same-sex unions for some time now," she told them during their initial meeting at her tidy church office. "We believe the universe should not be about exclusion."

"Would it be alright if we wrote our own special vows?" Leo said. "We want this to be uniquely ours and not some rote ritual that who knows who thought up a thousand or more years ago. For the record, we were both brought up as part of mainstream religion, but that just isn't working for us right now. We've set out on our own journey."

"I will be more than happy to use them. This is your day, and your words deserve to be heard."

With that, they shook hands, agreed upon a fee, and everything fell into place effortlessly.

Finally, June 21st, Summer Solstice of 1990, arrived. The weather at Wilkinson House at the Pool was typical of Maine in June—a bit overcast, the temperature barely reaching seventy degrees and a gentle breeze coming in off the nearby Atlantic. Of those who had been sent invitations, the following had found the time and incurred the expense to make the trip up: Terrence and Phil, Angelle and Chase, Lake and Ignacio all the way from Mexico City, Pauly Dixon, Mara Lehmann and Yolanda Delery, who had become an item, and, of course, Joseph and Louisa Marble. Uncle Brady Marble had not been able to get away but had sent along a fat check through his brother.

The evening before, there had been a rehearsal dinner of sorts where the in-laws had formally met, and the early arrivals had mingled at the long table that had been set up in the dining room.

"What about these sons of ours?" Louisa Marble had said to

Beth Wilkinson, Jay's Mum, who was seated next to her. "I never thought I'd be matron of honor at my own son's wedding. I guess you could say we raised 'em right."

"That, we did," Mum said after a sip of her white Zinfandel.

At his end of the table, Leo had pursued an earnest conversation with Ignacio Delgado, whose Spanish-flavored English was charming to say the least, as were his sharp, swarthy features.

"I see you're taking good care of our Lake here down in Mexico City," Leo said. "If there was one of those pageants for handsome international, male couples, you two would win it hands down."

"Ah, you flatter us," Ignacio said, lowering his thick, dark eyelashes.

"Our secret is that we get in long walks together most every day," Lake added. "At least a couple of miles or more. Exercise is the key. We highly recommend it. Word of advice: don't go soft on yourself."

After the extravagant lobster dinner was over, Leo stepped up to perform a trio of show tunes at the rented piano: "They Say That Falling In Love Is Wonderful" from *Annie Get Your Gun*; "Getting To Know You" from *The King And I*; and "People Will Say We're In Love" from *Oklahoma!* All three numbers established quite effectively the light-hearted, romantic tone that both Leo and Jay wanted as everyone gathered around attentively; and Leo had never been in better form.

The ceremony, itself, the next day was performed around noon out on the spacious deck without music, however, because the two men in tuxes wanted their original vows, which each recited in turn, to be the focal point:

I, Leo Marble/Jay Wilkinson, have lived for this day from the moment of my birth, and perhaps when I existed even before that. There are so many things we do not understand about the universe. We spend our entire lives trying to figure it all out. We cannot know for sure where we came from or where we are going. But we can know the value of loving deeply and putting someone else before ourselves. We can sense the growth that provides us, and to the extent we can, we can share it with others. We can live in a universe of endless possibilities, or we can live in one of fear and guilt. We can choose from strength or we can choose from weakness. I, Leo Marble/Jay Wilkinson choose to put my faith in my love for you, knowing that it belongs to us exclusively and that no one can take it away from us. As I have in the past, I choose to spend the rest of my life with you, holding you close to my heart for all time. As the universe and all that is behind it is my witness.

The two grooms kissed and hugged warmly after they were pronounced husband and husband to the applause of all the friends who had come from all over to bear witness. It was a moment Leo thought he would never live to see standing behind that louver door in Beau Pre and hearing his mother say that he couldn't be their son if he didn't like girls. But all of that hurt and doubt had long been resolved. Sometimes, life did let up on people.

The menu for the wedding was simple but wildly successful. It consisted of a two-tiered chocolate groom's cake—since both men were grooms—with mocha icing and Leo and Jay written in green cursive on top of that; lobster again, but in the form of rolls, the calling card of Maine's cuisine; an enormous bowl of green salad with feta cheese and black olives; and plenty of good champagne. It was anything but a traditional wedding, but it made perfect sense for Leo and Jay and to all of their guests as well.

"This is the most eclectic barrel of fun I think I've ever had," Lake told Leo, taking him aside out of Ignacio's earshot. "I'm envious, of course. Ignacio won't go against his church's position on gay marriage, but we haven't let that come between us. We're a forever couple, and that's what counts."

"Maine in June is a majestic revelation," Terrence told Leo a few minutes later. "It all feels so spontaneous, but I know it took you two fellas planning out the wazoo to pull this off. How many trips up did you guys have to make?"

"For the record—two."

Angelle was equally effusive with Jay. "Way to go, my beloved brother."

"So when are you and Chase gonna follow us down the aisle?"

Lowering her voice, she said, "We've just about decided to come up here next year and do something like this. Naturally, we didn't want to steal your thunder by bringing any of it up. That would be very bad form."

"I appreciate that very much," he said, and then brother and sister hugged tightly.

After most of the champagne was consumed as it always is at weddings, there were more than a few robust calls for Leo to do an encore at the piano. Perhaps it was the bubbly or the adrenaline that came with the ceremony, but Leo decided on the spur-of-the-moment to depart radically from his R&H predilection and offered up instead a bit of Lerner & Loewer for once. "Get Me To The Church On Time" and "I Could Have Danced All Night" from *My Fair Lady* were the rousing, well-known, but entirely appropriate, numbers he chose.

Everyone again applauded enthusiastically, recognizing the implicit humor of it all, but Jay sidled up to his husband, put his arms around his waist and nearly in a whisper said, "Do you think R&H will ever forgive you? You've rarely abandoned them over the years."

"Oh, I think they'll understand," Leo answered. "No one has sung as many of their songs as I have in one lifetime. I suspect I hold the all-time record, though some Broadway rehearsal accompanist has probably already beat me out. Those people do what I do every now and then every single day."

Jay gave his husband a peck on the cheek and smiled. "I can picture us in old age a few decades from now. You still at the piano, playing and singing away, while I turn up my hearing aid to soak it all in."

"If hearing aids are the worst we have to deal with, I'll settle for that picture any day. As for R&H being upset with me, the skinny is that I've always had this strange little suspicion in the back of my mind that I was partial to them even before I was born."

THE END

About the Author

R. J. Lee was born and grew up in Natchez, Mississippi, and graduated from Sewanee (University of the South) with a B.A. in English and Creative Writing. Though he now lives in Oxford, Mississippi, he lived for thirty years in New Orleans during which he worked in journalism, advertising, and tourist commission work writing and publishing 16 novels from 1992 to the present. *The Majestic Leo Marble* is his 17th book.